D0296478

Give a Little Love

Also by Jackie Clune:

I'm Just a Teenage Punchbag (2020)

Give a Little Love

JACKIE CLUNE

CORONET

A CIP catalogue record for this title is available from the British Library

Hardback ISBN 9781529353853
Trade Paperback ISBN 9781529353860
eBook ISBN 9781529353877

Typeset in Celeste by Hewer Text UK Ltd, Edinburgh
Printed and bound in Great Britain by Clays Ltd, Elcograf S.p.A.

Hodder & Stoughton policy is to use papers that are natural, renewable and recyclable products and made from wood grown in sustainable forests. The logging and manufacturing processes are expected to conform to the environmental regulations of the country of origin.

Hodder & Stoughton Ltd
Carmelite House
50 Victoria Embankment
London EC4Y 0DZ

www.hodder.co.uk

Heartfelt thanks to Hannah Black at Hodder for her continued guidance and help, and to the excellent structural editing skills of Kirsty Crawford.

Big love to my agent Robert Caskie.

Huge thanks to all the people I felt privileged to volunteer with – Christelle, Suzi, Michelle, Lizi, John, Jason, Claire, Nicky, Liz, Elsa and Mark on The Kindness Project, Ash, Caroline, Kate and Charlotte. Thanks to The Cornerhouse Project, Wanstead. Great big hearts, all of you, who made 2020 at least a bit more bearable for some.

Respect and love to Jane and everyone at the real Magpie Project. Look them up. They are warriors: www.themagpieproject.org.

Thanks to the Co-operative in Wanstead for helping us feed all those families at The Courtney Hotel. Such a small thing – such a big thing.

For my kids Saoirse, Thady, Frank & Orla

For Richard

For my dear departed Mum and Dad

For my brother Ray, a writer, who died 10th February 2020

For Maggie & Adrian

And for Deborah

1

1st January 2020

'How long have we got left – twenty, thirty years? And the last ten of them will be crap.'

'Happy New Year to you too!' I say, pulling my sparkly top off and climbing into bed. I can't be bothered to take my mascara off. 1 a.m. A late night for us, but worth it. Brendan and Erin are still out, but they at least stayed long enough to have dinner with us before heading into town to join Uni mates in crowded, noisy pubs. I've never been one for New Year's Eve, so a cosy night in, with the kids home and the nest full again, has been heaven. Outside the fireworks are still going off, but my brushed cotton nightie is thrill enough for me. I watch as Robert pulls at his cardigan, struggles with the buttons, undoes his cuffs. His pot belly protrudes over the top of his belt as he raises his arms, and his last few remaining wisps of hair stand on end as the clothes drag a static charge over his head. Where is the slim, slicked-back man I married all those years ago? If I had known then how he would end up – portly, often grumpy, prone to occasional bullishness – would I still have gone for it? And does the memory of his former, hotter self make it possible to still desire him despite the ravages of the years? We all sag, wrinkle and expand, but at least we do it alongside each other in mutual acceptance of the inevitable decline. Imagine having to start with someone new now! Nightmare.

'Aren't you getting in?' I say, pulling the duvet down in a

feeble attempt at seduction. Hopefully he won't make a caustic joke about it tonight.

'It's not my birthday, is it?' says Robert, mock confused.

'Oh shut up!' I say, a tight little laugh choking my words. Oh well, I was willing.

Robert stands at the end of the bed in his pants and a dirty vest. I can't remember now how much wine he's had. A lot, no doubt, shuffling between the sofa and the fridge while me and the kids chatted at the table. He's been moody for days – one of his existential funks that comes to visit every so often like an uninvited dinner guest – 'What's wrong?' I say, doing my best to swallow the irritation bubbling up inside me. I try to be patient, but Robert can be a little bit infuriating sometimes. 'Come on, get into bed. I'll suffer all day tomorrow after this late night as it is.'

'Wait a minute! I'm trying to get my socks off!' He wobbles, balancing himself on the bed post.

'Get into bed. Come on.'

He climbs in beside me but sits up, wrangling his special goose down pillows into place behind him. The bed shakes as he arranges himself.

'Angela . . .'

I turn towards him and place my hand on his belly.

'. . . What would you say if I told you I want things to change this year? That I think we could do things a bit differently?'

He's got my attention now. I feel instantly anxious.

'What do you mean?' I say, taking my hand away. 'Don't tell me you want to start going to ballroom dancing classes!'

He tuts, irritated.

'No. I don't know. I just mean it's a funny time, isn't it, this time of life. The kids more or less off our hands. I'll be retiring in a couple of years. You're at home all the time . . . I keep thinking about that song – "Is That All There Is?".' To my surprise he starts to sing. Robert doesn't sing. Not even Happy Birthday.

> 'Is that all there is, is that all there is?
> If that's all there is, my friends, then let's keep dancing
> Let's break out the booze and have a ball
> If that's all there is . . .'

I'm stunned. Robert, for all his occasional moodiness and snappiness at home, never talks like this. Normally it's me asking the big questions – and getting flap all in return. I'm still smarting about the conversation we had just last month about whether I should start learning the piano now that I'm on my own so much. I told him I was lonely, that I lacked purpose, that I felt whatever confidence I had left seeping down the plughole day by day. I must have talked for ten minutes while he gazed at his phone before muttering something like 'You wouldn't have the brain cells now. Impossible.' So what on earth has got into him tonight?

'What's brought this on? You've certainly "broken out the booze". It's just New Year – it makes you maudlin.'

'No, it doesn't!' he snaps, and I know to leave it or things will escalate and I'll be in the dog house for New Year's Day. I've made a trifle, so I don't want to spoil things.

I take his hand.

'It was always going to be like this, Robert. No surprise. We'll be fine. We'll be just fine. We'll just keep jogging along, you and me. Now go to sleep.'

'Good night, Ang,' he says, switching off the bedside light but still upright against his pillows.

As I turn my back to him and hunker down, mildly blindsided by this late-night apparent discontentment, I am oblivious to the fact that in ten weeks' time Robert will be dead.

2

23rd April 2020

It's amazing what a gaping hole one person can leave – even a person who was absent a lot of the time. He was often physically present but mentally elsewhere, and yet the definitive, abrupt *goneness* of him reverberates around the house, lurking in unexpected corners, ready to pounce as I open a drawer and find a golf tee, or pull his dusty old sock from behind a radiator. It's been just over six weeks since Robert died. It feels at once like yesterday – the raw, startling rudeness of it – and also a million years ago. I feel old. Tired. Sore. I'm afraid. I don't know how to read the meters. Jump-start the car. Change a fuse. I'm lonely. Even though I sometimes felt that gnawing loneliness that only the long-term married truly know – how disconnected from a person you can feel despite sharing your whole life with them – this new loneliness has no hope of a warmer, more connected tomorrow. I miss him. The kids miss him. He never called them once they went away, but he was always there. Always Dad. Always ready to drive them somewhere when they came home, or begrudgingly pay for nights out when cash was scarce.

He was so solid. How can he be gone? For years Robert's demographic had been on top of the pile, at least economically. Middle-aged white man, comfortable income, semi-retired, mortgage running down nicely, a new car every five years. Surely all that privilege should shield you from the ignominy of death? Seemingly not. Even winners fail at immortality. Of course, he'd received the usual mild bollockings from the practice nurse at the GP's surgery, which he'd always tried to josh and flirt his way out of.

'Your BMI is over thirty, Robert!'

'That's not fat, that's contentment!'

'I thought you were joining the gym?'

'I walk to the pub!'

'It's much more than thirty units of alcohol a week, isn't it?'

'Oh you mean a *week?!*'

Even though all the alarm bells were ringing, and even though he refused to listen to them, we thought he would live to a ripe old age, calling the shots from his armchair while I scuttled around after him. Nothing prepared us for what came next. I'd always feared that his biggest enemy was his heart. That he'd drop down in the booze aisle at Sainsbury's, clutching his left arm. Ambulance. Concerned onlookers. Me crying and pumping his chest. Robert breathing his last in his favourite place, surrounded by Three-for-£10 Shiraz. I always imagined it would happen like that.

But not this.

This silent assassin coming in from left field, its opening gambit a tickly cough and a slight fever, its surprise move a hospital admission on a calm Tuesday morning, its final aria a plastic tube forced into his lungs and him lying face down, prone, hovered over by gowned and visored blurry figures. He'd been so unlucky. A skiing trip with a couple of the golf guys. Came back really tired, so he slept in the spare room. I thought nothing of it. Then the cough. The temperature. The flu, or so we thought. I was irritable – he'd just been away and left me on my own for a week, only to come back and be completely out of action, leaving me to flick through the TV channels on my own. Again. I hid my resentment and ferried liquids and soothing sweets up and down the stairs, and he was rallying after a week or so, the assassin slinking off in search of another, weaker victim.

But then he turned grey in the face. He was struggling to breathe. It was terrifying. I called the ambulance and they took him in. After a week on oxygen he wasn't getting any better. That's when they told me it was Coronavirus. We had heard of it, of course, but it was so far away. China. And yes, we knew it had arrived in the UK, but so had SARS – and we managed that all right. These things don't get out of hand in developed countries, and Spanish flu was a century ago – before antibiotics! How little we knew then, and how different the world looks just a month later. Covid-19 took over like a global coup. Robert submitted. Finally he was sedated. Intubated. He lasted a few days more.

Then.

A young nurse calling me from her own phone.

'It's about Robert . . .' she said. I could tell she was crying, so I instantly became brave.

'I'm afraid he is not coping at all well with the intubation, and I'm so sorry but we think we might be near the end of what we can do for him.'

'OK,' I said, too numb to be able to come up with anything else. 'Shall I come in?'

'I'm so sorry but we just can't have anyone here who doesn't absolutely have to be here. I'm so so sorry. I know this is awful.'

'OK,' I said again, sitting down heavily. So this is it? This is how it ends?

'I'm with him now. You can speak to him. They say hearing is the last thing to go, so he may well be able to hear you . . .' she said between small, exhausted sobs. She'd held the phone to him to let me say goodbye, but it seemed absurd. How could this be happening? Why wasn't I there? Somehow I had escaped infection myself. Surely to God they would allow me in to hold his hand to say goodbye? And how *do you* say goodbye to someone who you've been married to for nigh on thirty years, whose muddy wellies are still by the front door, whose slippers are still under his side of the bed, whose coat is still hanging on the banister, full of tissues and boiled sweets?

'Robert? Robert, can you hear me? It's Angela. I want you to know we love you. Thank you. Thank you for being a good husband and a great dad. We love you.'

Afterwards I wept alone in the hallway. Stupidly I picked up my phone to text him. Pointless, but I had to do something.

> Robert please try to fight this. Don't die. Please don't die. What will I do without you? Angela xxx

I sat for two hours talking out loud. The dog came and sat by my feet, staring up quizzically every time I wept.

'Robert, please fight this. Please wake up. I love you. I love you.' The words felt strange in my mouth. Like dry pebbles. It had been a long time since I had told him I loved him. I just assumed he knew. I hope he knew. The kids were home. I had called them when I feared the worst and they had come back, missing out on the end-of-term parties – the shots, the kebabs, the laughs. Instead they had been sitting with me worrying all day. Typically when the hospital called to say Robert was on his way out, they had gone for a bike ride to ease the pain of waiting. They never got to say goodbye. When they returned and I told them, it was just awful. We tried calling back, but things were so chaotic.

The nurse had told me someone would be in touch shortly but they didn't expect him to last the night. The call came at

4.40 a.m. Surprisingly I was in a deep sleep when the phone rang, and I woke with a start. I received the news much like I'd just been woken up by my airport taxi. Shock.

'Thank you,' I'd said. 'Thank you for trying.' Then the surreal tea in the chilly kitchen, the dog surprised and vaguely irritated by my early appearance, the wondering when to wake the kids and tell them he had gone. I waited until eight in the morning. That seemed the kindest of cruel awakenings. I held Erin as she sobbed, and Brendan hugged me tight, the man of the house now. We had breakfast.

In hindsight it seems so cruel that on the surface it looked as though we were carrying on as normal. We didn't run into the street tearing at our clothes, publicly displaying our pain. I made a fry-up. At the time we didn't know what else to do. That's what grief is, I suppose. Walking, but wounded. Staggering from one moment to the next, until before you know it an hour has passed. A day. A week. A month. We watched the news and felt a small, morbid surge of pride that our family was now a featured extra in this unfolding disaster. Unbelievable now. If I'd been watching myself as a character in a drama I'd have turned to Robert and said, 'That's ridiculous – people don't act like that! Doesn't she love him or something??' But nevertheless there I was, carrying on like he was at B&Q buying paint, or outside mowing the lawn, and not lying dead in a flimsy gown, waiting to be cremated. Sometimes I amuse myself by imagining him in full rant about the current situation. It's oddly comforting. He would have hated the lockdown. I would have had to listen to him rage about the infringement of his civil liberties, the nanny state, the fact that 'to live is to risk', and how the economy would crumble and be brought to its knees all because of an overprotective liberal elite. How ironic that he was one of the first to go down. Well, a little more than irony, the poor man. If only we had known then what we know now. Although I doubt Robert would have heeded the advice. He always prided himself on his strong constitution, despite his expanding waistline. He was never ill. We had no idea about his type 2 diabetes until he was already on his way out. He would have hated it. Weakness. If he had survived, would he have managed his diabetes? I heard once that there are two types of diabetes and two different types of diabetes patients – those who count every carbohydrate and are constantly monitoring their blood sugar levels, and those who eat sticky toffee pudding for breakfast. I fear Robert would have been one of the latter. I wonder about how it would have played out if he had survived, newly diagnosed with a potentially life-threatening disease. Would he have changed his ways? Started eating healthily, cut down on the booze, done some exercise? Or would we have been hurled into the terrible diabetic downward spiral – blindness, nerve damage, silent heart disease, amputation.

We will never know, because he didn't get the chance to try. I shock myself when I find myself thinking so coolly about what might have been. If anyone could hear my thoughts they might be forgiven for thinking there is a little relief that he is gone. What a wicked thought.

But there it is. And here I am now, a month later, sitting at the kitchen table at 2 p.m. on a sunny Thursday wondering when I should get them up. When your kids have sort of left home, at least for most of the year, are you still allowed to go in at midday, pull the curtains open and declare that it's a disgrace they are wasting the day, and that their rooms smell like a rancid badger has died under the pile of washing on the floor? Are you allowed to insist on them going to bed at a decent hour, eating regular meals and getting some fresh air every day? Or do you just have to accept they have crossed that young adult rubicon into self-determination, no longer under your jurisdiction even though it's YOU paying the bills, YOU providing the Honey Nut Clusters, and YOU still drying their smalls on the radiators? Whatever the answer, it looks like they are here for the foreseeable future anyway. The world is shut. There is nowhere to go and nothing to get up for. What's the point in doing anything today when it could just as easily be done tomorrow or the day after? They have work to do – essays on Gothic literature, dissertations on coding and secrecy. They are showing no inclination to do it. Who can blame them, when they have no idea if their next year will even happen and their dad has just died? They are doing OK otherwise – sad, quiet, but getting on with little things. That's the everyday business of grieving after a while.

The news is full of grim predictions – two years, ten years, a generation before we recover. How did they get through the Blitz? It went on for eight months. Eight months of going to sleep not knowing if you'd be bombed in your bed. And yet they always look so plucky and upbeat in the old photos. The photos they show, anyway. Maybe because they didn't have rolling news, instant access to the morbid daily roll call. We know too much. It makes grieving so much harder. It's not like I can distract myself with other news – Covid is everywhere. Imagine your husband has been knocked down and killed by a big green van, and every time you switch on the news, pick up a paper or scroll through the internet, you are bombarded by pictures of people lying under big green vans. It's, as Erin would say, 'triggering'. Hard to get through an hour without being reminded. Occasionally in the past week I have been brought up short – I'll hear a news story about the virus, feel my stomach lurch in pain then realise I have been totally absorbed in something else for twenty minutes or so and had almost forgotten. Then the guilt comes. Isn't the human heart strange? So heavy and so sore and yet capable of fleeting joy. Like the soldiers' truce for football on Christmas Day.

My phone rings. I pick it up with dread. Someone wants to 'support' me, 'through this difficult time'. It's Denise. Of course it's Denise. She calls me every day, at least once. She is one of those uber carers. She should have a delivery service – Deliver-ooh-poor-you. I shouldn't be mean, but it gets a bit much. She's there for everyone, *anyone* in a crisis. I feel vaguely guilty about why I find that so suspect.

'Hi Denise,' I say, trying to modulate my voice to the perfect pitch of recently-widowed-yet-doing-OK-but-not-so-OK-it's-disturbing.

'Angela,' she coos. 'How *are* you?'

'Oh you know, just sitting here trying not to bake.' Baking has become my new obsession. Lemon drizzle, coffee and walnut, banana bread. Robert loved cake.

'Well look, if you want to bake, if that helps, then do it. You should be doing things that soothe you at this time.'

'Oh I know. It's just that I've only got half a packet of flour left and the shops are sold out, so I'm on rations.'

'It's ridiculous, isn't it? I went to the shops this morning – it was my daily exercise and we needed an urgent shop, we've run out of granola, and I wore a mask, one of the *twenty* I made yesterday – and the shelves were bare! I mean, why are people panic-buying flour? I had to try four shops before I could even find one kilo – and that was organic.'

'Are you planning on doing some baking yourself?' I ask. This is news. Denise has the most beautiful kitchen but rarely cooks in it because she doesn't want 'to spoil it'.

'No,' she says, bemused, like that's the most ridiculous conclusion to draw from someone buying flour.

'Oh. OK.'

'I just wanted it because – you know – just in case.'

'In case . . .?'

'In case I needed it.'

'Yes, I see,' I say. 'For a rainy day. Maybe that's what everyone else is doing.'

'Anyway, I saw so many people in the park! It's like they don't care! People have gone mad! They've taped off the benches, so people were just *sitting on the grass!* Jodi in the greengrocer's says she sees the same people every day with their shopping bag – just 'popping out' to buy silly things – kumquats, pickled walnuts – I mean, that's taking the Mickey, isn't it? "Essentials", they said. I've never *needed* a kumquat.'

'Well quite,' I say, not knowing how to respond.

'So you're doing OK?'

'Yes, yes, you know I've been sorting a few things out.'

'His clothes? Oh poor you . . .'

'No, the finances. Pensions and life insurance and so on. It's quite complicated.'

'Well listen – if you need any help with anything just shout, OK? Not much I can do from a distance, but I can ask Paul if he can call you or something? He's good at all that.'

Oh dear God, spare me the bone-aching tedium of one of Paul's financial planning talks.

'No no, I should be fine, thanks. We have Oscar, Robert's friend. Robert wouldn't want anyone else looking at his finances.'

'Of course. Yes. The kids OK?'

'I think so. Erin keeps me busy with her Instagram-inspired cookery experiments. Brendan sleeps all day. They're OK. I mean, they are very sad, of course, but it's sort of nice that we have been forced together.'

'Yes, it must be nice having them home, you know, for the company. That's one positive to come out of all this, isn't it? People are spending more time together as families, you know, rediscovering their bonds.'

I resist the urge to point out to Denise that, in effect, what she has just said is that there's a sunny upside to losing your husband at the age of fifty-nine to a deadly virus, and that upside is being slam-dunked back into the dreadful teenage years with your now grown-up children, with the exception that there's no one to slag off Kirstie's *Keep Crafting and Carry On* with of an evening. How am I ever going to get her off the phone? *A Place in the Sun* starts in five minutes. I want to zone out watching indecisive Brummies wandering dazed and confused around three Spanish villas saying 'Ooh this is nice' then going home empty-handed.

I know.

I need to get real with her. She can't handle it. She only wants to hear 'I'm OK' so that she can move on to her next 'Poor you' recipient – I've heard someone has lost their cat in our street, and she has probably got some 'Missing' posters to laminate.

I start by sighing. That makes her nervous.

'I don't know, Denise, I am doing my best, but I'm awake from about four a.m. and I lie there – still on my side of the bed, it seems wrong to spread out just yet – wondering what the hell I'm meant to do now, you know? We were going to go to Australia. I can't stand to think of going there alone. What about the summer? Who is going to do the lawn? I don't know how to use the lawn-mower, or even get it out of the shed from underneath all the ladders and old hoses. What about when I get ill? What if I get dementia? There'll be no one there to remind me about the past, and I won't remember really important things like the kids' birthdays and what order to put my clothes on, so I'll probably be found wandering up and down the high street with my pants on over my trousers. And will the kids even come to see me? They always preferred Robert anyway, if I'm honest, because he never pushed them and made better dinners. And if I'm honest it's hard to get up and start the day once that's all gone through my head.'

There's an uncomfortable pause.

'Oh God, sorry, Angela, I have to go – the Ocado delivery is here. I booked it three weeks ago – lucked out on a slot. I'll call you later!' And she's gone.

Back of the net. As Robert would have said. I don't know why she irritates me so much. She means well. I just wish she didn't mean well right in my face. Robert didn't like her much. He called her 'that bloody awful curtain-twitcher'. If only she knew.

Two hours later there's a knock on the door and when I open it there's Denise at the end of the path, wearing what looks like a homemade Hazmat suit and a Cath Kidston face mask. She points to a large dish covered in clingfilm sitting at my feet.

'Lasagne! For later!' she shouts, her voice muffled by the carefully pleated and top-stitched flap of fabric covering her mouth.

'Thank you!' I say. She blows a kiss and rustles off, happier now.

I go back inside and scrape it straight into the bin.

Robert loved lasagne. We wouldn't be able to swallow it now. One day maybe. But not now.

Is it too early for gin? Surely the lockdown sun is over the yardarm by four o'clock?

3

1st May 2020

'Mum – has my Amazon delivery arrived yet?'

Erin has appeared in the kitchen. It's 6 p.m. and I haven't seen her all day. Her long blonde hair has been dyed Lockdown Pink, her strong body encased in Lycra sportswear, ready for a run that never quite happens.

'Good morning!' I say, mock reproachful.

'I've been up since about one, Mum, calm down.'

'Have you? What have you been doing up there? Don't you get hungry?'

'I've got some vegan bars in my room.'

Of course she has. She'll have a vegan bar, declare that she is 'juicing' for the rest of the day then eat ice cream straight from the tub at midnight.

'No, there's been no deliveries. I went out for a quick walk with Mona this morning, but these days they just leave stuff at the door anyway. Heaven for your opportunist thieves.'

'Oh bloody hell!' she says, staring into the fridge as if it can tell her where her delivery is.

'What are you expecting?'

'I ordered some rice paper to make spring rolls with.'

'Sounds nice.'

'Yeah, I saw it on Instagram. Have we got, like, any prawns?'

'Maybe. Have a look in the freezer?'

She rummages for a few seconds.

'No, we haven't.'

'Get out of the way and let me have a look!' I say. Nobody ever looks for anything properly.

I pull icy packets of peas, oven chips and ready meals from the freezer's jaws. Towards the back there is a tub – probably an old Chinese takeaway container – holding some left-overs from a meal long gone. I must do a clear-out. Who knows what's lurking in there. I pull the tub out.

I stop dead. Scrawled on the lid, in Robert's unmistakeable hand, are the words 'Fish Stew 20.01.2020'. I remember him making it. It was delicious. I don't like freezing fish – don't know why, I just don't trust reheated prawns – but Robert never threw anything away. I won't eat it, but I can't throw it away.

I shove it back into the icy depths. I fumble around for a few unnecessary moments, waiting for the tears to sink back down into the well.

'I think we may have run out of prawns,' I manage.

'Oh bloody hell! When are you going shopping again?'

'Erm . . . tomorrow?'

'OK. Maybe the rice paper will be here by then. But can you get king prawns – like Dad used to get – not those small irritating ones that don't taste of anything?'

'Yes. OK.'

'Thanks.' She eyes me for a moment.

'You OK, Mum? What have you been up to today?' I feel vaguely patronised.

'Oh this and that.'

'Are you OK, though? Are you having a down day? I've been having a down day too. It just hits me sometimes. I was straightening my hair and then I said to myself – out loud in the mirror – "Your dad's dead."' She comes and puts a hand on my arm, concerned. My lovely girl.

'Oh I'm OK. Just trying to get on with things. We need to keep on keeping on, love. That linen cupboard won't fold itself!'

'Yes. Best to keep busy, Mum. Dad wouldn't want me sitting around moping, would he, Mum? Or you!'

'No, I suppose not . . .' I say.

Wouldn't he? It feels wrong to be 'getting on with things' and 'keeping busy' – why do people say that? Like grief is something you have to actively guard against? Like pain is a bullet you have to dodge by tidying up, running half marathons, cooking, doing the garden? Be a moving target if grief comes your way, which it surely will. As sure as eggs is eggs, as Robert would say. Is this what I'm doing – running away from the pain? Getting on with things can look suspiciously like a hardened heart.

Erin pours herself a large glass of apple juice and wanders out of the kitchen.

'Where's Brendan? Is he still in bed?' I ask.

'I don't know,' she shouts over her shoulder.

Brendan is nocturnal. He always has been. He'd cry all night and sleep all day as a baby, which was hard with a toddler as well. But 6 p.m.? That's no time to wake up. Not unless you've been on a night shift in a hospital, a supermarket or a care home. I head up to his room. It's dark and smells of boy. The blind is down, and he is wrapped in his duvet. I asked him to change his bedding yesterday and he has. Obviously he didn't look in the linen cupboard properly, because his duvet cover is the Spider-Man one he loved when he was a kid. He's nineteen. He doesn't care. Oh well, at least it's clean. I should have thrown it away long ago, but I couldn't bring myself to do it. I even gave it to the charity shop once – then regretted it, went in the following week and bought it back again. How mad is that? Robert was furious! Now I'll have to refold everything – Brendan's pulled the whole cupboardful out onto the landing and it's still there. We've all stepped over it since yesterday morning.

'Brendan? Brendan?'

I shake his shoulder gently. Nothing.

How can he sleep so soundly? Someone only has to turn over in bed three streets away and I'm wide awake.

I shake him some more.

Nothing.

'Bah!' he says, suddenly springing up and almost rugby-tackling me onto the bed with him.

'Jesus, you frightened the life out of me!' I shout.

He is laughing. His puts his arm around my shoulder and pulls me close. I can smell his sour breath, his fetid armpits.

'Sorry, Mummy!' he says, still laughing.

I smack him playfully on the arm and wriggle free. Despite the stinkiness of him it's nice to be touched again. Not that Robert was the most tactile person, but still.

'Don't you think it's time you got up, love? It's six o'clock! *IN THE EVENING!*'

He rubs his eyes like a bear at the end of hibernation. His hair is starting to grow back now, thank God. Last week he begged me to use Robert's beard trimmer to shave his head. I was tentative at first, taking off the smallest amount of his thick dark hair, but he kept egging me on, telling me to go shorter. Eventually I grew gung-ho and pushed the clippers right into the nape of his neck. A huge bald patch. Whoops. He insisted on a mirror, but when he saw it he just laughed.

'Give me a mullet, Mum!' he'd said, finding the whole thing hilarious.

'No!'

'Do it! When else am I going to get to have a mullet?'

So I did. And now my lovely boy is sporting the most horrendous haircut – the sides shaved from the front to the back, leaving a neat stripe of hair down the middle. He's even started growing a hideous '80s moustache to go with it. He thinks it's hilarious. His girlfriend Sindy is less impressed. She's still in Birmingham, but they spend most of the night talking on Zoom or House Party or whichever virtual thingy is working best that night with my 'crap wi-fi'. I hear them when I'm lying awake wondering if I should just chuck the towel in and go downstairs for a biscuit.

'Get up, Brendan. I'm cooking dinner for seven o'clock. So you've got an hour to have breakfast *and* lunch first.'

'Cool,' he says, seeing this not as a reprimand but a challenge.

Dinner. What to cook for dinner? Erin is off the carbs to get rid of the 'Covid 10' she has gained in lockdown. Except she hasn't gained ten pounds – more like two or three, but she can 'feel it' on her body and is starting each day with a new regime. I'm dizzy with trying to follow if she's doing intermittent fasting, no carbs, vegan, juice cleanse or paleo. Brendan will eat anything. Everything. And still maintain his whippet-like thinness. Lucky sod. I don't know where he gets that from. Robert was stout, or 'well upholstered' as he liked to say. But he liked me to be slim. And mostly I have been. Slimmish. Because I wanted to be, not because he liked it. How have I dieted? Let me count the ways. All my life I've been half a stone heavier than the bastard charts suggest I should be. Even when I claim to be an inch and a half taller than I am. But since Robert died I've been eating and drinking more than ever. The Merry Widow. Except it's not pleasure, it's more like a compulsion. Fill the void, stuff it down, push the emptiness to the bottom with endless supplies of cake, biscuits, crisps, wine, hunks of fresh bread smothered in butter and the packets of toffee popcorn that I buy 'for the kids' and put at the back of the highest cupboard out of sight, only to find myself dragging a kitchen chair out at 1 a.m. to retrieve them and pour them down my throat. I don't know if I've gained weight, because I can't bring myself to face it. 'Give yourself the gift of the truth' one slimming consultant once told me. No, thanks. There's been too much reality around here lately. I'm down for some cosy comfort, that false sense of security courtesy of the elasticated waistband, the 'sod it' kickback of the trackie bottoms. Who needs the truth at a time like this? Most widows lose weight, apparently, and in fact the first few days did see my usually voracious appetite disappear. I couldn't swallow. The grief stuck in my throat like a boulder in a dam. I was almost mute. Nothing was going either way – in or out. But slowly the boulder started to erode, until its sides, worn away by my attempts at sobbing, corroded enough for it to plummet down my oesophagus and find permanent lodging in the pit of my stomach. And then I started to eat. And eat. I could sit for hours watching TV and discover that an entire packet of Malted Milk biscuits had disappeared. I'd make huge casseroles with lots of creamy mash, serve myself a large portion then still go back for more. Bake endless cakes with interesting ingredients – rosemary, beetroot, sorrel – and take slice after slice as I walked past on some made-up errand or other. I've stuffed the bathroom scales behind the sink's pipe, where they jut out accusingly, daring me to pull them out and face the music. Yesterday I told them to shut up. Out loud. Every morning I open the wardrobe, look at the neat day dresses and tailored trousers Robert liked me in, but instead find myself reaching for the leggings I left on the floor the night before. Who is looking at me anyway? I'm not going anywhere – only to Asda, and in Asda you're practically haute couture if you've remembered to put a bra on.

Dinner. I open the fridge and stare into it, looking for salvation. The fridge door is my wardrobe into Narnia. Except since Robert died it's always winter *and* also Christmas. He loved food, loved to cook, but always made me feel a bit guilty for eating what he made. 'Little pickers wear bigger knickers!' he'd laugh, whenever he saw me at the fridge. Now it's heaving with cheese, deli meats, luxury yogurts, cream, olives, left-over bowls of curry, chilli con carne, half-eaten cheesecake and, of course, vegetables (which largely go uneaten and lie in a green spongy sludge at the bottom of the crisper section). There's a chicken. Maybe I could do that one-pot chicken casserole with leeks and mushrooms and cream? Robert made it at least once a week. The kids love it. He always cooked it for their welcome home dinner. Have I got any wine? I shake the box I keep in the fridge, the tap overhanging the shelf for convenient pouring. Yes, I am a wine box person now. It's come to this. There's about a glass left. That should be enough. I pull a wilting leek and some withered carrots from the drawer and set about piling everything into the big pot. I put the radio on. More death. I switch it off again. Robert would whistle as he cooked. He would be uncharacteristically jolly, filling his glass often and whistling along to the radio. Fun Robert. He always despaired of my more anxious attitude. It's a class hangover. I may be educated and go on foreign holidays and occasionally go to the theatre, but there's a large part of me that is still the girl on the council estate whose every meal came out of a packet or a tin. Food was fuel – not love, not skill, not status. Nowadays – largely thanks to Robert, who came from a family where they had pasta that didn't come out of a tin – I know what I'm doing and I even enjoy it.

I put the TV on in an effort to stall the inevitable first gin and tonic. Again nothing but death, virus, lockdown, closed, closed, closed signs everywhere. I feel closed. My heart is in lockdown. Shame my stomach isn't. I switch it off again. I turn the heat down on the hob.

'Come on, Mona – time for a walk!'

Mona, our elderly fat Scottie, gets up from her default position on the arm of the sofa – sentinel for any cats or squirrels that might dare cross her turf – and flops semi-willingly down onto the floor. She gives herself a little shake and stretches – first forwards and then backwards. She waddles to the front door and waits patiently. I get the long lead and attach it to her collar, before putting on one of the face masks Denise dropped in last week. I don't know where she managed to get the elastic from. There's been a run on elastic – imagine! If this was the war, Denise would be the one with real eggs, oranges and nylons. It feels ridiculous to wear a mask, but I feel judged if I don't wear one. 'Look at her – that woman's husband died of it and she's prancing about like there's no danger! You'd think she'd know better!'

The park is busy. I keep my distance and stand waiting patiently for parents with entitled children to go through gates and cross paths in front of me. Mona sniffs everything, pulling me from pillar to post. It's a beautiful evening. The bluebells have died off early this year, due no doubt to the warm spring, but now the horse chestnut trees are in full bloom, yesterday's wind having blown their blossom all over the paths, making them look as though a wedding party has just passed through. I duck out of the park and let Mona lead me slowly around the streets. Families sit watching TV in front rooms. The streets around here are so pretty – rows of well cared-for Victorian terraces with loft extensions and nice curtains. Teddy bears stare balefully out of windows, pulled from their cosy beds and put on display to signify, what? Hope? I play a cruel game of judging the standard of the many rainbows displayed alongside the bears, drawn by eager children in the first weeks of lockdown. 'That's pretty, number forty-two – I like the use of post-it notes in rainbow colours. Oh dear, number forty-four – that's a bit rubbish, isn't it? It's not even an arc – just some scribble in different colours. Must do better.' I toy with the idea of knocking and telling them, just to see their horrified faces. But of course, I don't. It's just my little game. Something to shake things up a bit – the sweet, slightly cloying optimism of it, like a bear or a rainbow can do anything. If only it could.

We head home. The chicken will be soft and succulent now. I'll take it out and leave it to rest while I add some cream to the vegetables and the sauce. But first I'll pour a large gin. As I turn into our street I see Brendan on his bike at the end of our path.

'Hi Mum! I'm just off for a cycle.' My heart sinks.

'Dinner's ready. Go after dinner.'

'Nah, I'm not really hungry. I just had some cereal. Laters!'

'But I cooked the one-pot chicken!' I shout to his retreating Lycra-clad back.

He waves without turning around. 'I'll have some later.'

Oh well. Just me and Erin, then. I wish they would be a bit more considerate. I suppose we all deal with grief in different ways, and it's been hard on them having to stay home all the time. I can feel myself starting to panic. Am I disappearing? At least when Robert was alive he was . . . well, *there*. I knew where I was in relation to where he was.

Erin is already in the kitchen.

'Hi,' I say as I walk in, throwing the keys onto the island Robert loved. She can't hear me because the NutriBullet is on full blast. She switches it off and pours some green slime into a pint glass.

'Oh hi Mum!' she says. 'Want some?'

'No, thanks. I made chicken. Drink that, then set the table, would you?'

'Oh I'm cleansing today, Mum. Sorry.'

'Well, you might have told me!' I sigh, turning off the hob and reaching for a glass.

'Sorry. I'll have some tomorrow. I've got a Zoom pub quiz now, Mum. Do you want to join?' She is very sweet, but I know she doesn't want me to really.

'No, I'll just . . . do some more of the jigsaw. Or something,' I say, carefully measuring out the gin then adding a generous splash straight from the bottle.

Mona is standing by her bowl waiting for her dinner. I check the pot, and pull the chicken out with two forks. It sags, defeated, pale and flabby on the chopping board. I know how it feels. I pull off a large chunk of breast and toss it into Mona's bowl. 'Merry Christmas,' I say. And I stand picking at the buttery carrots, slugging my gin and wondering how I will make it from now until bedtime without running out into the street naked shouting 'The End is Nigh! The End is Nigh!', *anything* just to feel something apart from loneliness and fear.

I can't carry on like this for months.

Something has to change.

4

10th May 2020

'Flobber, piffle waffle, splutter, obscure Latin reference, purple prose, wrestle it to the ground, flobber flobber!' says Erin, doing her best Boris impression.

We are watching the latest governmental briefing. Or 'Number Piffle' as Erin likes to call it. She's not a fan of the government's handling of the situation.

'Ssh! I can't hear what he's saying!'

'He's not saying anything, Mum. It's all a load of shit. They fucked it in February and now they are gaslighting us all with baby slogans and "*What* deaths in care homes?" and total nonsensical rubbish.'

'Stay Alert? What does that even mean?' adds Brendan, coming in from the kitchen.

'Yeah, like if you catch the virus from now on it's because you were stupid and looked the wrong way? Like it's somehow your fault? It makes me so angry!'

'I know, love. I know,' I say, rubbing Erin's back as she starts to cry. She misses her dad more than Brendan, I think. Daddy's girl.

'Poor Dad! Every day these numbers! Like it's all just a silly equation they are trying to solve before rugger practice! These numbers are people, you assholes. People you sold down the river because of some fucked-up Nazi Herd Immunity flirtation.'

'They are doing their best, love. It's a difficult time for everyone.'

'Mum! Listen to yourself!' says Erin. 'They didn't tell us the truth! Remember when Bojo made that dark, Gothic statement about how we were all going to lose loved ones? That was POLICY back then. "Let the vulnerable die!" And now look at us? They shut the stable door after the horse had bolted and they can't even admit it. Scum.'

Brendan chips in. 'And now they're saying that Black and Asian people are three times more likely to die from it. They must be chuffed with that. Ethnic cleansing anyone?'

'You can't say that, Brendan. That's just not fair,' I say. Time was I was quite left wing myself, but years of losing arguments with Robert over economic policy has left me a bit shaky ideologically.

'Why not?' Erin asks. 'He's right. They don't care about the Black and Brown people! They're cannon fodder!'

I turn off the TV and we sit in the living room – a rare occurrence these days – and an uneasy silence descends. Outside a blackbird warbles into the dusk. It's blustery and cold. Like autumn.

'Drink anyone?' I ask.

'Mum, what are you going to do?' asks Erin.

'What, now? Pour myself a glass of that nice Sancerre,' I say.

Erin darts a conspiratorial glance at Brendan. He shifts uncomfortably on the edge of the sofa.

'I mean . . . in the future? Now that you are on your own?' Her eyes prick with tears again.

'I'll be OK. Don't worry about me.'

'Mum,' says Brendan. 'We are worried about you. It's OK now – we're here – but we won't be for much longer.'

'I don't think you'll be back at Uni any time soon, Brendan,' I say, resisting the urge to add that they might as well be, for all the time we spend together.

'But what about the future, Mum? Eventually we will be gone, and you won't want to sit around here doing nothing all day, will you?'

'I'm used to it! I've done it for thirty years!' I laugh. But I know what they mean. Even after they left I had Robert to look after. Although he could be – exacting at times, at least we had each other for company. A key in the door at the end of a long day alone. Isn't that the most we can hope for as we grow old? It doesn't matter so much that your heart doesn't flutter and your pulse doesn't race, just so long as there is someone else to finish the crossword for you or make a cup of tea for. I was getting used to my new quieter life. And since he died the kids have both been here, so I haven't yet had to face the house totally on my own. They have recognised this, of course, damn them. I've been trying not to think about it.

'We were thinking . . .' says Erin. 'Maybe you could . . . get a job? Just, you know, to get out and about?'

I blink at them, stunned.

'Why would I get a job? The insurance has paid the mortgage. I have the pension. Your dad provided for us very well. I'm perfectly comfortable. I don't need to work.'

'But maybe it would be good for you?'

'Where's all this come from?!' I ask, laughing.

Brendan looks embarrassed. 'Mum, we're not trying to be mean. But I can hear you. Up and about half the night. Talking to the dog all day. You need to start thinking about what your future holds. We won't be here forever!'

I let out a derisive snort. 'I'm getting a drink,' I say, and I head into the kitchen, smarting. Do they think I'm mad? Or just a saddo?

A job? Me? For a start they are touchingly naive about the employment situation at the moment. People are being laid off left, right and centre, but sure, yeah, there will be someone out there looking for a fifty-six-year-old ex-primary-school teacher who hasn't worked in twenty-five years and who is Hobnob dependent. A fuzzy-haired, grey-rooted middle-aged woman with a Wine Baby stomach, who is so short-sighted she can't see her beard hairs any more, who is barely computer literate and who thinks Social Media is sharing a copy of *Woman's Own* at the hairdresser's. They'd be queuing up to offer me a job. And if by some miracle I did get a job, I'd be taking it away from someone who really needed it. Besides, it's been two months since Robert died. Just two months. Even in today's fast-paced world that's an indecent amount of time to be starting to think about 'the future'. I'm getting through this hour by hour. I don't want to look up. I have no interest in the path ahead. It scares me. If I can just keep plodding along until all this – *all this* – has passed . . . then . . . what? I stand at the sink and stare at the grey grouting. It was on Robert's To Do list. We were living the dream.

'All right, Mum?' says Erin, appearing at the kitchen door. 'We're not being mean – we know how hard it is. We just don't want you to get depressed.'

'I know. I'm fine. Really. I will be fine.'

But the 'fine' catches in my throat. Will I? What does 'fine' mean? Happy? Content at least? Is it enough – 'fine'?

I stuff that thought down for another day. The phone rings. Saved by the bell. It's Jenni. I like Jenni. She lives opposite and she doesn't give a shit. I have been scandalised by her on a few occasions – our Christmas drinks for the neighbours where she climbed up onto the kitchen cabinets to get our expensive wine (carefully placed out of reach by Robert), the street party for the Royal Wedding where she turned up in a Union Jack bikini, got drunk on vodka-laced Pimm's and challenged the local youths to a dance-off, the night I saw her snogging her friend Pam in the park. She's 'a bit of a one' as Robert would say. She's married to a really nice guy called Ellis, who adores her even though she's a nightmare. He's tall, black, very kind and has a habit of tilting his head when he listens, which makes you feel special. Robert always said Ellis had the patience of a saint. Whenever Jenni gets too much Ellis just smiles, puts his arm around her and takes her home. They look so happy together, although she moans about him so much. They look perfect to me, but I suppose you never can tell . . . I'm sure me and Robert looked perfect too. Jenni's the closest I've got to a really good friend around here, and she has always been there, just across the road, when I've needed to borrow something or just fancied a chat. They have a daughter called Rachel, who is married with a young baby. Jenni loves her granddaughter but body-swerves any kind of responsibility for her – 'I've done my bit! Not going through all that again!' I admire Jenni. I feel very comfortable with her. She tells it like it is, says what I think but would never dream of saying out loud. She's been a real godsend in these past few weeks, even though I hadn't seen so much of her in the past year or so. It's been hard for me to open up to someone outside of the family. I've never been good at that.

'How are you doing, Angela?' she asks breezily. 'Is there poo up the walls yet?'

'Not quite,' I laugh. 'We're still relatively sane.'

'Oh God, I'm going mad in here. Ellis has started another fucking jigsaw. Baked beans! For fuck's sake! One thousand pieces! All over the dining table. We're having our dinner on our knees because the table is always covered in Scenes from the Cotswolds or bloody Pies and Puddings of England or something. I'm desperate for him to go back to work, but he says he's "vulnerable"! He's not vulnerable! He once had an allergic reaction to a bee sting, that's all! I told him, "You're more fucking vulnerable sat there with that jigsaw – I might ram it piece by piece up your arse, then you'd know what vulnerable is!" Ha ha ha, only joking – I love him really, you know I do! We're actually getting on really well – he can't answer back from under the patio! Ha ha ha!'

'Poor Ellis,' I laugh. I can just imagine the conversation.

'Poor Ellis?! He's lucky he's not six feet under with his skull caved in!'

'You're terrible,' I say. 'Just be kind to one another.'

There's a short pause.

'Oh God, I'm sorry, Angela. Me and my big mouth.'

'It's OK!' I say. 'I didn't mean to—'

'No, I should be more sensitive. Why don't you come over for Bin Drinks?'

This is Jenni's new thing. I see her outside in her front garden, sat on a camping chair with a bottle of wine in the evening, sometimes joined by a friend perched on a stool next to Jenni's bins, the requisite two metres apart. It's social distancing – of sorts – but some of the other neighbours have started WhatsApp tutting about it.

'Oh I don't know . . .' I say, panicking. What will the neighbours think? I can't be seen having anything approaching *fun* yet, can I?

'Come on! It will do you good!'

'It's pretty chilly this evening . . .'

'Bring a cardigan! Come on!'

'I feel a bit . . . you know . . .'

'Is it those other fuckers in the street? I've seen them twitching their curtains. None of their business. I'm not hurting anyone!'

'I know, it's just – with Robert dying and everything, I think people would think it was a bit . . . you know . . .?'

'Sod them. Come on. I'll see you in five.'

She hangs up. Oh God. I stand in the hallway wondering what to do. I never really understood why she sought me out back when they moved in across the street. We're very different, and I've often felt a bit dull around her. She's almost sixty, but you'd never know. She's trim, fit, always fully made up and wears clothes that Erin compliments her on. Brendan pads down the stairs, rubbing his eyes. It's six thirty in the evening. Breakfast time.

'You all right, Mum?' he asks, hugging me from behind. His hair is growing back, thank God, but he is still sporting the ridiculous porn star moustache.

'Yes. Jenni has invited me out.'

'Out?! What, you just going to go for some Tapas, cheeky bottle of Cava at El Toro Loco?'

'Don't be daft. Bin Drinks.'

He laughs. 'Do it, Mum!'

'Seriously? What will people think?'

'They won't think anything. And if they do, then they won't say anything. And if they say anything, just tell them your husband died and you need to get out of the house for five minutes before you kill yourself. That should put them straight.'

'Jesus, Brendan,' I say, but I can't help feeling a bit . . . tempted. I haven't sat opposite anyone in weeks, months, and I admit – I'm lonely. It's not an unfamiliar feeling. I have felt lonely before, especially when the kids left for college, but there was always Robert – although there were times when I felt lonely with him too. But that was just ordinary *married* lonely. This is different. More . . . permanent. I stand in the hall looking at my reflection in the mirror. I look pale. Puffy. Maybe I should put some lipstick on? I reach for the first tube I can find and drag it across my lips. It's a jaunty summer coral – the one I bought for my sister Sally's wedding two years ago. It looks a bit garish, but I stick my feet into my trainers and open the front door anyway. Jenni is already in situ on her front path.

'Yoo hoo!' she waves, brandishing a full wine glass in her other hand.

I take a deep breath and head out for the first time in two months (apart from the supermarket, walking the dog and the funeral, which doesn't count at all). I look both ways before crossing the quiet street – there are no speeding cars to run me over, but I could be *judged* at sixty miles an hour.

'Take a pew next to the bins – they've just been emptied!' says Jenni, placing an over-full wine glass halfway up the path.

I giggle as I reach forward in that exaggerated way that we have all learnt in order to maintain a two-metre distance these days.

'Cheers!' says Jenni, downing the rest of her glass and topping herself up theatrically. 'And bugger anyone who doesn't like it!'

Bang on cue, Denise appears. She's like the shopkeeper in *Mr Benn* – if you've run out of dog poo bags and are attempting to kick the evidence under a bush, she'll be there. If you put your bins out on a bank holiday, she'll spring out from behind a tree to remind you there's no collection and your bins are an eyesore. And God forbid if you park even an inch over her dropped kerb, she'll slap a restraining order on you before you've even put the handbrake on.

She reaches the end of the path.

'Hello, ladies,' she coos, backing away in a pantomime of fear and propriety. 'This looks cosy.' She adjusts her floral, homemade face mask.

'Doesn't it just! Pull up a flower pot and join us!' says Jenni, getting up to fetch another glass.

Denise visibly reddens. I'm sure her cheeks are puce, but all we can see is her red, blotchy neck.

'Oh no no no, not for me. I'm keeping well away from everyone. As advised. If it's not essential, then I'm not doing it.'

'Very wise,' says Jenni, sitting down again. 'Cheers!'

I'm embarrassed. I feel caught red-handed by the headmistress. Ridiculous. I'm a grown woman. She's not the boss of me. But I feel ashamed.

'Did I see you out and about yesterday, Denise – in your car?' asks Jenni pointedly.

'Yesterday? Erm . . . yes.'

'It's just that I saw on the WhatsApp you were so pleased to get the last Ocado delivery slot, so I was intrigued as to where you were going – obviously not to the shops! Have you got a secret lover you're not telling us about?'

Denise attempts a laugh, but it comes out more like she's being choked with an electric cable.

'Oh I was just going to pick up some more fabric from a lady in Walthamstow. It was only a couple of miles away. So. You know. That's OK. I'm helping to make scrubs for the local hospital.'

'Of course you are!' says Jenni, not unkindly. Denise glows.

'Oh well done, Denise,' I manage, not able to meet her gaze.

'You used to sew, didn't you, Angela?' she asks.

'Well, a long time ago . . . I made clothes for the kids. Not that they ever wanted to wear them.'

'Why don't you get involved? There's a real shortage of scrubs. I managed to source some pretty fabrics, so I'm making ten sets this week for the ICU women. I'd be happy to send you the pattern if you can get hold of some fabric.'

I squirm. I always try to resist being swept up in Denise's pet projects. Maybe I shouldn't. It's just that there's always something – she's always 'helping' and although I feel like an absolute monster for saying this, it makes me feel dubious about her. It's like she's trying to get all the Brownie badges all at once. Somehow she hasn't realised that they stop giving you badges when you're an adult, and Brown Owl dropped off the perch years ago. That's when I'm feeling kind. When I'm in one of my dark moods I think she's a bloody annoying virtue-signalling bore with too much time on her hands. That's awful of me, isn't it?

'I don't know, Denise . . . I don't even know where my sewing machine is.'

'In the loft, maybe? You could get Brendan to get it down for you?'

She's not going to give up.

'Go on, Angela!' says Jenni, enjoying my predicament. 'You could give it a go!'

I smile a thin smile.

'OK,' I find myself saying. 'Though God only knows if they will be any good.'

'I'm sure they'll be very much appreciated. It's our chance to give something back, isn't it? Not all heroes wear capes!'

And not all bullies wear Bovver Boots. Some sport fluffy slippers.

'I'll send the pattern on the WhatsApp. Maybe more of the street will get involved!' She smiles, looking pointedly at Jenni.

'Oh no, not me! The last time I tried to make something was in school and unless they are employing midgets with three arms, I don't think they'd want my efforts.'

Denise smiles. This is her comfort zone – being better than people at things.

'Well, perhaps you could bake? I'm involved in this Bake for Heroes thing – I take cakes to the hospital on a Tuesday and Friday.'

'No, I'm hopeless at cakes. Sorry.'

'I can bake,' I offer, but she's on Jenni now.

'How about the homeless clothes project? You could donate clothes?'

'I had a clear out while the charity shops were still open. I was going to offer to be the collection point for the food bank donations, but I see you've got that covered, Denise.'

'Yes, I'm doing that. You can't do that. There's no point having two collections on the same street, so I might as well carry on – less confusing for everyone.'

'Yes sure. No worries,' says Jenni, smiling sweetly.

'But I'm sure there's something you can do! Why don't we say I'll collect the food and you can take it to the food bank?'

'Sure,' says Jenni. 'I'm not much of an organiser, but I'm a very willing foot soldier.'

'Perfect! When this is all over we will want to look back and say "What did I do during the crisis to make things better?"'

'Yes, we will. But I prefer to take things a bit further back than that, like, around 12th December 2019. Or actually 8th June

2017. I know what I did on those two days. I voted for a party that wasn't interested in asset-stripping the NHS, criminally underpaying its workers and making secret plans to privatise it for profit. I voted for a party that wanted to put an end to shocking poverty and deprivation, the normalised use of food banks for people on shitty zero-hours contracts, the racism of Brexit, the appalling treatment of Black and Brown people who rebuilt this country and are still serving on all the front lines we clap for every Thursday night, but who are dying in huge numbers in the line of duty. That's what I'll look back on, Denise.'

Denise is stunned. She opens her mouth a few times, closes it again and blinks dumbly. Denise's Vote Conservative poster was the talk of our mainly liberal leftie street. The only person who defended her, at least privately, was Robert. He was 'a fiscal Tory', much to Erin's disgust. 'Is there any other kind?' she'd say. 'A fiscal Tory is just a Tory, Dad.'

Finally Denise manages to regroup. Her neck is crimson.

'This is no time for politics, Jenni,' she says, fussing with her mask.

'Oh I think it's the ideal time for politics!' says Jenni brightly.

'This is a global pandemic, Jenni – it's got nothing to do with the current government, and in my view you are not helping by dragging down everything they are trying to do to save the NHS. It's – *unpatriotic*!'

Jenni smiles. Denise is fervently royalist, freakishly sentimental for an England that never really existed (and certainly not in her lifetime), and has a real thing for the Union Jack – at the VE Day street party last Friday apparently she refused to take part because, even though it was properly organised and socially distanced, she felt it was 'wrong'. Instead she stood at her front door in a dress made out of Union Jack tea towels. My only regret about not going is that I didn't get to see her little round body wrapped in towelling flags, her face a mask of disapproval.

'Ah. Unpatriotic. I can assure you I sing 'God Save the Queen' every time I wash my hands, Denise!' laughs Jenni, not remotely flustered. I can feel my own cheeks joining Denise's in a full flush. I hate conflict. I always got Robert to do any complaining – he was good at it. Enjoyed it even. He could make people laugh, even when he was complaining, by jollying them along and making stupid dad jokes.

'Anyway, I'll send you the details for the scrubs, Angela. It's really easy. Take care.' And she marches off, her Doing Good fluffy slippers slapping fiercely along the street.

'She's marvellous really, isn't she? I mean – I know, a bit annoying, and it does irritate me a little bit how she's got a hand in everything, and always has to know best, but she does so much for so many people!' I jabber, desperate to dispel the bad atmosphere.

Jenni takes a long slug from her glass. She sets it down on the floor.

'She,' says Jenni, wiping her mouth with the back of her hand, 'is a cunt.'

And for the first time in about two months I burst out laughing.

5

14th May 2020

It's 6 a.m. on . . . Wednesday, is it? No, Thursday. It must be Thursday because I've just received the helpful reminder about the Clap for the NHS at 8 p.m. tonight. It was stuffed through the letterbox just now – probably by Denise.

As good as her word, she's also posted the pattern for the scrubs, plus a few metres of dark navy cotton ready cut into pieces. I'll be able to make one set out of that apparently. Brendan lugged my old machine downstairs last night and I am sitting in front of it now, trying to remember how to use the needle threader. The instructions are long gone, together with my eyesight, so the chances of me managing to thread the needle are slim. To get to this stage has already taken twelve hours – but here I am. Ready to sew. If only I could get the bloody needle threaded. I lick the end of the dark cotton and stab at the invisible tiny hole in the machine's needle. Why do they make them so bloody small? Surely the sewing demographic is largely older ladies like myself with diminished visual capability? I try again. Nope. The cotton bounces cheerfully off the edge like it's all a great game. I try again. Miss the hole completely. I feel like a cartoon drunk trying to get the key in the door. I try again. Miss the hole the other side. How the hell can I tell Denise I couldn't do it because I couldn't thread the bloody machine? She'll laugh in my face – or worse, purse her lips in that pitying way she has, making me feel even more pointless than I already do. Why can't I find just one of the thirty pairs of reading glasses scattered all over the house? Robert would be going berserk about now. 'You keep buying them every time we go to the wholesaler's, but I can never find a pair! I think you hide them just to annoy me!' he'd say, pulling every drawer and cupboard apart trying to find a pair to use for his sudoku.

I slump back in the chair. It's only six fifteen in the morning. The day extends before me like a road in the outback – dry, deserted, the destination of bedtime depressingly miles and miles out of reach, and even then just a short pitstop before resuming the same never-ending journey tomorrow.

I'll never even get to Australia now. Sally's so happy out there with Husband Number Three and has even started suggesting I go over there to 'find the next one' – as if.

I reach into my dressing-gown pocket for a tissue to mop up the first self-pitying tear of the day. My hand catches on something – glasses! I must have stashed a pair there last week when I attempted to read in bed. They were the ones the hospital returned in the pathetic little plastic bag containing Robert's few belongings. His watch, his phone, his clothes and his reading glasses. He couldn't write or read texts without them, so thank God I'd had the foresight to stuff them in his cardigan pocket as he shuffled to the ambulance. Incredible to think he walked out of the house. Unbelievable how cheery his last text had been – 'Don't panic Mr Mainwaring!'

Then nothing. I haven't had the heart to switch his phone on since he died. What would be the point? Just to stare at it, watch it aggressively NOT ringing?

* * *

I give the glasses a quick wipe to rid them of the biscuit crumbs gathered there and put them on.

I look the needle right in the eye. 'OK you tiny, evil little shit, I'm going to get this cotton in if it kills me!'

I stab the cotton assertively at the needle and BOOM! It goes in first time.

I take the front and back of the top and tentatively stitch them together at the shoulders. So far so good. All I've done is sew two straight lines, but I feel a huge sense of achievement. Now comes the tricky part – the V-neck interfacing. I pin it laboriously in place. It's tricky. If you don't get the alignment right the V will be off-centre and it won't sit flat when you turn it inside. This much I know from the four hundred and seventy-two YouTube tutorials I watched last night. Suddenly everyone is Coco Chanel. It's quite daunting. Still, the journey of a thousand scrubs starts with one single top. I set the stitch speed to 'Tortoise' on the sweet but slightly patronising speed dial and press my foot on the pedal. The needle creeps in and out, in and out, inching along the neckline interfacing. It looks neat. I feel insanely proud. I have to snip into the V on the wrong side to make sure it's not bulky on the right side. This is the tricky bit. I take the tiniest pair of scissors I have – I think they are the old baby scissors I used to cut the children's toenails – and place the tips gingerly into the V. I close the blades around the fabric, but they are far too old and blunt. Nothing happens. It will have to be the sewing scissors, which are huge but at least relatively sharp. I place the very tips into the V and snip. It's close to the stitching but not quite close enough. I turn it the right way out and there is a little lump of fabric still visible. I'll need to go again. I take up the scissors once more and snip – right through the stitching.

A small but totally devastating cut appears on the front panel right in the middle of the V.

'Oh bloody HELL!' I shout. Mona raises her head from the sofa where she is doing some important sleeping and inwardly tuts.

What to do? Do I unpick the whole thing, cut a new front and start all over again? I can't bear it. The only other option is to extend the V a bit lower and restitch past the cut. I unpick the interfacing just above the cut and restitch about an inch past it. This time when I make the slit into the V I hold my breath and bring the blades together in slo-mo. It works. The front looks neat and sharp. I make myself a celebratory mug of tea and sit stroking Mona for a few minutes. The sun is pouring in through the back door and the geraniums are starting to flower. I'm aware I have a creeping sense of something approaching wellbeing for the first time in months. Instantly I feel guilty. What is this – survivor's guilt? How can I be sitting sipping tea, feeling at one with the world, when poor Robert is dead and gone? Gone. Even though it's been over two months now, the finality of that has not sunk in yet. I keep expecting to hear his key in the door, him grunting as he bends down to take his shoes off in the hallway, his weary sigh as he takes his coat off after a hard day in the local government planning department. But I will never hear those things again. Never. Again. I practise thinking this, to get it into my head. But it just doesn't compute.

I finish my tea and start on the trousers. These are much easier and by midday – slowly but surely – I am pulling the drawstring through the waistband and pressing them flat. I set the top and the trousers out on the table. They look good. Six hours. Not too bad. How the hell do people make five sets a day? I'm going to have to speed up. Erin comes down for her green tea.

'Ooh someone's been busy!' she says. 'Wow, Mum, they look so cute!'

'They do, don't they?' I say, unable to stop smiling.

'Get you! Well done, Mum! Are you going to make some more?'

'Oh I don't know. I mean, yes, maybe. Look at the neckline – can you see anything . . . weird?'

'No . . .? Why?'

'Nothing. Good. Yes, I think I would like to make some more!'

I feel a bit excited. I can do something. Suddenly the empty weeks ahead seem full of possibility, creativity, *purpose*. I will need to get ordering more fabric – it's in short supply apparently. Maybe I could start experimenting with pockets? In contrasting patterns and colours? I've heard pockets are very useful.

I message Denise to let her know I have finished my first set. She had a lead on some fabric locally, so she should be able to get hold of it in time for my second set tomorrow. I could order my own online, but I'm impatient now to crack on, and I'm sure now that I know what I'm doing I'll be able to get through two sets tomorrow. Ten minutes later she messages me to say she is outside and that I should bring the scrubs to her 'for inspection'. I assume this is tongue-in-cheek, but you never know with Denise. I feel shy and nervous as I open the door.

'Hi Angela!' she says from behind another mask, this one with a smiley face drawn on it.

'Here they are!' I say, leaving them on the gate post and backing away. Denise says nothing but puts on some surgical gloves and advances as if she is about to defuse a bomb, not check out some overlocking.

She picks up the bottoms first, tries the drawstring for stability, gives a barely perceptible and somewhat begrudging nod, then inspects the hem. It seems to pass muster. She puts the trousers back and picks up the top. The arm holes are given the once over, as is the hem. Then she turns to the neck. I hold my breath. She peers at the stitching before coming to rest at the bottom of the V. She holds the garment out in front of her, then without saying a word pulls a tape measure from her pocket. She measures the neckline and despite her mask I can tell she is smirking.

'Had a bit of an accident, did we?' she coos, every inch the Bond villain.

'Oh well – yes! Ha ha, I got a bit overzealous with the trimming and had to make the V a bit deeper I'm afraid!'

'A *bit* deeper? This neckline is a good centimetre too low. I don't think female staff would be very comfortable flashing their bras in this!'

She laughs a horrible little tinkly laugh. I am dejected.

'Oh don't worry, Angela – we all make mistakes first time! My first set were pretty awful! You'll get the hang of it!'

I try to smile, but to my absolute mortification my bottom lip starts to wobble. This was meant to be my new thing, my way out of this pointless existence, and Denise has just cut me down at the knees.

'Oh Angela!' says Denise, genuinely concerned, 'I didn't mean to be harsh! It's just they have to be very sturdy, these scrubs, or they can't be used, and the last thing they need is the bother of having to get rid of unusable donations.'

'No, it's OK, I'm just – don't worry, I just – look I have to go, thank you, sorry!' I say, as I grab my sub-standard sewing and rush back inside.

'I'll order you some more fabric!' shouts Denise as I slam the door closed behind me.

The hall is quiet and dark. I lower my head and let the tears fall. I feel absurd. Why has this managed to reduce me to such a snotty wreck? I slide down the front door and sit in a heap on the floor. This is a familiar feeling – what Robert would call my 'Pity Party'. He always said that I was too easily deterred, that I let people push me around when I should stand up for myself more. He said it was my fatal flaw, and that it was 'very unappealing'. I can't deny it hurt to hear him say that, but he was right. I've never been able to fight back. If someone is mean or rude I just sort of freeze, go bright red and become completely mute. It's not like I don't know what to say – in my head I am a raging, self-righteous, eloquent defence barrister – but in the moment I can't summon a single squeak. Sometimes I've woken up in the middle of the night and brainstormed elaborate, excoriating diatribes against people who have upset me. I'm really good at it. Just useless in the actual moment. And it's no good being good at it after the event – everyone just moves on with their lives and carries on thinking of you as a sad sack who doesn't think much of herself and probably deserves to be spoken to as if she is worthless.

'Mum?' says Erin, coming out from the kitchen, 'What are you doing on the floor? Are you OK?'

I wipe my face with the scrubs and start to get up.

'Yes, I'm just being silly. Come on. Let's have some tea.'

'What's happened? What's wrong?'

Erin always hates to see me upset.

'Just . . . nothing, it doesn't matter, sweetheart.'

'Mum, you're upset! What did that cow say?'

'She's not a cow, she just said they were not up to standard.'

'What?! They are brilliant, Mum! What's wrong with them?'

'She said the neckline is too low and that nurses and doctors wouldn't want to show their bras.'

'Oh come on! They wear bloody aprons over the top anyway! You know what this is, don't you? It's jealousy. She can't bear that you've managed to do it. She wants to be the Mother Theresa of Scrubs. She doesn't want anyone else to help.'

'She does, Erin. She asked me.'

'She only asked you because she was pitying you, Mum.'

'Thanks!'

'No, I don't mean it like that – I mean, she likes it when people are down. It makes her feel better. Come on.'

Erin helps me up and we go towards the kitchen. As we pass the cupboard under the stairs I snatch at the handle and push the useless scrubs into a bin bag of Robert's clothes – we cleared them last week, ready for when the charity shops reopen. Perhaps they won't want Robert's old clothes. Too many dying. I picture the British Heart Foundation's rails groaning under the weight of fat old men's trousers.

'Oh no you don't!' says Erin, retrieving the scrubs from the bag.

'They're useless, Erin!' I say.

'No, they're not. I might wear them.'

I laugh. 'What, like pyjamas?'

'No. Might help get me into the supermarkets ahead of the queue.'

I laugh despite myself.

Sewing will not save me from disappearing, it seems. I'm going to have to find some other way out of this. Sorry, Robert. I don't have the strength to fight Denise.

* * *

The day rushes past and seems to last forever, like all these days. Before we know it, it's time for the weekly clap. I've started to dread it, mostly because of all the attention I get. People smile sad little smiles, raise their hands in salute and go back inside shaking their heads about the 'poor Covid Widow'. I hate it, not least because most of them never acknowledged us much when Robert was alive. Although he liked to talk to shop assistants and waiters, he liked to keep himself to himself on the street, just in case there was any conflict with parking or rubbish or noise. 'It doesn't pay to be too close to your neighbours, Angela,' he'd say if he saw me chatting too long to Jenni, or Denise, or Baljit at number twenty-seven. 'You never know when you might need to draw a line in the sand.' He was friendly enough if he was in charge – loved to shoot the breeze if he was giving hedge-trimming advice, or tips on how to complain about parking tickets – but not so much if they tried to connect with him in an everyday way. I don't know if he'd be thrilled or appalled to be the new local celebrity, even if it is only by virtue of his death. I think he'd be secretly chuffed.

There's talk of stopping the weekly clap for carers. No danger of our street giving up – Denise just would not allow it. She has been known to doorstep people and ask them why they did not come out. She's stopped doing that now because in the second week she banged on the door of someone's house at ten in the morning and when they answered, bleary-eyed, she tore a strip off them for not being out on the street clapping the previous night. The young woman listened politely before replying that she'd just gone to bed after a long night shift – in the local hospital. Denise now points her claps to that house specifically. Clapping is now a competitive sport riddled with complex social and moral codes – who can clap the loudest? The longest? If you stop clapping before everyone else does that mean you are not as supportive of the NHS as everyone else in the country? If you don't come out at all does that basically make you a narcissistic psychopath? If you just use your hands and not a pot, a drum, a vuvuzela, does that mean you are only mildly impressed by the men and women working on the front line in hot, deathly Covid wards up and down the land? If the clapping carries on until the end of lockdown, I think Denise will be driving a bloody clown car with honking horns, flashing lights and wheels that fall off with a loud bang.

We stand at the end of our path and nod to all the neighbours. Even though I have misgivings about the whole thing, I always find myself moved by the clapping – the ripple that starts bang on eight at Denise's end of the street and grows to a hearty crescendo as it reaches us. I wave to Jenni, who is also out despite her cynicism.

'How did it go?' she shouts as the applause dies down.

'What?'

'The sewing!'

'Oh . . . don't ask!' I shout back. Like it was only ever a bit of a laugh. Like I didn't spend all day ruminating and berating myself for not being grown-up enough to just take it on the chin and sew another set. Like the whole episode hasn't thrown me into a pit of self-loathing and despair.

And we go inside for another week, wondering when this will stop and real life will start again. What will that real life look like? I try not to think about it. Soon the kids will go – just as soon as they are allowed to travel they will be off on European adventures,, crossing the borders freely for the last summer before Brexit slams the shutters down – and I will be left here. On my own. Me and the dog. And Denise down the road. Thank God for Jenni.

What the hell am I going to do?

I haven't had to think about anything for years. Not really. Robert worked high up in planning at the Council, I looked after the kids; we went on holiday once a year, mostly camping in France – 'You might still have to do the washing-up, but at least it's a different sink!' – and when the kids left, Robert always found ways of breaking up the months – he'd started to take me on city breaks, sometimes in foreign countries but mostly in the UK. He drove us to Cardiff, marched around the castle then booked us into a budget hotel for the night. We had a hearty fry-up in a greasy spoon because Robert said it was always better than the extortionate hotel buffet, which in fairness neither of us ever ate much of. Then we drove home. We went to Oxford. We walked around the gardens of Worcester College, had an 'overpriced' cream tea then decided to drive home. Twice we flew to European cities – not places I would have chosen myself, but still. I would have loved to revisit Barcelona, which I haven't seen since my student days, or the Coliseum in Rome, which I have never seen, and sit in a piazza with a gelato listening to the beautiful music of the Italian language all round me. But Robert was a big fan of the Second World War, so we spent a weekend in Hanover, walking the Red Line, a tourist walk which takes you around all the areas that were razed to the ground in bombing missions. Robert didn't want to join the guided tours – 'Too expensive! Too many inaccuracies!' – so we bought a map for three euros and Robert told me all about it. It was actually quite interesting – for the first day. The second day my new sandals had started to rub and I kept forgetting things in Robert's quiz, and he had grown impatient with me. By the time we got on the plane home he was tetchy and my heels were bleeding. But mostly it was nice to get away and see different things. Our big trip was meant to be this year. Robert wanted to visit his brother in Brisbane, and my sister in Melbourne. It was going to be our big pre-retirement trip. He had saved up all his holidays for this year. We had bought the tickets. A thirty-hour journey due to a long stop-over in Singapore airport which saved us three hundred pounds. I haven't had the energy to find out if we can get a refund. Probably not. Force Majeure – is that what they call it? Who knows if we'd have been able to go anyway, with everything that's going on. Maybe people won't ever fly long haul again. Maybe the continents will all build walls, and the UK will once again be the magnificent island paradise of yore. Robert would be happy with that. He was a Brexiteer, after all. I fill up the dishwasher and hit 'Go' – it's the most powerful I've felt all day.

6

11th July 2020

The weeks start to fly past. At first I felt every moment of every waking minute, like a dyslexic in a spelling test. The days seemed to last an eternity and the nights were even longer. I would have to try to construct ways through each hour of the day, setting them out like lily pads I could jump between to stop myself from sinking into the murky depths. Cooking. Baking. Walk the Great Wall of China in Your Living Room. Gardening. Clearing cupboards. Baking again. TV. Obsessing about the news. Avoiding the news. Feeling scared. Feeling OK for fleeting moments. Feeling guilty. Feeling guilty about feeling OK. Feeling strangely comforted by the quiet streets, the low-level hum of the nearby roads reduced to a murmur, even at rush hour. Stop all the clocks. The world had come to rest, had been forced to rest. Foxes became bolder, wandering along our quiet streets at midday. Birds seemed to chirp louder, as if to tell us they have always been there but we could never hear them properly before. Elsewhere in the world goats went on the rampage in lockdown Llandudno, dolphins swam in Venetian canals, monkeys played on deserted roads in Ahmedabad and jackals howled in suburban Tel Aviv.

As I walk the dog in the mornings, I notice the unfurling. Almost four months since Robert died. I wish he was here with me now.

We could go and have a coffee on the high street like all the other couples seem to be doing every day. Not that we ever did that. I made him sit outside one of the many new cafes that have sprung up locally once, about a year ago, but he moaned that it was cold and too expensive. 'Why are we freezing our bollocks off out here and paying ten quid for the privilege when we have a perfectly good coffee machine at home?' Funny – as time goes on these little memories keep surfacing, it wasn't all rosy in our garden. I guess it never is, not for anyone. I play Whack-a-Mole with these little negative memories, and knock them back down. He was a good man.

The lockdown has started to lift. At first people were timid – meeting in small groups outdoors, standing at exaggerated distances from each other, not touching or hugging. The restaurants on the high street began to open up for takeaway only, shyly at first, almost apologetically. The people trickled in, looking every inch like naughty school children bunking off to drink warm cider in the woods. Is this really allowed? People started to meet in parks for bottles of wine and socially-distant, anxious picnics. Strange how quickly we became acclimatised to the dramatic reduction in socialising. I can't think now what you are supposed to talk about with other people. The weather? It's been nice. The news? No, thanks. Politics? Definitely not.

It's Saturday morning. 7 a.m. I am sitting in the garden with a cup of tea, Mona snoozing at my feet with one ear on high alert for the clear and present danger of any neighbourhood cats that might have the nerve to cross her patch. The French lavender is buzzing with bees, and the blue tit family are busy flitting in and out of the bird box where I suspect their young are about to fledge. They're late this year. Nature's been in lockdown too. The sun is strong for this time of day, and it's too early for the neighbours to have thrown open their back doors and unleashed their mornings onto the quiet world. No loud radios, no children screeching and fighting, cooped up for too long in unnatural sibling proximity. It's extremely peaceful. I sigh. I am sitting exactly where I want to be. I am alone. I have tea. The sun is shining.

The thing is. The thing is. I'm wrestling with this weird little feeling. It's sitting somewhere in my chest, like an exotic moth, one of those ones with huge wings and incredible colours, waiting for some light to fly towards. I can feel it. It's waiting. Waiting for someone to switch on the light and bring it to life. I'm dimly aware of it. I don't know what it is. But I know it must stay there – for now. I empty the dregs of my tea into the flower bed and remember planting that azalea the day after a horrible night out. I try to push the memory down, but it's strong, this one.

It was mostly when he was drunk. And in all probability he felt driven to it. He always said I was too meek, and that I should stand up for myself more, so it's most likely that when he had been drinking a bit more than usual his guard came down and he couldn't hold it in any longer. On the fairly rare occasions that we were out to dinner with other people – his friend John and his loud wife Andrea, or Justin from the pub quiz team Robert was in – I would find myself feeling anxious as we arrived. I could never quite name it, this sense of unease and foreboding, but it was in the pit of my stomach and reminded me of the time in sixth form I was going through a brief flirtation with arty clothes. I had taken to wearing my dad's old trench coat, fondly imagining it made me look like Bananarama. I wore it into school one day and was followed around by a much younger girl who had taken against my self-conscious attempt at individuality. She taunted me all day about my 'Chazza shop coat', even devoting most of her lunchtime to the pursuit of my humiliation. It worked. I went home and threw the coat to the back of my dad's wardrobe. The next day I went to school in my normal navy-blue anorak. At break the girl appeared, eager for a new onslaught of abuse – and when she saw me her face kind of fell. She looked . . . not jubilant but . . . sad. She opened her mouth to speak but thought better of it and walked away without saying a word. Even after the embarrassment and strangeness of the previous day – it's quite something to be taunted by someone two or three years below you at school – even after her cruelty, I felt bad. I felt as though I had let her down in some way by bowing to her judgement.

Sometimes it felt a bit like that with Robert. John and Andrea had invited us to their house for a barbecue. It had been a hot, sultry day and the idea of sitting in their lovely back garden eating chicken kebabs was appealing. I always used to take the dog with us – Mona hated most other dogs but was quite taken with their Cockapoo Bella. Robert liked John, and they enjoyed lots of 'banter', which as far as I could see involved trying to top each other with bad jokes and intimations of the other's perceived lack of masculinity. I didn't mind. Andrea was nice to talk to – or rather listen to. She talked in long, rambling, gossipy anecdotes which spiralled outwards from a starting point that soon disappeared into the distance as she free-associated and referenced ever more people I had never met or heard of. I didn't mind. She was friendly, and it meant I could just smile and nod without any fear that I would be called upon to start a conversation about anything. I never felt I had much to talk about that anyone would be interested in. Mostly I read, watched TV and looked after the kids. So it was nice to sit there in the dying heat of the day, glass in hand, letting Andrea's affable monologue wash over me like a warm breeze while Mona and Bella played 'chase me' games on the lawn. Robert and John poked at the meat on the coals and chatted, swigging beer straight from the bottle, trying to look at ease and Australian. We ate with plates on our knees, the salad dropping onto the floor, where Mona sat waiting for scraps from my plate and Bella retreated to the shade.

'Get down, Mona!' I had chided, embarrassed at Mona's insistent pawing at my skirt.

'I told her not to bring the dog,' said Robert, stuffing a bread roll into his mouth. 'She spoils it.'

'She's OK, aren't you, sweetheart?' said Andrea kindly, rubbing the back of one of Mona's fine ears. Mona shrugged her off, eyes on the prize of my burger.

'She's spoilt rotten,' Robert repeated. 'I keep telling Angela to train her.'

'You can't train a Scottie, Robert – they don't know they're dogs!' I remember saying, reaching down to rub Mona's beard.

'That's the trouble with some dogs – especially female dogs – untrainable!' said John, jabbing Robert in the ribs.

'That's no way to talk about my good lady wife!' said Robert, mock offended.

'Robert . . .' I gently chided.

I remember Andrea rolled her eyes and smiled at me.

'Have you tried a reward system, Robert? Give her a treat every time she behaves herself?' said John, warming to his extended gag.

Robert laughed too heartily.

'What do you suggest, John? What's worked for you?' he asked.

'If my bitch is good, I let her sleep on the bed and give her a nice bit of sausage!' said John, grabbing a banger from the barbecue for emphasis.

Robert roared. I drained my glass and managed a thin smile.

'And if she doesn't behave herself?' asked Robert.

'I get the slipper out, give her a belt across the backside and make her sleep in the shed!'

Both men roared at this, and Andrea threw her napkin at John, who came and hugged her. I sat still.

'I'll have to try that with my bitch – she can be way out of line sometimes, looking at me with those sad puppy-dog eyes like butter wouldn't melt, trying to make me feel guilty for something I haven't even done, her stupid little face begging for approval!' said Robert, attempting a humorous response. It came out several shades darker than anything that had come before, and the atmosphere took a slight chill. He looked instantly mortified.

'Angela – have some more Sancerre – it's on offer in Lidl and it's fabulous!' said Andrea, topping up my glass.

'I'm driving, Andrea,' I muttered.

'Driving me round the bend!' said Robert, laughing, trying to dig himself out of the manhole he'd created. He had the same expression as the girl at school – what was it? Pity? Pity that I couldn't take it, didn't fight back?

I remember looking at Robert as he and John resumed their banter – football this time – and thinking, 'Why does he do that? He's perfectly nice to me most of the time, but when we are out and he's drinking, he starts to act like he secretly hates me, and seems to enjoy nothing more than trying to humiliate me in public.' I knew it was an overreaction to silly male joshing but still . . . it had stung.

The rest of the evening had passed without any more incident. At ten thirty I tapped Robert's arm and mouthed 'Home', and he made a great show of being 'under the thumb'. In the car he attempted to chat about the evening. He could tell I was upset, but his way was to ignore it and hope that I'd get over it. Mostly I did, but too often his attempts at humour were at my expense, and sometimes I had trouble letting it go. Eventually he realised there was nothing coming back over the net in our conversation and he went silent. We got into bed without speaking, and as I turned the light out he said, 'It was only a bit of a joke.'

I wasn't laughing. I was upset. Disproportionately upset, like all those little jokes and tiny smears were coming home to roost. Death by a million tiny cuts. Stamp-collecting all my petty grievances over the years and turning them into one big ball of hurt. At least, that's what Robert said I did. And I did, I suppose. I was incapable of answering back, speaking up for myself. Anything for a peaceful life.

The next day he had apologised. It took me by surprise as he always found saying sorry very hard. He said he'd been drunk and carried away with the banter, and that he'd hate for me to feel so upset. He had taken me to a garden centre and insisted on buying the azalea that had caught my eye. I was reluctant to accept it – I didn't want him to think I was so basic a woman, such a sitcom cliché of a wife, that my injury could be easily healed with the purchase of a pot plant. But sitting here now in the early-morning sun, I marvel at its lurid pink blooms and its lush green foliage. Robert is gone, but this plant lives on, testimony to his better nature and a reminder that he had a softer side.

Is this what 'moving on' feels like? You start to process memories and they don't make you cry any more? You are able to think about the person in all their warty reality – not the deified version of eulogies and orders of service. Robert could be grumpy, rude and insensitive. In public he was surprisingly popular – charming, almost charismatic – but at home he was often monosyllabic and unavailable. I put it down to him being able to fully relax at home. That's what families are for, isn't it? I can't deny it irritated me a bit, to see the disparity between his public face and his private moodiness, but if he was a grouch he was my grouch, and I do miss him. Not as keenly as the first three months, but I miss him.

Maybe it's time I started to let things go. Maybe this feeling marks a new phase. A phase I can't fully enter until I leave some things behind. I could donate his clothes to Denise's homeless project. I could move the furniture around, get rid of that horrible wardrobe Robert always insisted we kept because it had belonged to his mother. Give his phone to Brendan, who always coveted it. I get up and go inside, filled with a sense of purpose. I can do this. It's OK. He is not his possessions. Long after his stuff has found a new home he will live on in the very bricks of this house. And in my heart, of course. Of course in my heart.

I drag the bin-bags from under the stairs and with a huge effort resist the urge to go through them again. No good will come of that. Time to let go. I throw them into the back of my car, ready to deliver them to the local pub acting as one of Denise's collection points. Back inside I go upstairs and glare at the ugly brown mahogany beast. Its legs have dug grimly into the carpet. I think it has grown roots. It's going to be hard to take it apart – it won't get down the stairs in one piece, and it's incredibly heavy. This was always Robert's last defence whenever I tried to replace it. But if I can get help to dismantle it carefully, I can perhaps sell it? Donate it somewhere? Although I'm not sure anyone would want it. It's the antithesis of Ikea sleekness. Apparently you're supposed to declutter by deciding whether an item is either very useful or very beautiful. This thing is neither. You're also supposed to thank it before you get rid of it.

'Thank you, ugly and space-devouring monstrosity that I never ever liked and that I never got to use anyway because Robert said you were for suit hanging only. Thanks.' It glares sullenly back at me, but I know I've won now. Its days are numbered.

Now for the phone. Brendan has had the same iPhone for three years, which is apparently an actual contravention of his basic human rights. Of course, Robert had the latest model. He liked a bit of tech, and guarded it ferociously. The only time I remember him not being interested in it was when the nurse called me on FaceTime to speak to him before he was intubated. He batted the phone away. That was the last time I saw him. He was exhausted, I think.

I take it from the drawer where it has lain since I emptied his hospital bag. It feels cool in my hand. I'm going to have to ask Brendan to reset it – I have no idea. I switch it on to see if it needs charging, but the bright white Apple logo springs willingly into life. I shut my eyes and wait for the image to fade from my startled retinas. When I open them, the security code boxes are on the screen. I have hardly ever used Robert's phone – occasionally he'd pass it to me to share some funny video from John or a stream of banter with his pub quiz crowd – but it's easy to guess his password; for a somewhat private and security-conscious man he was worrying predictable with passwords. It was always either his birth date or mine. I enter his date of birth – 250760 – but the screen shakes its head. I try mine – 110163 – and I'm in. There is a little battery life left, which I'm sure will be enough for Brendan to wipe the phone, but I plug it in to charge it anyway. Now that I've switched it on it would feel awful to switch it off again – like switching off Robert.

I set about tidying the bed. Various books, magazines and tissues lie scattered all over the duvet, evidence of another restless and mostly sleepless menopausal journey through the night. My phone pings. I take it from my pocket, but there's nothing there. Odd. Oh. It must be Robert's phone, just coming to life after reconnecting with the wi-fi. Of course he will have had messages before he died. For some reason I hadn't thought of this. It pings again. And again. Everyone knew he was in hospital. I kept them abreast of his condition right up until the last two days. I didn't know they were to be his last two days, but once intubated it felt too serious to message people about. I feel suddenly guilty – how can I read messages for a dying man? Dead men deserve privacy, don't they? The phone pings several more times. What to do? I creep towards it like it's a sleeping child. Just as I reach to pick it up it vibrates, and scuttles a few centimetres across the bedside table. I jump back, spooked by the life of its own it seems to have. Clutching my heart, I start to laugh. Imagine being frightened by a phone? Must be the lack of sleep. I pick it up and look at the text message app. He has seven new text messages. Dare I read them? It will probably upset me all over again. I was just starting to feel vaguely calm and accepting. I toy with the idea of switching the phone off and just letting Brendan wipe it. What's the point in destabilising myself? But even as I go to press the 'off' button, I know I will have to read them. It's a connection. A final contact across time and space.

I click on the icon and look at the list of messages. Two from Erin. I let out a little sob.

'Dad – if you're awake text me back. Just wanted to say LOVE YOU!'

The next one is a little more heartbreaking.

'DAD! I know you're not busy so LOOK AT YOUR BLOODY PHONE! You'd better get out of there soon, you lazy old codger! Xxx'

It was sent on the Saturday morning. He was dead not twenty-four hours later. I sit on the bed and read the next message. It's from John.

'Come on mate – everyone's rooting for you!' it says. No kisses. Of course.

Then there's a number with no name. Four messages all from the same number. Weird. I tap on the first one.

'HELLO?!!!' it says.

Then underneath it –

'Where are you? Why aren't you replying to me?'

I feel a bit sick. Someone doesn't know. Who did I miss? Everyone who knew him had found out, I'm sure. He was one of the first hundred people to die in England. A grim sort of anonymous celebrity.

I scroll down further.

'This isn't funny any more. I've called and called but nothing. I had to call this number because you're not answering the other phone. What's happened? How can you treat me like this! We were doing so well.'

My stomach freezes. What the hell is this? My hands start to shake, but I have to see what the last message is. I note with a queasy clarity that it was sent a month ago.

'OK Bob You clearly don't want to talk. I'm not going to chase you any more. Be nice to your poor wife x'

I'm frozen. I can't move, and my eyes seem to have lost the ability to focus. The room is swimming before me. I try to settle my vision on familiar objects – the vase, the clock, the bin – but I can't see anything. My heart is in my throat and my stomach somewhere near the floor. What is this? My brain tries to grab at anything it can find – a work colleague? Someone he owed money to? But why 'the other phone'? Who has another phone apart from drug dealers and people having affairs?

There it is. The word burns in neon before my eyes.

He was having an affair. Robert. My Robert, who stomped around this house with all the entitlement of someone who was written into every brick of it, who had mended guttering, cleared drains, grumbled about new appliances and painstakingly painted banisters on warm bank holidays, was seeing another woman. My Robert. My tubby, balding husband was, for someone else, 'Bob'. I want to laugh. It can't be true. There must be some other explanation. My brain is racing, but my body moves as if underwater. I find myself lurching towards the bin. My stomach empties the quiet tea of an hour ago neatly into the plastic bag lining the wicker. I'm spinning. The world has turned on its axis – four short messages written weeks ago, that have lain in waiting for the moment I switched the phone back on, like a cancer cell ripping through my lymph system. Ridiculously I grab at the phone, switch it off and bury it in the back of the bedside table drawer. If I cannot see it, does it even exist? That's how he did it. In plain sight. He was doing it all along, but he buried it. A different phone. Late home from work. The dedicated employee. The upright father. The devoted husband. All so obvious as to be laughable now. Too obvious. I wrack my brains for any clue that I might have doubted him. I must have been dimly aware, surely? Or just dim? Surely not? He can't have been having an affair. Not Robert. This sort of thing only happens in books, in dramas, in other people's lives. Yes, he was often grumpy, sometimes mysteriously so. I just thought he was stressed and tired. The planning office was under pressure quite a lot of the time and he had always been slightly prone to visitations from the Black Dog, as he called it. He didn't have a sex drive to speak of either.

At least, not with me.

Oh God. Maybe that's it? Maybe he got it elsewhere. Maybe I had become the over-familiar, non-sexual mother figure – good for pushing out babies and tidying up, not to be tainted with the dark forces of desire.

Who is she? Who the hell is she? I'm suddenly furious. Who the FUCK is she? To play around with our family then dump it on my door three months after he has died and can't answer for himself? How can I get any kind of explanation now? The images of him smiling out from the memorial page we set up for his tiny funeral swim before my eyes. What secrets those twinkling eyes were keeping. How can I face the kids? I can't tell them. They will want to remember their dad as the affable old grouch they have always relied on. I can't take that away from them – they have already lost him in the flesh, I can't destroy their idealised memory of him.

I am racing ahead. Wait. Breathe. Maybe this is all a huge misunderstanding on my part. I am putting two and two together and making five hundred. This is not my Robert. It can't be. My reliable, dependable man. Maybe it was a wrong number. I could call it and find out that those messages were from his garage mechanic, annoyed at a non-payment of an MOT test bill. Robert was very loyal to his mechanic.

But what self-respecting mechanic would sign off with a disgruntled kiss? 'Be nice to your poor wife'? And why the different phone?

No. This is what I think it is. My mother used to say 'If it looks like a fish and smells like a fish – it is probably a fish.'

I wish with all my heart I had not switched his phone on. I could be downstairs now, planning lunch, and not sitting here sick to my soul trying to compute the unthinkable, wondering how I am going to get my legs to take me downstairs to get some water. I have to get it together. I can't let anyone know. There is no other way. I will have to will it out of my head. What good can come of any delving now? Only pain and madness lie that way. There be dragons. I must steer clear, pretend I had never seen it. I can do that. I have pushed things down all my life. This is no different. The sneaking suspicion – because yes, yes it was there – that Robert secretly despised me, that I irritated him into deep silent troughs, that I repulsed him physically and disappointed him intellectually. I have sublimated that for years. The day trips and weekends away he took us on, when he would return not refreshed and energised but cross and irritable, having proved to himself that wherever you go you take yourself – and your dull wife – with you. Of course. Of course he was having an affair. How pathetic of me not to have known. How dare he. How dare the dead have secrets. How dare they have made themselves immune to the wrath of their discovery? My mind flips from despair, to rage, to steely resolve beat by beat. It feels like I am turning a kaleidoscope in my brain, the colours and shapes shifting with each new thought to reveal a new pattern, a different, more torturous perspective.

Enough. Stop. This isn't happening. I won't let it happen. I take a deep breath and force my body to carry its raging cargo down the stairs, the same stairs that he had walked up and down a million times, into the same hallway that was there just a few minutes ago before the ground fell away beneath my feet, and into the kitchen where the same old dog has been all this time, unaware of the human storm raging above her head. I open the back door and let her out. It's an impulse. She rushes to the back fence and barks ferociously at invisible interlopers. The image of a woman – what does she look like? – being ripped to pieces on the lawn flashes across my mind. I push it out. I push it out. No. I will not go there.

Without thinking, I go to the booze cupboard. It's 8 a.m. – too early for wine – so I reach for the whisky. Robert loved his whisky. I pick the really expensive one he was given at work – Japanese, still in its box. I rip at the lid, peel off the foil top and uncork it. The smoky fumes fill my nostrils and my stomach lurches. I pour a modest measure – 'Two fingers, please!' as Robert would say – two fingers. Yes, two fingers to you, Robert.

Bob. How could he? He was my husband. We had a deal. I put up with him because I loved him and he tolerated me because . . .? Did he ever love me?

I down it in one and pour another two fingers. My throat burns and then warms. I pour another. And another. Within five short minutes my edges are smoother and I can think. I sit at the kitchen island – the same island that has for years been host to family gatherings, serious discussions about school choices, 'must do better' reports and admonishments about overspending. So familiar, this island, but here I sit all at sea. I smile a wry smile – of course I couldn't have those curtains from John Lewis – 'What's wrong with Ikea? Throwing your money away on posh nonsense you will only want to change in a few years anyway!' – because he must have been spaffing half his money – OUR money – on his tart!

Oh God, I have turned into a vengeful harpy already. Stop it. How undignified.

Of course we could only go camping – even after the kids had left – because he had to take his bit-on-the-side out for expensive lunches and dirty weekends away.

Stop it.

That golf trip to Portugal last year? Was it really with 'the lads from the pub'? He hated golf. Oh yes, it's all becoming way too clear now. I was sitting at home trying to move the furniture to hide the sun-bleached spots on the carpet while he was shagging his slapper in some Algarve boutique hotel. I'm shocked at my language. Spaffing? Tart? Slapper? Look what you have done, Robert. Look what you have turned me into. The sort of shrieking harridan who uses this sort of vocabulary about another woman. I'm drunk.

Who is she?

I wrack my brains. Someone from work? He never mentioned any women except Anne-Marie, the office manager who he hated. He was always ranting about her sanctimonious emails and her control of the parking permits. He despised her. Or did he? Was his anger an elaborate smoke screen? Surely not. She's older and fatter than me, and I'm quite old and fat. No, it can't be Anne-Marie. She knows he's dead. Of course she knows he's dead. She arranged the collection for the flowers. I'm going mad.

It must be someone he met at the pub. He knew I hated it there – he always wanted to prop up the bar, holding court and flirting with the tolerant barmaids. After the kids left for university he would always invite me anyway, and early on I sometimes went, just to stop feeling so bloody lonely. The few times I did go I insisted on sitting down and he begrudgingly sat at a table looking a bit miserable. He had drummed his fingers on his knees and looked like he was waiting for it to be over. Like we were at the dentist. If there had been magazines he probably would have picked one up. We always left after two drinks.

It couldn't have been one of the barmaids, could it? No. They were very young and always looked as though they pitied him when he attempted banter with them. They say young women like older, settled men with a bit of money, but I just cannot picture any of those pretty young things with Robert. An image of his hairy belly slapping against a toned, youthful stomach flashes across my mind. It sickens me. I push it away. Too obvious. Too clichéd. Was there anyone around here he could have been seeing? Margaret from the corner shop? He was always keen to pop out for the paper. Margaret? With the disabled husband and the missing tooth? No. Then who?

* * *

The first rush of whisky wears off like anaesthesia after a filling and the pain in my stomach returns. I cannot believe it. The fucker. The absolute fucker. Here was I thinking I had the perfect marriage, the perfect husband, and all the time he was playing away? It was all an elaborate facade.

I sit and let the cold, hard rain of disillusionment drench me to the bone.

Who was I trying to kid? The perfect marriage? The perfect husband? The facade wasn't even elaborate. No. This is the oldest story in the book. He got bored. Thought he could have one last ride on the merry-go-round. After over a quarter of a century sleeping next to the same woman, he felt it time to spread his wings before they were clipped forever. He cheated. He lied. He blamed me. He shut his children out of his mind. He carried on behind our backs. For how long? 'We were doing so well'? For how long?

And now the bastard is dead.

I don't even get to shout, scream, shred his clothes on the drive in front of him. He gets away with it. The perfect crime. You can't be held to account if you do the dirty then fucking DIE, can you? And no one will listen to those who speak ill of the dead.

I grab my laptop and start googling.

'Dead husband had affair.' There are hundreds of links. It's a whole world of hidden pain. My eyes struggle to focus on the words, which seem to jiggle and roll along the page.

'My husband had an affair and now he's dead.'
'How do I process the anger about my dead husband's affair?'
'Should I tell my children their late father had an affair?'

I feel sick to my stomach. How am I now in this tortured demographic of pathetic women all clawing at a shred of dignity with no recourse to revenge? An apology? An explanation? How can I be like them? These are letters on Agony Aunt pages in weekend newspapers, to be tutted at, flicked past and pitied. How am I now in their gang, identifying with every word they say?

'I feel so ashamed, and I did nothing wrong!'
'How can I have been so stupid?'
'How am I supposed to grieve when if he wasn't already dead I'd kill him?'

It's an odd sensation to feel at once soothed and in good company but at the same time desperate to get out of this claustrophobic pity party. I don't want to be in this group.

How can I not have known?

I google that. Hundreds of links. It's a bloody pandemic.

'10 Sure Shot Ways to Know Your Husband is Having an Affair'
'30 Subtle Signs Your Husband is Cheating'
'The SIX signs that point to an affair!'

I skim through them. There are common themes. I make a grim mental checklist as I go through.

'He becomes emotionally distant to mask his guilt.'

Check. Although ever since the children were born he became a lot more inscrutable. I would try to pre-empt his bad moods and tiptoe around him, asking if he was all right, buying his favourite biscuits, making sure the place was tidy. He hated mess. Although it's true – yes, I think it is – that since Erin and then Brendan left he became harder to read.

'He gaslights you if you bring up the subject.'

Well, I have never EVER suspected him of having an affair. More fool me. I never once brought it up. And yet the 'gaslighting' bit rings a large bell. A very literal bell. He had come into the kitchen late one autumn afternoon. I was reading and it had grown almost dark outside, so I had switched on the lights. Without speaking, or asking, he had switched them off.

'Hey! I'm reading!' I'd said.

'It's like Blackpool Illuminations in here!' he'd grumbled.

'It's getting dark outside! I need to be able to see the book!'

He had questioned my eyesight, questioned my seat choice – 'too far away from the window, no natural light'– then cast doubt on my understanding of the term 'dusk'. I had laughed, exasperated.

'You're like the man in that play – *Gas Light,*' I had said. 'He keeps dimming the lights and when his wife complains he tells her she's going mad and he's not doing anything with the lights!'

He had blinked, turned the lights back on and walked out.

I move on to the next 'sign'.

'Improvement to Appearance.'

I can't help but snort at this. He always took pride in his appearance even when it had become a lost cause. His shirts were good quality – not just M&S but a few designer ones, a couple from posh tailors in London, high quality and well cut. Until his stomach had grown too big and the buttons had started to strain to contain it. He didn't have a lot of clothes, but what he had were nice. Plain. Always well ironed. By me, of course. I can't say with any commitment that I had noticed him preening himself or altering his style. If anything, he had become less concerned with his appearance, maybe because he felt fat and ridiculous in anything a bit fancy. He was always clean – he showered twice a day – but that was nothing new. He'd always done that. It wasn't evidence of any attempt to wash off a recent tryst.

'Periods when he is unreachable.'

Check. How about twenty years?

'Secretive and/or increased computer/phone use.'

Yes. This. But ever since he first had a decent phone and laptop. Not that he hid them or locked them up or anything. He didn't even protect his security settings very well. I knew his passwords. Or could at least guess them. I feel vaguely insulted. Although he was often on his phone and would hold it close to his face, I used to think it was because he couldn't be bothered to get up and find his glasses. Now I know it was because he had so little respect for me that he felt comfortable hiding in plain sight. Ah, but of course there is the matter of the Other Phone. Where is it? Taped into the boot of his car, like in all the good drug cartel dramas? I will look for it. Not now. I'm drunk. I feel angry. Sad. Sick. I read on.

'They become hostile towards you and your relationship'

Oh yes. I read on.

'People who have affairs internally rationalise their behaviour. Normally they start by blaming YOU. They tell themselves that you don't look the way you did when they married you, or you're not adventurous enough in the bedroom, or you don't appreciate all the wonderful things they do for you, so they deserve to have a little fun elsewhere. Often, their internal justifications for cheating leak out, and they behave judgmentally toward you and your relationship. If it suddenly seems like nothing you do is right, or that things that used to not bother your partner suddenly do, or as if you're getting pushed away, that could be a strong indication of cheating.'

Hmmm. Yes. This. Probably this.

I'm furious. How dare he? How dare he blame me to cover his own guilt? Bitter tears spring to my eyes. All those years of selfless sacrifice, doing the right thing, trying to be what he wanted me to be, wearing what he liked me to wear, speaking at the level that didn't irritate his sensitive ears, buying the food he liked, socialising with his fucking awful friends – yes, they are AWFUL! – submitting to sex with him because I felt it was my duty as a wife. Jesus – all for nothing. All to have it thrown back in my face like this from the safety of the afterlife. His afterlife. Even in death he has all the say. What about my afterlife? What am I supposed to do now that I have learnt that everything that came before was an illusion? And yes, I am hotly aware of how fucking stupid and deluded and unliberated I have been. I know what I look like. The accidental Stepford Wife with egg all over her face. How did I get here?

* * *

I sit and sob for a good hour. I start to make strange guttural noises, so I stuff a tea towel into my mouth. I don't want to wake the kids. I do all the things you see good actors do when they are portraying mental breakdown. I rock. I silent scream. I pull at my hair and beat my fists on the table. When I am spent I stand up, get the kitchen broom, go into the back garden and beat the living daylights out of the azalea. The lurid red petals splatter all over the lawn, and the stems bend and break like so many bones. It's a crime scene. I sit on the steps not three hours since my peace epiphany and stare out at a whole new world.

This is my new normal.

7

'Mum, what the hell happened to that plant?'

It's four in the afternoon now. I have been sitting here a long time. The sun has been beating down and I let it scorch my arms, my forehead. I am in the desert. In exile. I could stay here for forty days.

'Lace bugs,' I say flatly, not turning around. Brendan comes to sit next to me.

'You OK?' he asks, wrapping his arm around my back. I lean on his shoulder and close my eyes.

'I'm fine,' I lie.

'I know it's tough some days, Mum. I know how much you must miss dad – we all do – but just try to take it one day at a time. Me and Erin are here. We're with you.'

I gulp. 'Do you? DO you miss him, Brendan?'

He looks at me, bemused. 'Of course I do. I may not always show it, but of course I do. I'm more worried about you right now.'

'Thanks, lovely,' I say, patting his hand. If only he knew.

'You must have really hated those bugs!' he laughs, picking up the broom and sweeping the decimated flowers into a pile.

'It's the most common blight. Little bugs growing on the underside of the leaves. You can't see them unless you look for them, and by then it's too late. They've wrecked the whole thing. They are very hard to get rid of once they set in. Best to just destroy the whole thing and start again,' I say.

I don't know if I'm talking about the plant any more.

'Fancy a trip out to the garden centre, Mum? Find something to replace it? You love the garden centre.'

My head is banging and my eyes are puffy and red. But I want to get out. Anywhere but here.

'OK.'

Brendan jumps and gets my keys.

'I'll drive!'

Even a white-knuckle ride with my speed freak son is preferable to sitting wondering how the hell to reconfigure the last thirty years of my life as an utter waste of time.

We ride through the empty backstreets, the traffic still gloriously dozy in the latter stages of post-lockdown. Brendan blares out his music from a small speaker on the dashboard. He takes it everywhere, like a patient with a drip on wheels. I'm grateful not to have to talk. The words sit in my throat like an infection – 'Your dad had a mistress. Your dad was having an affair. He was shagging someone else. I don't know for how long but probably ages. We didn't know him.' How can I speak and not say any of this?

Instead I stare bleakly out at the tiny gatherings of happy families as we pass every green area. Little children kick lamely at plastic footballs while young dads chase after them and mums laugh in cotton summer dresses. Old couples edge nervously along pavements, stepping into the road when other pedestrians cross their path. Teenagers sit in close circles, flirting and daring each other to break the physical distance. Are all these relationships, fledgling and well established, built on such shaky ground as mine apparently was? Is it all a big, fat lie, the love, romance and eternal monogamous commitment story?

*　*　*

We arrive at the garden centre. It's a Saturday afternoon and they've only just been allowed to open, so there is the inevitable queue. Yellow tape is marked out on the floor at two-metre distances, and around twenty people stand in quiet acceptance of the new regime. How quickly we adapt. A sign says there is a thirty-pound minimum spend in order to discourage casual browsers – gone are the days when mooching about in the aisles of perennials and bedding plants without any intention to buy was an acceptable way to spend a bored Saturday afternoon. Robert and I came here whenever he would allow. He hated it but saw it as a pay-off for all the evenings he would disappear to meet up with his cronies. Of course, now I know it is unlikely that all of those evenings were in fact with his cronies. I never dreamt of questioning him.

Brendan chatters on while we queue. I stare at all the older couples, gruesome-looking twosomes in beige anoraks, looking for all the world like they are in line hoping for a miracle cure at Lourdes. What's their sickness? Boredom? Irritation? The realisation that *this is it?* I often let that thought bubble up to the surface – the thought that we were just waiting out our days now. Retirement. Illness. Death. But I squashed it back down again. There were many good things. The kids. The garden. Crosswords. Baking. Cake always made everything better. But now? That landscape – bleak though it sometimes looked – has vanished, like a watercolour left out in the rain.

Finally we get to the front of the queue and a masked assistant hands us an anti-bacterial wipe for the trolley – I haven't come here to buy anything, but Brendan has got us one anyway. We stroll through the aisles of begonias, perennials, trays of geraniums wilting under the polythene roof. Fruit trees, shrubs, climbers and evergreens. I see everything as a blur of green, red, purple. Nothing interests me. How many times have I stalked this labyrinth full of energy and purpose, dragging a reluctant Robert behind me, refusing to let his moodiness bring me down? Now I can scarcely bring myself to approach a single plant. Time was when I would have been eagerly inspecting every label – 'full sun/ partial shade', 'well-drained soil', 'superb colour all year round' – my mind awhirl with planting schemes and colour themes. Time was. All around us couples bicker sotto voce – 'We *haven't* got any of these, Simon!' 'I said get *four* Salvia!' – and I stare at the men, wondering if that one in the bad jeans is having an affair too, or if the stooped guy with the comb-over is getting his end away anywhere while his tidy wife in the capri pants sips Prosecco at Book Club. I slump over the trolley while Brendan inspects a bird bath. He must be bored if this is piquing his interest. Too many days all the same. It's nice of him to bring me here. He's always been sweet-natured, always gone along with me. We round another corner and come face to face with the garden ornament section. Robert always loathed the cute little statues of animals, children, toadstools and butterflies that sit silently waiting for some fool to re-home them on neat little patios. He'd always groan theatrically and head for the cafe if I dared venture into that section. It's not that I really liked them as such – most of them were repulsive – but I secretly resented not being allowed to look. Some of the animals were so adorable – three bunnies in various stages of leaping, a mole's head and claws seeming to poke above ground, a miniature single deer stooping to nibble the grass. They were quite beautiful in a grotesque kind of a way. I liked the fact that someone had made them, in all their naivety, to cheer people up. Old people. Or people with no taste. They were defiantly perky, determinedly lowbrow, unashamedly naff. I find myself tearing up looking at a perfectly revolting pair of stone children perched on a bench quietly reading. A boy and a girl. A cherub holding a plant pot. A small boy hugging a puppy. I stop in front of the bit where all the old-people ornaments are. An elderly couple perched on a swing – laughing, familiar, cuddled up close. An old man on a bench reading the paper while his bespectacled old wife peers over his shoulder. A fat old pair of grandparents giggling on a scooter. That's what old age is meant to look like. Not mine. Not any more. Just as well it was all a crock of lies, then.

Without thinking about it I pick up the statue of the children reading and place it in the trolley. It's surprisingly heavy, so I wrestle it onto the bottom shelf. Brendan laughs.

'Good one, Mum.'

He thinks it's a joke. I have no jokes. There are no smiles in my mouth.

'Shall I put it back for you?'

'No. I want it,' I reply, going back for more. I pick up the mole, then the deer, then a trio of frogs playing the banjo. They all go in the trolley.

'Mum! What are you doing?' Brendan is laughing, but there is slight fear in his eyes.

The trolley is full, so I grab a nearby spare and start loading it. A small stone wishing well, a gnome with a fishing rod, a concrete cockerel.

'Mum? Are you OK?' asks Brendan. He looks worried.

Finally my eyes rest on a solitary old lady holding out her hand to feed the birds. A little robin rests on her open palm. She's about three feet tall. Just how I feel. I take it.

'I'm fine,' I smile, starting to wheel the first trolley to the tills, 'I just feel like I want to brighten up the garden.'

'OK . . .' he says, falling into line behind me with the other trolley. 'But . . . why don't you just get some flowers, Mum? These are . . .'

'What? These are what, Brendan?'

'They are not . . . really . . .'

'Not really what?'

'Not really you, Mum.'

We stop in the middle of the path.

'Aren't they? How would you know? How would anyone know?' I'm aware that I must seem absolutely crazy. Brendan knows I used to tear out pictures of the dreadful 'art' on sale in the bag of colour supplements and stick them on the kitchen noticeboard just to make him laugh. Now here we are with two trolleys full of kitsch statuettes.

'OK, Mum. Chill!' he says, looking around anxiously. I'm aware that my voice, filled will suppressed rage, is too loud for this hushed, cosy place.

'It's just I thought you didn't like this sort of stuff. You and dad.'

I stare back at him, breathing hard, trying not to flinch at the mention of Robert.

Brendan puts his hand on my arm. Consoling. Reasoning with the mad.

'Dad would have hated these, Mum,' he says, playing his trump card.

'Well, that settles it, then!' I say, pushing my trolley with renewed determination. After a few beats I hear Brendan fall into line behind me, the wheels on his trolley squeaking under the weight of the half tonne of masonry it holds.

I stare straight ahead at the checkout. I'm aware of a few odd looks, but I don't care. I don't even know why I'm doing this, but I know that it feels good.

'These are nice!' says a lady with a bad perm on the till. She is wearing several gold necklaces and has a tattoo on her upper arm. She is what Robert would call 'common'. I love her already.

'Aren't they?' I say, reaching for the credit card.

'OK, that's four hundred and forty-eight pounds, please,' she says.

'Mum . . .' Brendan says, clearly concerned.

'Thank you,' I say, handing over the card. I punch in the security code and it's done. We wheel the trolleys to the car in silence and I watch as Brendan gamely wrestles each item into the boot. We strap the children into the back seat alongside the old lady with the robin and head home in silence.

Erin is at the front door when we get back. Brendan must have warned her somehow. She waves, trying to hide her anxious curiosity. I get out of the car and unbuckle the stone children and the old lady from the rear seats. I'm aware of some inter-sibling gesticulation behind my back – does Brendan make the 'crazy' sign by circling his finger next to his temple? Oh well. Maybe I am crazy. Who wouldn't be, after what I have been through today?

'Mum! You've been busy!' says Erin, coming to retrieve one of the statuettes. I can see she is trying not to laugh.

'Where are we putting these beauties?'

'Just take them through to the back garden,' I say, going to the boot. I can hear her and Brendan whispering as they go down the front path. The odd phrase floats on the breeze – 'losing it', 'absolutely hideous', 'couldn't stop her'. I don't care. I want to fill the house up with all the shit Robert hated.

Then burn it down.

*   *   *

Ten minutes later we are all sitting in the garden with a large gin and tonic. Our new friends are installed in various locations around the end of the lawn – the frogs in one corner, with the deer grazing nearby. The mole is popping up nearest to us, with the gnome (which really is awful), the cockerel and the wishing well arranged in a semi-circle on the left of the lawn. On the right, under the weeping willow, I have placed the children reading, and just behind them the old lady with the robin in her hand.

'It's kind of cool,' says Erin finally. She has always been nice, always encouraged me in her gentle way, despite her often scathing judgements on others. Perhaps she saw something in me that needed the boost.

'It's kind of like an installation. Like a sort of low-rent Grayson Perry.'

'Yeah, like a sort of meta-sculpture park depicting the conflicted interface between man and nature,' adds Brendan, always keen to flex his intellectual muscles. They both burst out laughing.

I say nothing.

'Mum? Come on. What's going on?' asks Erin finally. 'I've heard of widows collecting dolls, or teddy bears, but garden kitsch?'

'I like it,' I say, necking the rest of my gin. 'Can someone top me up?'

I haven't eaten all day and I'm feeling woozy.

Brendan shrugs, gets up and goes to refill my glass.

'Mum – are you OK?' asks Erin. 'You seem kind of – weird. I'm worried about you. We're worried about you. Is it Dad? Are you missing him today? I am. Some days are harder than others, I know.'

I take her hand and rub her fingers.

'I'm fine,' I say, totally unconvincingly. Then I burst into tears.

Erin puts her arms around me. It's been a long time since I've been held and I sob onto her shoulder. I hear Brendan come back and place the glass next to me. She shoos him away. I can hear him clattering about in the kitchen. Finally my heaving stops and Erin pitter-patters off to fetch me a tissue. I look down the garden at the ugly new residents. They truly are dreadful. What was I thinking? What is this – revenge? For all the years I never got my own way, always bowed to his taste in food, decor, holidays, friends, even what I wore on my own body? What a pitiful kind of fight back this is – drunk and betrayed, staring at five hundred quid's worth of bad garden art. Despite myself I start to laugh – small titters at first, then my shoulders go, and finally I am guffawing. Erin comes back and looks even more worried.

'Mum?'

'It's OK . . . it's just . . . they are bloody REVOLTING!' I roar. Erin relaxes, relieved I've apparently come to my senses.

'Thank God!' says Brendan.

'We thought you were losing your mind! It's so good to see you laugh, Mum,' says Erin, visibly relieved.

Am I laughing or crying? I don't even know any more.

We spend the rest of the evening drinking in the garden. At some point Brendan hands me a burger and I eat a little bit of it. By ten I'm pissed and queasy.

'Mum, maybe you should drink some water and go to bed,' says Brendan, picking up the dirty plates and glasses. Erin helps him inside and I drain my glass. It's almost dark now. My eye is drawn to the old woman. She looks a bit pathetic – too grateful to have the attention of the small bird resting on her upturned palm. But there is something different about her – her chest appears to be glowing. I stand, unsteady on my bare feet, and semi-stagger towards the tree. Yes, her chest seems to be red, on fire almost. What sort of drunken apparition is this? A miracle? Will my suburban back garden be the new pilgrimage destination for all the newly widowed women of the world?

I stand facing the old woman. I am not imagining it. Her chest – her heart – is radiating a faint red light.

'Mum – are you OK?' shouts Erin. She jogs down to join me.

'Look – LOOK!' I say, pointing to the old woman.

'Oh cool!' says Erin. 'She glows in the dark!'

'But – how? Why?' I stutter.

Erin inspects the label, still hanging from the old lady's wrist.

'"Solar-Powered Old Lady's Heart." It's the sun, Mum, it powers her heart during the day so it lights up at night. Cute.'

'Oh. I see,' I say, managing a weak laugh.

If only it were that simple.

They take me to my bedroom – our bedroom – walking me up the stairs, and setting water on the table. I glare at the four pillows, Robert's two still set out on his side. I throw myself onto the bed fully dressed, hurl his pillows onto the floor and fall asleep spread-eagled bang in the centre, my dreams a fitful melange of glowing phone screens and solar-powered hearts.

8

I wake at 4 a.m. My mouth is dry and my head is banging. I reach out in the dark for the glass of water – and knock it straight onto the floor. I can't be bothered to get up and clear the mess, so I lie there thinking about the phone shoved into the recesses of the drawer next to me. How can an inanimate object be the nodal point for such turmoil and despair? There it sits, behind all my tissues, bed socks and pillow spritzers, anonymously poisonous, mutely indifferent to the suffering it has caused. Should I switch it on? What if she has messaged again? Unlikely. The last message was a month ago. Why would she message again now? That's magical thinking. Unless. *Unless.* She will now be able to see that the messages have been read. How did I not think of this before? Phones let you know when the recipient has opened the message, don't they? Her messages will now be marked as read. I panic, lying still in the dark. If I switch the phone back on will she have written again, berating 'Bob' for his silence, his cruel treatment of her? I can't risk it. I already feel like I'm going crazy. I don't know who I am any more, or who he was. Could it be that he had a split personality? Was he one man with me – distant, moody, and yes, controlling – and another with her? Was he able to be the loving, kind and decent man in his other life? The name Utterson comes into my mind. Who is Utterson? Ah. Yes. Months spent helping Brendan revise for his English GCSE. *The Strange Case of Dr Jekyll and Mr Hyde.*

Utterson is the nice lawyer who is obsessed with his friend's weird association with the satanic, violent Mr Hyde. Little does he know that they are one and the same person, the result of a weird scientific experiment which turns the respectable Dr Jekyll into the murderous Mr Hyde. Was Robert a Jekyll and Hyde split personality? Could I have been enduring the Hyde while this other woman languished in the affections of the kind Dr Jekyll? How can my grumpy, fastidious husband have been able to sustain another woman? Who would put up with my Robert without the ties of the mortgage, the kids and the years of habitual erosion of any resistance I may have had? It must be that he was quite different with her. There's no other explanation. Utterson spends the whole book shoving wills and secret letters into the back of his safe, too afraid or 'noble' to read them. Now I understand why he infuriated me so much – just open the bloody things and give yourself the gift of the truth! I was in denial. I was Utterson, and I could not utter what my heart must have known. Clearly. From the cold, dark vantage point of the middle of this marital bed, with the stark, laser-like appraisal of a middle-of-the-night mind, I can now see my husband for what he was – a cold-blooded cheat, a pompous, self-aggrandising fool, an insidious drip-feeder to my self-doubt. And still . . . still I can't square this reappraisal with the upfront, upstanding man I knew. How can a person be so coldly duplicitous? Time to rethink it all. No more hiding. For years I have made excuses – to myself, to the kids, to neighbours in the street – 'He's just tired,' 'He's a private person,' 'He's had a few too many, ha ha ha!' – and even though at the time I convinced myself they bought it, if I'm honest I always caught the slight twinkle of pity in their eyes. Even the kids. Brendan would never say anything, but he would often hug me for no reason. Erin would always be over-jolly if there was an atmosphere. All of the tiny adjustments we made to excuse Robert's sometimes cold behaviour, adaptations to let him carry on riding roughshod over our family life. How damaged our perfect little nuclear family sounds. How awful. I'm fuming. And I feel terrible. How can I have let it happen? I am weak. He was right. He was right to despise me. And what of this other woman? If I am weak, she must be strong. Why would he choose another sap for his bit on the side? Surely she must be everything I'm not – strong, confident, sexy, independent. Maybe she argued back? Maybe she gave as good as she got and he liked it? Maybe he metaphorically knocked the stuffing out of me and then hated the pathetic monster he created? Maybe he's not Dr Jekyll, but Dr Frankenstein – he created a monster and needed to destroy it.

My Gothic roll is interrupted by Brendan going to the bathroom next door. He's probably still playing games on his computer. I listen while he pees, flushes the chain and washes his hands. He's a good boy. He has always been a good boy. Did I let him down? We have never once spoken about his dad, even though I sometimes detected a slight longing for a warmer father–son bond. I swatted it down. Like so many things.

On his way back to his room I hear Brendan pause outside my door. He pushes it open a few inches and sticks his head in to check on me.

'Hi,' I whisper, 'I'm awake.'

Without saying a word he tiptoes to the bed and crawls in beside me, just like he used to do whenever Robert was away. Brendan always said our bed was the comfiest place in the world, and although Robert never allowed the children in our bed, even when they were tiny, I always loved it when Brendan crept in beside me during the night. Waking up with his gentle warm breath on my neck was so lovely. As he got older he used to come in and lie beside me for a chat if Robert was out at the pub and I was lying reading. We'd always have such good chats. I always marvelled at the sweet young man he was becoming.

'You OK, Mum,' he asks quietly in the dark.

'Yes. Just thinking.'

'About . . .?'

'Dad.'

I always refer to Robert as 'dad' with the kids. Not 'your dad' but 'Dad', like he was my dad too. In many ways it felt like it. He was certainly the Man of the House, and in charge of most things.

'What about Dad?' asks Brendan.

I sigh. What to say? Just because your children are grown-up it doesn't mean you can be totally open with them about your feelings. The maternal instinct – the Mother's Oath – is to protect your children from all harm. That includes the truth, if necessary.

'Just about how weird it feels that he's not here. Death is so weird. Just a permanent and ongoing absence.'

Brendan is silent in the dark. When he finally speaks his voice is hesitant, boyish.

'Yeah . . . I guess, for me anyway, it doesn't feel . . . like he's gone . . .?'

'How do you mean? Like you don't believe it yet? It hasn't sunk in?'

'No, I believe it, I just . . . I don't know, I suppose it's because I never really felt he was there anyway. I mean, he *was* there but kind of *not there* as well. If that makes sense.'

I gulp. So it wasn't just me. Robert had a defensive aura, a 'don't come too close' electric field around himself. The first day we dropped Brendan at Uni I remember wincing as Robert roughly patted him on the back during an awkward hug. Brendan had gone in hard for a big embrace and Robert just froze. None of us said anything, but we all felt it – 'Don't let's be silly'. It's what Robert always said if the kids were affectionate. Even with me he would often shrug my arm away from his side if we were walking anywhere and I reached for him.

I reach across the duvet and pat Brendan's hand.

'I think I know what you mean,' I say.

'I'm not trying to be horrible – I loved him and I miss him – but I wish we'd been closer. I always wanted him to hang out with us. I mean, I wanted him to *want* to hang out with us. But he seemed far away. Like he lived in a different reality but under the same roof.'

I say nothing, but I squeeze his hand. Tears start to roll silently down my cheeks. I wonder if Brendan knows I always felt exactly the same way? I can't tell him. Even now, after all I have come to know and realise in the last twenty-four hours, I feel a sense of loyalty. It's not a choice – it's become an instinct. Don't speak ill of the dead – even if that dead person has since revealed themselves to be a lying, cheating bastard who, if you're brutally honest, was a bit of a control freak who routinely withheld affection. Why? To what end?

'How about Erin?' I ask. 'How does she feel? Have you talked to her about it?' Maybe it was easier with Erin – a dad and his daughter can have a special bond that a son can't get near.

'A bit. She was a bit closer to him than me, I guess. But she always worried about you.'

'Me?' I try not to sound panicked.

'Yeah. She says that you always looked a bit . . . sad.'

I flinch silently.

'Sad? Me? About what?' I say finally, trying to sound nonplussed.

'She said she never knew. She just thought you looked sad. That's why she is always so cheerful, she reckons. To cheer you up. To stop you looking so worried.'

Oh great. So not only was he a liar and a philanderer, but he has now left me to pick up the pieces of the emotional damage he's caused to our two children – a son who felt paternal indifference and a daughter who has become co-dependent with her depressed mum. Really winning at Dead Father of the Year, Robert.

We lie in silence listening to the wind in the trees outside. The weather is turning, the unusually glorious English summer reverting to type. Brendan is the first to break the silence. I can sense his anxiety. Has he said too much?

'Mum?'

'Yes?'

'I know he loved us. I know he loved you.'

'Do you?' I ask.

'Yeah.'

A few moments later he starts snoring gently. I curl my fingers around his and close my eyes. All these years I wasn't alone. They knew. They sensed it too. Of course they did. I think about the word 'bubble'. The government has just announced further unlocking of social distancing measures. You can now form a 'bubble' with another household. The trouble with our family is we always lived in our own singular bubbles anyway. Try as we might, Robert kept himself so secure inside his own space that we all silently retreated into ours. There was no family bubble. How can four people live under the same roof in such a divided way? We were experts at social distancing long before the virus. Oh the irony.

I don't know how I manage it, but I fall asleep and when I wake up it's morning. I try to shake off the night horrors and head downstairs, my head thick with gin and sleep, my legs wobbly. Brendan is playing loud music now and has set the table for breakfast.

'Morning, Mumsicle!' shouts Brendan above the music.

'TURN IT DOWN!' I shout, taking a glass from the sink and filling it with water.

'Someone's got a sore head today!'

He turns the music off and hands me a glass of orange juice. I wave it away, queasy.

'ERIN!' shouts Brendan up the stairs, 'BREAKFAST!'

Erin shuffles in, rubbing her eyes like a cartoon bear and yawning elaborately.

'What time is it?' she asks, squinting at the clock.

'Breakfast time!' says Brendan, taking a tray of bacon, sausages, tomatoes and mushrooms from the oven where they have been keeping warm. 'Fried or scrambled?' he asks, poised at the hob.

'I don't want eggs,' I mutter. I don't want any of it, but I'll have to try.

'Brendan, it's Shit O'Clock! Why have you dragged me out of bed?!' wails Erin, whacking him as she goes to the fridge.

'I just thought it would be nice to have breakfast together. You know, at BREAKFAST TIME, like the good old days!'

I shoot him a look. He catches my eye and smiles. Robert once literally dragged him out of bed at midday on a Sunday, ranting that it was a disgraceful waste of time to spend 'the best part of the day festering in your pit!' Does Brendan remember our conversation in the middle of the night? He is whistling now, seemingly oblivious.

We sit and eat, me forcing tiny pieces of bacon into my mouth while the kids stuff loaded forks into theirs.

'Oh by the way, Mum, Jenni says can she bubble with us,' Erin says.

'What?' I ask, trying to soften the blow of food into my gurgling stomach by slathering jam on my toast.

'The two-household bubble thing. She came over last night, but you were sparko. She was pretty pissed. She said something about she can't stand another day couped up with her husband – but Ellis is so lovely! – and her car won't start, so she can't drive anywhere to see anyone else and it would make sense to bubble with us?'

'Fine,' I say. 'Whatever.' The only bubble I can focus on right now is in my stomach. The bacon is making me queasy.

'Yeah, I said it was OK if she comes round this morning.'

'Did you? Why?' I'm in a panic now. I don't want anyone coming in here today. I have nothing to say to anyone. I'm in shock. In mourning. In mourning for a life I never really had.

'Chill, Mum. Jenni is cool,' says Brendan, mopping up the grease on his plate with a slice of bread. I think I might vomit.

'I don't want to be in a bubble with anyone today!' I say, getting up and going to the toilet.

'OK. Don't worry, Mum,' says Erin, shooting Brendan another concerned look.

In the loo I splash my face with water. It is saggy, exhausted. A bubble? I can just about hold it together with my children. The tension of not saying what I have just recently discovered is unbearable – I want to scream 'Your father had an affair!', and it's taking all my mental energy not to. How will I be able to hold it in in front of anyone else?

There's a knock at the front door and I hear Erin jog into the hallway to answer it.

'Hi Jenni!' says Erin, like they are long-lost relatives.

Oh Christ. She's keen.

'Hi hi hi! Is this a good time?'

'Yeah, come in – we just had breakfast.'

'Oh, I can come back later if you like? I'm just desperate to get out of the house, ha ha ha!'

Please please please tell her to come back later. Don't let her in, don't let her in, don't let her in.

'No, don't be daft, come in!'

Shit shit shit.

'Thanks! I brought some croissants – the farmers' market is back on, so I beat a path through all the bastards buying sourdough for ten quid.'

'Ooh lovely. I'll pop them in the oven.'

'Are we supposed to be in the garden? Shall I go through?'

Please no, don't let her go into the garden. The statues. She'll see all the statues. I can't cope with that. Not right now.

'Yes, go through – I'll bring some coffee out.'

I hear Jenni open the back door as Erin fills the kettle. Brendan mutters something, but I can't catch it. Could I just stay in here? I could pretend I've fainted? Make out the key has jammed in the lock and I can't get out? I could live in here, if I can make a bed out of the laundry in the utility room adjoining the loo. I could totally live in here. They could slide toast under the door, and there's a tap for water. I could do cave art with jam and butter. I'd get hairy and pale, but at this point in time the life of a hermit seems infinitely preferable to the imminent humiliation of seeing Jenni doubled up in mirth at my expense. I stare at myself in the mirror. Last night's mascara is streaked down my cheeks, my face looks at least a decade older than yesterday and my mousey hair is now streaked with lockdown grey.

It's no good. I will have to face it. I could claim it was all ironic. I could pretend I had a mini stroke. I could say it's a memorial garden for Robert – she wouldn't dare laugh then.

Gingerly, I unlock the door and creep into the kitchen. Through the back-door window I can see Jenni, Erin and Brendan. They are standing like the three wise monkeys facing my statue park. Worryingly, no one is laughing. I can tell by their backs – straight, still, serious. Maybe they are discussing who is going to call the funny farm? Am I going mad? Just like Robert to leave me with that conundrum and no one to put me straight.

I take a deep breath and compose my face into a mask of amused indifference. I go outside.

'Morning!' I say breezily. 'I see you're admiring my new purchases?'

Jenni turns and surveys me quizzically. Maybe she will be gentle with me.

She considers her position for a moment.

'What the ACTUAL fuck?' she says, bursting out laughing.

I smile a Mona Lisa smile. I say nothing.

'Mum went a bit mad with the old plastic, didn't you, Mum?' says Brendan, coming and putting his arm around me.

'Yes, looks like it!' I laugh. 'I don't know what came over me!'

Jenni doesn't wait for an invitation – she sets off down the patio steps to inspect everything. She has no boundaries. None.

'I mean . . . these are just . . . I had no idea . . . that you were such a collector . . .'

'Well, I'm not really, it's kind of a joke really—'

'. . . of ABSOLUTE SHITE!'

Jenni laughs so hard I can't help but join in.

'I mean, these are just – extraordinary! Look at this mole! Hello, little moley, peeping up out of the ground. You're revolting! And the deer – how twee! The frogs with – what are they, guitars? No, they're banjos! Of course! A frog wouldn't play a guitar – a banjo is far more folksy!'

I chuckle indulgently. But who am I indulging?

Erin comes to stand next to me. I can sense her protectiveness.

'Mum likes them, don't you, Mum? I mean, it's funny, she thinks they're funny, don't you, Mum?'

She's always tried to protect me.

'Yes, I mean I know they're silly, grotesque even. But I felt I had to have them.'

'Really?' Jenni stops her inspection for a moment and takes a long hard look at me. She registers something. I'm not sure what. Maybe I look pleading, but she stops laughing and softens. She wanders over to the children and the old lady.

'Well, these are nice . . .' she says in a placatory tone.

'Oh not really, I just—'

'No, they are, they are really sweet actually. I can see what you've done here.'

I can't.

'What have I done?' I ask.

'It's you. You and Brendan and Erin. And the robin in her hand – is that Robert?'

A wave of horror washes through me. Oh God. She's right. It is me. Me and the kids. But the robin? It's not Robert. The robin is me as well.

'Yes, yes, I just thought they looked sweet together,' I lie. 'A way for us all to remember him but let him go.'

Erin and Brendan go to put the croissants in the oven and make coffee. Jenni doesn't wait for an invitation to sit down and heads straight for the garden bench, beckoning me to join her.

'Is this two metres apart?' says Jenni, brushing some fallen leaves off the seat. 'Sod it, who cares? It's all a load of bullshit anyway. Totally arbitrary. They are just trying to make us all think it's that easily controlled – "As long as you stay precisely two metres apart and sing the national anthem every time you wash your hands you'll be absolutely fine – probably! The kids can't go back to school, but we can open the shops because it's all about money money money – we never liked state education much anyway!"'

Jenni is settling in for a long rant. Time was I'd have joined her. I'd have been so switched on to it all. I was a card-carrying Labour member for years. Even flirted with the Socialist Workers for a while at college – they just seemed so *sure*. And I liked that. It's all changed now. I wasn't really allowed to be 'loony-leftie'. I try to nod my approval, but my head is full of Robert. His other woman. Did they ever come here while I was out? Maybe they sat, hands entwined, on this very bench, wondering when they could break it to me?

'I mean, ridiculous. I heard from someone's sister-in-law who works on the underground that they're going to reduce it to one metre soon anyway – "When the science allows" – load of bollocks, "the science"! All those bald buggers looking shifty and shitting themselves at the daily briefings – all in the government's pocket! There is no independent science now! It's not a thing any more! They sack anyone who isn't strictly on message! It's a junta!'

I swallow hard, trying to push down my rising fury. How could he?

'It's all about the shops, the pubs, the restaurants, the tourist industry. They don't care if people drop down dead in the street as long as they're in a queue for Primark. It's not about public health. It's a cull. A Gammon Cull. Kill off all the old bastards, save a fortune in social care. All those poor old people in care homes – sitting ducks. Wouldn't surprise me if we find out they knew all along and deliberately withheld positive test results when they sent the elderly back – super spreaders in hot little sitting rooms. Makes me so angry!'

Jenni takes a breath long enough to look at me. With a jolt I realise I am crying.

'Oh God, sorry, Angela – I'm being really insensitive.'

I say nothing. 'It's not that. It's got nothing to do with what you're saying,' I want to say.

She goes on.

'I'm sorry. Typical me – banging on about politics, not thinking about the person in front of me who has actually been through all this first hand. Sorry. Here I am barging in on a Sunday, desperate to see someone who isn't him indoors, adorable though he is, and ranting about the government when you are still in the depths of grief about Robert. Of course you are. It's still very new. You must miss him so much.'

'He had an affair.'

It's out of my mouth before I even know it. No going back now.

Jenni freezes. What have I done? She doesn't want to hear all this.

'Someone has been messaging him. I switched his phone on yesterday morning,' (is it only yesterday morning? Feels like a year) '. . . and some woman had left messages. She doesn't know he's dead. He had another phone apparently. He was cheating on me.'

Jenni blinks a few times. She opens her mouth to say something, but I can see she is struggling for words. She cannot compute that dull old boorish Robert, the man she has seen dutifully washing his car every Saturday morning, had it in him to find another woman.

Finally she speaks.

'Well. What a cunt,' she says.

Bang on cue Erin and Brendan arrive with a plate of warm croissants.

'Breakfast Number Two!' says Brendan, setting the plates down on the garden table.

Jenni keeps her eyes on me. 'You know what? I don't actually feel that hungry. I was just coming to ask your mum if she fancies a walk?' Jenni's eyes burn into mine, willing me to pick up her hint.

'Oh that would be nice,' I say, eager to get out of the garden and let rip. Now that the cat is out of the bag I want to let it run amok. 'Let me just throw some joggers on.'

I need to talk to someone. I can't call Sally. She'll just say 'I told you so!' – I don't think she ever liked Robert. I feel rage and shame and hurt bubbling up inside me and I can't let it erupt all over our garden. I don't even care who I tell – I'd go to the corner shop and tell Margaret. I might rent a billboard outside. 'Local Covid Victim in Love Rat Shocker!' I'd even use a photo. Just so that everyone knew. If it wasn't for the kids.

Upstairs I'm breathing hard. What have I just done? My hand hovers uncertainly over the drawer. The phone. Should I take the phone and show Jenni? Maybe there will be a new message? I pull the drawer open and throw all the contents onto the bed, stuffing the silent poison into my pocket. In for a penny. I feel full of energy. It's new.

I tumble down the stairs and call through the hallway. I don't want Erin and Brendan to see me. Who knows what I might say?

'Mona! Walkies!' I shout, trying to sound vaguely sane. Mona, who has been snoring away, oblivious to my troubles, comes trotting out, excited and ready to go. Jenni follows her and fusses over her to fill the silence. We can't speak yet.

Outside we walk for a couple of minutes without saying anything much apart from to remark that everyone is making much more effort with their front gardens since lockdown. Smart paving and blousy window boxes have replaced patchy lawns and overgrown borders. How obsessed we are with how we appear from the outside. Instinctively Jenni seems to sense my need to put some distance between myself and ground zero. I don't want to say any more until we are in the neutral territory of the park. Once we pass through the gates, Jenni speaks.

'Right. Tell me everything. Who when where why how!'

'I don't know,' I say. 'He was very careful.'

'How long have you known?'

'Twenty-seven hours,' I say. Not that each minute has been a torture or anything.

'What? Only since yesterday? I mean, are you a hundred per cent sure?'

'What would you think?' I say, taking the phone from my pocket and switching it on. I feel emboldened by having Jenni with me. We will do this together.

The phone lights up and we both stare at the screen waiting for the evidence to surface. No new messages. I select the texts in question and hand the phone back to her. She reads them silently, shaking her head slowly.

'Well . . . yes, I must admit, it looks like he had someone else on the go. What a bastard.'

I don't say anything. It stings to hear her appraisal. Maybe a part of me had hoped she would come up with another story, and infuriating as it is, I can't help but feel a tiny bit protective. What am I protecting – Robert? Or my version of him? Our fake life? Our sham marriage?

'So. What are you going to do?' Jenni asks as we walk on. Mona sniffs every tree, every bench, every blade of grass. I tug at her lead, keen to keep moving.

'Do?' I ask. 'What do you mean "do"? What can I do? He's dead. I can't kick him out. I don't even get the pleasure of that.'

'But what about this woman – don't you want to find out who she is? What the story is?'

'I don't know. No. Yes. Not really. No. What's the point?' The idea of a confrontation – online or otherwise – with this mystery woman fills me with dread.

'Well, don't you think she should at least know he's dead?'

I stare at Jenni. 'Why? Why should I dignify her? I didn't get to know she existed – why should I tell her he no longer does? Let her stew. I can at least have that power.'

'I suppose so. It's just – it might help you to . . . move on?'

'I have moved on. He's gone.'

'I know but – this is a big deal, Angela. This is huge. You two were always so . . .'

'What? What were we? "Stable"? "Strong"?'

'Well . . . yes, I suppose so.' Jenni looks like she's starting to regret this.

'You can never tell, can you? That's what I've been thinking these past twenty-seven hours. Nobody can ever tell. It might have looked like it was all sunshine and roses, but deep down it was actually a pretty uncomfortable, distant, disappointing marriage. He wasn't very nice to me. I can see it now. He treated me like an irritation. I was an irrelevance. Even when he tried – guilt probably – it felt like he was being charitable. He made me feel like I was begging for even a small scrap of respect. His moods. His fussiness.'

'What they call coercive control,' says Jenni flatly.

'What?'

'That's what it's called – coercive control.'

I blink. 'What do you mean?' I know what she means. I know what it is. I know she's right.

'I mean, I'm not saying he was an abuser but . . .' says Jenni gently.

She leaves a space for me to speak, but I am suddenly mute. I don't want to acknowledge this. Not with a name. The ground starts to crack under my feet. The horizon shudders. My vision is blurry. I feel like I might faint.

'Shall we sit down?' asks Jenni, gently steering me to the

nearest bench. Mona pulls on the lead, refusing to budge. Jenni takes her from me and tugs us both to a seat.

We sit and I gather myself. Something is shifting inside me. I can feel ice melting and falling in sheets from my highest peaks, scales flaking from my eyelids and shafts of light shining onto my darkest corners. I want it to stop. Rewind the clock.

'I did notice, you know,' says Jenni finally.

I say nothing. I feel like a suspect in an interrogation. No comment.

'It was subtle at first. Most couples bicker and tease each other, but with you I always felt uncomfortable – like it wasn't a level playing field. I hate to say this when the man isn't here any more to defend himself, but I always thought he was a bit of a bastard to you. Sorry.'

I remain silent. I want to hear more.

'. . . and I suppose because I've been doing this work with Women's Aid I became a bit more sensitive to it. The little things. Not every abuser is a puncher. Some prefer to dominate in ways that aren't physically obvious. No bruises. Limiting your social circle, putting you down in front of other people, controlling your access to money, isolating you from support. Did you never wonder why I stopped coming over?'

I can't remember her 'stopping' – we just sort of grew apart. Didn't we?

'He didn't like me,' says Jenni.

'Don't be ridiculous! Of course he did!' I say, surprised at her neediness. She seemed stronger than this.

'No, he didn't, but it's OK. I think he knew I saw him.'

'What do you mean?'

'He came over on Boxing Day last year, after we'd been round for drinks on Christmas Eve. He brought an earring I'd lost in your kitchen.'

'Yes, I remember.' Why is she talking about this now?

'He didn't come in – said you were busy and he had to get back – but he stood on the doorstep and said that you had been so drunk with me on Christmas Eve that Christmas Day had been all but ruined. I laughed, but he looked really cross.'

What?

'I wasn't drunk on Christmas Eve, I only ever have two glasses on Christmas Eve maximum, precisely because Robert liked a tight ship on Christmas Day!' I protest.

'I know. I said that. I said you weren't drunk at all. He said I gave you Baileys and that it sent you over the edge.'

'Oh yes, I did have a Baileys. So what?'

I may be stalling, but I remember how moody he was on Christmas Day that year. It was the first year the kids had had to 'come home' for Christmas and I had wanted it to be special, but it was a bit of a let-down. They had slept in and not shown the usual excitement over their stockings. I just put it down to them being grown-ups, but Robert had had an outburst (alcohol, I assumed) just after the Queen's speech in which he said that it 'wasn't the same this year' and that he hadn't enjoyed his lunch. I'd made an extra effort with tea, and he did perk up when everyone praised his Christmas cake.

'Angela – he told me that he thought it would be best if I didn't come over again.'

I'm stunned. She must have misunderstood him.

'What did he say? He was probably joking!' People often misunderstood his dark sense of humour. I know I did.

'He wasn't joking, Angela. He looked me in the eye and said, "Perhaps it would be best if you made other friends in the street" – and I was so shocked I just said OK.'

I can't think of what to say, so I just say, 'Right.'

'So it's not so much of a surprise to me that he might have been cheating too. It fits the pattern. It's coercive control and it's a hidden crime.'

'Hang on!' I say, unable to stay silent any longer. 'He may have been a liar and a cheat and a bit bloody horrible sometimes, but I think it's a bit of a stretch to say he was a criminal!'

I don't know why I feel the urge to defend him. Shame? My cheeks are burning. I know she's right. Deep in my heart I know she's right.

'OK. Sorry. I don't mean that. I didn't want to upset you. I'm not saying he was a criminal – I just want you to know that it is taken seriously – by me, anyway. People like that – like Robert – men like Robert can get worse. It's a spectrum. That's all I'm saying. I'm sorry. I'll shut up now. It's just kind of been my thing recently.'

We don't speak for a few minutes. I'm angry and confused and scared. I feel exposed. Am I that weak, pathetic woman that is open to bullying and intimidation?

'And no,' says Jenni finally, breaking the tension, 'it's not your fault.' It's like she can read my mind. 'You didn't deserve it, invite it or provoke it.'

We sit in silence for a long minute.

'So are you going to call her?' says Jenni, changing the subject.

'No. I don't know. Maybe.'

Perhaps I should?

'I'll do it if you like,' says Jenni. 'On my phone. Then she won't know who it is calling. I can even block my caller ID.'

Right now I don't care about her. Right now all I can think of is the marriage, my life, disintegrating before my eyes.

'Look, I'm sorry. I don't want to push you. I just think you need support. But what do I know? Let's go and get a drink, eh?

The pizza place on the corner is open for take-outs – they do beer in plastic glasses. You've had a big shock. Come on.'

I follow Jenni reluctantly through the park. Coercive control. These sorts of things happen to other women. Women in poverty on council estates. Women with tattoos and several children with different fathers. Women with little education and no self-esteem. Well, I might be a bit lacking in the confidence department, but I have a university degree in Politics, Philosophy and Economics, I've been married for over a quarter of a century and we had plenty of money and our own home. I am not the sort of woman who ends up in an abusive relationship, coercive or otherwise.

So how did I? The answer is I don't know. Robert was there for me at a time when I was struggling, I suppose. It wasn't really a breakdown, just emotional exhaustion. Teaching was hard work, and I put a lot into those kids. Plus, I'd always been a bit shaky if I'm honest – a bit emotionally weak. Robert pitched up at a time in my life when I couldn't make decisions. He was so sure. He decided we should get married and I was relieved. He was good to me, took on all the things I hated doing – paperwork, DIY, finances – and he could be funny. Early on he was attentive – so much so that people would remark upon it. It was only after a few years that his attention started to become more negative and critical. Little things at first. The way I stacked the dishwasher. The inaccuracy of my reverse parking. My inability to iron a decent crease in his favourite trousers. Normal stuff. Inconsequential. I didn't really mind because he was mostly right. It was much later that the meaner things started – the ridicule in public, the tighter control of money, the social isolation – and by then I just put it down to grumpy middle age. I still remembered the protective man I married all those years ago. But what was he protecting?

Jenni buys us a pint of lager each and we sit on the grass in the sunshine. The bins are overflowing with pizza boxes. Despite my hangover I gulp the beer down, keen to take the edges off my nerves. I finish my drink in a couple of minutes and wait for it to do its work.

'Let's do it,' I say. 'You're right. I want to know who she is.'

Jenni looks surprised.

'Really? I don't want you to do anything you don't want to do.'

I hand her the phone.

'The number is in the missed calls section. She tried to ring him first.'

Jenni, despite her protestations, seems exhilarated. Is she getting some vicarious thrill from this?

She hides her caller ID then taps the number into her phone. She pauses, looks at me. Her finger hovers over the green 'call' icon. I nod and she presses it. She maintains eye contact while waiting for The Woman to answer the phone. It rings and rings. She's not answering. Maybe she's a serial cheat and never answers unless she knows who it is? Maybe this is a normal day for her – receiving anonymous calls from angry wives?

Jenni is just about to hang up when the ring tone ends and someone answers.

'Hello?' asks the disembodied voice of my dead husband's mistress. Jenni puts her on loudspeaker.

'Hello – who is this?' asks Jenni.

There is a brief pause.

'Sorry, I don't know who *you* are – your number didn't come up,' says the woman. She's clearly shifty. She sounds young. The Younger Woman. What a cliché.

'Oh it's just, you don't know me, it's just – I'm doing a survey in the area on . . . litter collection and wondered if you had any thoughts?'

'Sorry is this a cold call? Because I'm busy,' says the woman briskly.

What the hell is Jenni doing? Who would believe that? I shake my head at her and gesture for her to hang up. I've heard enough. Despite the fact I haven't met her and she doesn't even know I am listening I feel cheapened and dirty. I don't want any contact with her. It just makes it all more sordid. And real.

'No, it's not a cold call, we're not selling anything!' says Jenni, adding a nervous laugh. 'So, shall we start with which area you are based in, Miss . . .?'

'Philips,' says the woman, clearly distracted. A baby cries somewhere near her.

'Sorry, I'm going to have to go – the baby needs feeding and I don't really have time for this right now, thanks.'

She hangs up.

'Did you hear what I heard?' Jenni asks.

'The baby?'

'Yes.'

'She's got a baby. Maybe she needed someone with money.'

'Maybe the baby is . . .'

'No! You don't think? Oh God. Oh bloody hell.' Could he be the father? It doesn't bear thinking about.

'Jesus. I'm sorry Angela. Maybe that wasn't such a good idea.'

Great. Now I have to withhold not only the fact that their dad was a cheat but also the existence of a potential half sibling from Brendan and Erin.

'At least we know her surname. Philips,' says Jenni. 'Do you want me to write it down?'

'Oh I think I'll remember,' I say.

'What do we do now – call back and tell her? I mean, if she's got a baby – I'm not saying it is his, maybe it's not, who knows, we just can't guess that, I mean—'

But we both know what we heard and what this looks like.

'Jenni,' I say, not really knowing how I am going to end the sentence. 'He had an affair, with what sounds like a young woman, he got her pregnant then disappeared. During that disappearance he conveniently contracted Covid-19 and died. Sadly. I mean sadly for her, not for me. Sadly for the baby, who no doubt now has no means of support. I need to think about this. I'm going to get another drink.'

I head back to the pizza place and order two more pints. What to do? I'm so angry. It would have been easy to yank the phone from Jenni's hands and shout 'He's dead! Sorry! I know about you, but it's too late now because he's DEAD, so don't bother calling back!' But then the baby cried. The baby. I didn't factor in a baby. Not in my wildest middle-of-the-night raging did I imagine that Robert, nearer grandpa age than doting dad, could have fathered another child. This feels like the biggest betrayal of all.

We drink our beer and Jenni tries to lift my spirits by telling me about Denise's latest charity drive – she's holding a socially distanced tea party in the street with bunting, a jazz singer and a Bake Off.

'It's to raise money for the NHS wobble rooms – some of the staff have been so traumatised by watching people die alone in

Intensive Care Units that they are suffering a kind of PTSD, so Denise is going to raise enough money to buy them all hand cream and a *Woman's Weekly* for their tea breaks.'

Jenni lets out a derisive laugh.

I don't respond. Jenni puts her hand on my arm.

'Look, Angela – I'm really sorry, OK. I can only imagine what you're feeling right now. Makes me realise how bloody good Ellis is.'

'It's just . . . you know when you have a nightmare and it's so real, so incredibly believable and detailed, then you wake up and you have to spend several moments telling yourself that it was just a dream? It feels like that – but the opposite way round. I'm waking up and finding that what I thought was good was just . . . not.' Jenni rubs my arm.

'Look at it this way, Ang – you're free. Now he's gone you're free to work out what it is YOU want to do – without someone breathing so hard down your neck that you don't know what you want any more.'

I don't feel free. I don't know what to do. I am exploding inside, but meanwhile life goes on. Children nag their parents to let them go in the taped-off playground, teenagers skateboard up and down the paths, terrifying the already petrified older people out for their one-hour respite from shielding. The shops are cautiously open and there is a sense of normality returning. Not for me. Normality is a million miles away on another planet in another epoch.

'I'm going home,' I say, suddenly agoraphobic. I can't stand the breeze on my skin all of a sudden.

'OK, let's go,' says Jenni, jumping up to walk alongside me. Mona stretches then tugs on the lead.

'Come on!' I bark, yanking her hard. She rolls her eyes at me and trots behind us.

We arrive back in the street and walk past Denise's front garden. She is dead-heading the geraniums placed in a sterile row along her pathway.

'Hi girls!' she says gamely.

'Hi,' says Jenni in a 'don't mess with us' way. Denise clocks it but carries on regardless, flinging her gardening tools down and grabbing her face mask.

'What are you two doing out and about?'

I swear any minute she's going to ask to see our papers then arrest us.

'We've just had a couple of pints on the green from the pizza place,' says Jenni. She knows this will scandalise Denise, but she doesn't care.

'Ooh that's . . .' She can't think what to say that won't sound horribly judgemental, so she just leaves it hanging.

'Busy, was it?' she asks nervously, tugging at her mask which has slipped down from her nose.

'Packed. People queuing round the block at the pizza place. Most people didn't even want pizza. They're just there for the beer!' says Jenni, clearly goading now.

'Ooh I know – it's awful, isn't it? What's wrong with people? We order our wine from Ocado. There's no need for dangerous behaviour – queuing for beer, honestly!'

'It is totally reprehensible. Me and Angela were saying that, while we sat on the grass with our beers. We didn't have a pizza either. But still, it's the principle, isn't it?'

Denise looks confused. 'Well quite,' she says uncertainly.

She narrows her eyes and changes the subject, focusing on me.

'And how are *you* doing?' she asks, tilting her head to one side and adopting the same tone of voice she uses for toddlers.

'I'm OK,' I say, resisting the Tourette's urge to scream 'My husband was shagging someone else!' just to make her jump.

'Well, I'm always here – *at home* – if you need me. Unless I'm doing a cake drop-off at the hospital. Just give me a shout if you need anything.' She smiles. I actually envy Denise. She is loving Lockdown Life. She has a renewed sense of purpose.

'Don't forget your food bank donations, ladies!' says Denise, gesturing to the basket on her front window. 'We especially need pasta, tinned vegetables and fruit, lentils etc. But please – no junk food! Last week someone actually put in a large packet of Belgian chocolate biscuits – from Marks and Spencer! I mean, honestly!'

'Seriously?' says Jenni sarcastically. Denise doesn't catch it and carries on.

'Yes! I mean, these people are on the breadline! They need the very basics, not fancy chocolate snacks!'

'I quite agree, Denise. Why anyone would want a delicious treat to dunk in their pauper's tea every once in a while is beyond me.'

Denise frowns. 'You know what I mean. It's not essential. It's frivolous. Plus, the poor are more inclined to develop type two diabetes, which is a key co-morbidity in Covid cases,' she finishes smugly. I can't stop my eyes flicking to Denise's generous belly and well upholstered arms.

'You know what, Denise, you are all heart!' says Jenni, pulling me away.

Jenni tells me to call her later, and not to do anything silly. I'm not sure what she means – don't top yourself or don't stand on the roof in a hula hula skirt singing 'Una Paloma Blanca'? 'Don't do anything silly . . .' I think she's worried I'm going to call the woman again and shout obscenities at her. I won't. I don't want to hear her voice again. I'll be sick. I go in and head straight upstairs. No sign of Erin or Brendan. Thank God. I lie on the bed with the phone in my hand. Should I tell her? Miss Philips? I have to. It's only fair. If I were her, I would want to know. I can barely believe that not two days ago my biggest worry was how I was going to get rid of my Covid weight gain without dying of sober lockdown boredom, and now here I am lying on the bed wondering whether I should tell my husband's mistress – and possibly *their baby* – that he is dead. Funny old world.

I pick up the phone and write an experimental text.

'This is Robert's wife,' I type. Robert? Didn't she call him Bob? I can't refer to him as Bob. I carry on.

'I don't know who you are or what you think you were doing with my husband but I feel I ought to let you know that Robert died over three months ago. Please do not contact this number again. Leave me and my family alone to grieve in peace.'

It's abrupt, but it says everything – well almost everything – I want to say right now. I hit the send button. Lying back on the bed I realise I have been holding my breath. I let out a long exhale and close my eyes. Done. Surely to God she won't have the nerve to answer that? Tomorrow I will take the phone into the shed – Robert's shed – and smash it to pieces with a hammer.

9

17th July 2020

It has been a very hot day, and the evening sighs in relief as the sun slides behind the Victorian chimney stacks. It's the end of the school term today, but the parks, which would normally be filled with over-excited kids throwing water balloons at each other, are strangely quiet. This virus has taken so many milestone moments. When I was teaching, I always loved the last day of term. I'd come home laden with chocolates and cards and bouquets of flowers. Not any more.

Me and Jenni are having a glass of wine in the back garden. The statues have started to look at home in the garden now, the daisies sprouting around their feet, their claws, their paws and hooves.

'What was all that about?' says Jenni, gesturing at the frogs. She particularly dislikes the frogs, who are, in fairness, bloody grotesque.

'I don't know. I think I was going mad. I bought them the day I found out.'

I don't have to say any more. She knows what I am talking about. It's the first time either of us has raised the subject since that day in the park almost a week ago. I'm sure Jenni is much more in the 'let's talk this out' brigade than my 'bury it so far down then fill it with concrete' gang, but she is respectful and never forces me to confront it.

She considers me for a long beat.

'You know what you need?'

'No, but I have a feeling you're going to tell me . . .' I say.

'You need a date.'

I laugh. 'I need a date like I need a hole in the head.'

'Seriously. You should try to have some fun. There are loads of online dates happening. I saw it on the news. It's like the war – but without the bombing.'

'That's offensive! In what way is this like the war?'

'Well, the shortage of eggs and flour—'

'That's just because people have been going mental with banana bread, not because of a real supply chain issue!'

'OK, but still! And people having to pull together to get through against a fatal enemy, a brush with the old mortality and all that. It makes people horny.'

'Does it?'

'Well, it's done wonders for me and Ellis – not that we needed any help in that department.'

'Too much information, Jenni.'

'I'm serious – you should open yourself up to it! Just because we're older doesn't mean we should shut up shop sexually! It could be just what you need!'

'Seriously?' I ask. 'He's only been dead four months. People would talk.' I marvel at the casual way I can just say it like that – 'dead four months'.

'Sod them. They'll talk about you whatever you do.'

'What would Denise say?' I can get at least a five-minute break from scrutiny by allowing Jenni a comic rant about her nemesis.

'Ugh, that woman. The bloody tea party is tomorrow. She's been sending a dress code out via WhatsApp. Red, white and blue. Wimbledon theme. Strawberries and cream. It would have bloody ended last week! I thought she'd forgotten but oh no – "Because we didn't get to cheer on *our* Andy this year!" Still. At least we can have a laugh. Chat to a few people. Have a cake. Blimey, my fun bar has slipped dangerously low. I sound like you!'

I laugh.

'Seriously, though – why not? No one need ever know and it might actually give you a feeling of . . .'

'Revenge?' I say. Do I want revenge?

'Maybe. Why not? It can be very liberating. I once shagged an ex-boyfriend's brother the day after he dumped me.'

'Jenni!' I say, although she has ceased to shock me.

'I know. Terrible. Actually it might have been the day before he dumped me. I can't remember. The point is . . . it might make you feel better about yourself.'

'You think? Putting a profile picture up with the lighting low enough to make me look less than a thousand years old then waiting to be overlooked by men fatter and more boring than me? Yes, I can see what you're driving at.'

'They're not all like that. There are sites for . . . the more mature lady.'

'Yes, and they're full of deluded women like me, refusing to accept that men our age don't trade in one old banger for another, they want a younger model with a smooth face and fully functioning womb.'

'That's a cliché. A lot of men are clear that they definitely DON'T want more kids. There are lots of lovely men out there who are just like you – divorced, recently widowed, looking for someone nice to have a drink with, talk to . . .'

'I'm sure there are, but nice men my age who aren't married are either gay or serial killers.'

'Don't be ridiculous!' laughs Jenni. 'You should give it a go! I'll help you!'

I change the subject.

'What are you wearing to the tea party?' I ask. We'll have to dress up or we'll get sent home by Denise.

'I was thinking a pair of crotchless knickers and a sequinned boob tube. You?'

'I've got a blue dress somewhere, and I'm making scones with strawberry jam and cream, so that's the Union Jack sorted.'

'That's cheating! Oh God, it's going to be awful. Let's get pissed on Pimm's!'

'No alcohol. Denise says that if we are to maintain social distancing for the whole time, then we have to be sober. Haven't you seen her latest epistle on the WhatsApp?'

'I don't read it any more. I get the rage if I read it.'

'So no, we can't get pissed. Maybe we can sneak off before the singalong? Come round the back and we'll have some wine in the garden.'

Lying in bed I start to think about what Jenni has said. Maybe it would be good to get back on the scene? What's the old saying – if you can't get over one, get under another? I shudder. I have no urge to get under anything except my duvet. Wouldn't it be good, though, to get back at him? I'm also dimly aware that a part of me might like to meet somebody else for the company, the cosy winter walks, the romance – as well as to stick two fingers up at Robert, who never missed an opportunity to tell me just how lucky I was to have him. 'She says she's going to leave!' he'd always joke whenever we were in public. 'But she knows no one else would have her!' Ha ha ha ha. Wouldn't it be good to prove him wrong?

I lie awake wondering what became of me. Time was I was a modestly attractive woman with a decent enough figure and just enough self-confidence to dress nicely and flirt a little bit in the staffroom at school. Whenever a young male teacher joined us – which wasn't very often, as male primary school teachers are as rare as hand sanitiser at Tesco's – I would stand back and watch as all the other women vied for his attention. Even the older married ladies would enjoy the little frisson they got when he opened a door for them, offered to make them tea or asked for their help on sports day. I would always get my fair share of attention, without even trying. What happened to that woman? She had a life wobble at precisely the moment a knight in shining armour was passing by; he scooped her up and told her he would be in charge from now on. And she let him. And it was nice for a while. And then she realised he wasn't a knight at all. Just a grumpy man who liked to be in charge. So she made the best of it.

An hour goes by. Two. I can't sleep. I give in and get up to make cocoa. Downstairs the house is quiet. Both Erin and Brendan have taken advantage of the partial unlocking to go to visit friends for the weekend. Who knows whether they will observe the guidance on limited numbers and staying outside. They took tents, but I doubt they'll use them. Images of illegal raves and street parties have been all over the news this weekend as young people, no doubt feeling untouchable and immune, gather to shake off the confines of the past four months. I can't blame them – I probably thought I was immortal at their age, and recent events have made it all too clear to me how caution and playing it safe have limited my life. I pour the milk into a saucepan and watch it start to simmer. Youth. Possibility. Excitement.

What harm could it do just to look?

I consider my laptop sitting innocently on the kitchen island, unaware of the Pandora's box it may be about to open. I snap the screen up and type 'Fifty plus dating,' already thrilling at the possibility of at least a vicarious romance.

Several sites pop up straight away. Silver Surfers. Match. eHarmony. Ourtime. Elite. All of them have the slight whiff of desperation. Or maybe that's just me. My finger hovers over the button on one site. I answer the initial questions. I am a woman. I am looking for a man. Simple. Then it asks me to enter my email and set a password. I pause. Dare I? Come on. Why not? Is this how Robert did it? Furtive middle of the night emails and texts on his secret burner phone? I input my first name, hair and eye colour (sort of beige and kind of grey), build ('curvy' – does 'curvy' mean having a fat belly? I don't really have boobs or a bum. Every time the daily Covid briefings talked about 'flattening the curve' I'd imagine a couple of pairs of Spanx), height (only five foot three – but men like shorter women, don't they? Robert always did. I wonder if she is short? Stop it. Let's not go there.) Profile picture. Hmmm. I search for the darkest, least recognisable image I have. Unfortunately, the only half decent one is a picture of me and Robert at a wedding last year. He hadn't wanted to go but I had made an effort, got my hair done and bought a dress. He had moaned about the money I'd 'wasted' – 'You've got five dresses in the wardrobe! Why do you need a new one every time we go anywhere? Look at this suit – I wear it to everything!' After the wedding he had cut my housekeeping back by twenty pounds a week for a whole month 'so that we can catch up' on the 'overspend.' I stare at his image for a few seconds – where is the man I thought I knew? Gone. I feel absolutely no guilt in cropping him out of the frame until all that is left of him is the hint of his shoulder. If only we could crop people out of our psyches so easily. The section where you describe your status is interesting. I tick 'widow', and it's a first. What a sad little word. But I don't feel the tears spring to my eyes anymore. Widow. Sounds like 'hello.' There is an option for people who are married 'unhappily', which strikes me as a bit like having your cake and eating it – who isn't unhappily married really? I can't think of any happily married couples. Apart from maybe Jenni and Ellis. It seems to me that boredom and drudgery come with the territory. That's what I always thought. Maybe I was wrong. Maybe I could have had a bit on the side too? It's not as easy for women, though, is it? Who would descale the kettle if both husband and wife were dipping out here, there and everywhere for dangerous liaisons? The 'Interests' checklist is the toughest. What to click? Cinema? Never go. Theatre? Ditto – unless you count the time Robert splashed out on the *Top Gear* live show. I half-heartedly add 'Gardening' and 'Cooking' to my profile, and it's done. That's it. I am now a merry widow looking for love with a full online profile. Is that how easy it is? No elaborate underwear, blow-dry and new frock for a night out on the tiles hoping to attract the attention of some drunk bloke at the bar? That's how we did it in my day. Nowadays it seems you can get anything online – tinned tomatoes, a degree, a husband. Do I take the next step and sign up with my bank details? I can't deny the feelings in my body – I feel giddy with excitement! I fumble around in my purse looking for my bank card, hands shaking. A hissing sound distracts me, and I remember the milk. It has boiled and is surging up over the rim of the pan. I lunge at the hob and switch it off. The cocoa can wait. In the time it has taken me to take the milk off the boil I have had three views on my profile page. Three! I panic. Instantly I want to take it down. My hand is shaking as I click on the three men who are up in the middle of the night, like me, looking for – what? Love? Companionship? Someone to talk to?

The first man is 'Mark, 57, Enfield' – his profile picture shows him splayed out across an unmade bed in what appears to be a plaid dressing gown. His eyes are approximating what I assume he thinks is a 'come hither' expression, which sadly gives him the appearance of being constipated. He probably is. No thanks. The next is George, 62, Turnham Green. George has a tooth missing at the front but doesn't mind because he grins broadly in his profile pic, which is taken in bad lighting and shot from under one of his many chins. I bypass George, 62, Turnham Green and click on Eric, 51, Broadstairs – not so much his location as an indication of how he manages to leave the house because he's about thirty stone. Bloody hell. Slim pickings in my age bracket. I bet none of the women on this site look as bad as any of these three men. Maybe I shouldn't have signed up to this 'seniors' site? I read in the paper once that even these flabby, balding and well past their sell-by date men will be searching for women half their age with twice their IQ. Depressing. I also read that, conversely, the younger man seeking an experienced older woman – a cougar? Is that what they're called? – is an actual thing and not just the stuff of romantic fiction wishful thinking. I close my seniors' profile and google 'Cougar dating'. Loads of sites. Blimey. Dating a younger man? I can't imagine anything more embarrassing than having to reveal my sagging, crêpey skin with its stretch marks, rogue hairs and southwards gravitational trajectory to a young, firm man used to airbrushed porn stars with no pubes and boobs like hot air balloons. Who are these women who have no such fears? I've always thought they are another figment of the male imagination – the sexy older woman who has somehow managed to maintain a supermodel figure, glossy hair and perfect nails as well as a rampant libido despite the ravages of age, life and loss? I don't know any women like that. None. All the women I know are either plump and sweetly matronly (Denise) or thin and hilariously caustic (Jenni). I'm definitely in the former category, and I can't imagine any young man getting his rocks off over my beige M&S waist-high 'Full Briefs' struggling to contain the wispy white pubic hairs which pop out on either side of the forgiving elastic, nor my greying full-cup bra with thick straps that dig in, and cups which are too small and bisect my boobs into four. Still, I'll never know if I don't try. Maybe the best way of getting over Robert's betrayal with a younger model is to get one myself. Why not?

I go through the same process of signing up, this time on a website called Cougars4You – for younger men looking for older women. The welcome page has a photo of a woman roughly a decade younger than me pulling her red top down to reveal her (probably enhanced) cleavage. She looks well up for it. I am nothing like her. I haven't got a red top, a cleavage, or indeed any desire to speak of, if you don't count Victoria sponge. I upload my photo and details, but when I reach the section on interests I am gobsmacked. The tick boxes are nothing like I have ever seen before. I don't even know what some of them are.

Fun with Food
Water sports
Rimming – giving
Rimming – receiving
Dogging
Anal
Adult Play

What the hell is Adult Play? Do you go round to their house and apply for a mortgage together? File a tax return? Take a trip to B&Q for some grout? Anal and dogging – I've heard of them of course. Rimming – I'm guessing it's got nothing to do with toilet bleach. Water sports? We once went to the Lake District and I had a go on a jet ski, but I fell in and had to be towed back with suspected whiplash. I'm not sure this is the site for me. It can't ALL be about sex, can it? Maybe I just need to navigate away from this page. I leave all the boxes blank and proceed to the profiles of the young men. Weird. A long line of profile pictures, names and ages. Most of the men are in their fifties, some in their sixties. I thought this was supposed to be for younger men and older women? Can't the wrinklies like me find what they want on the 'silver websites'? I don't want them clogging up my inbox with their hypertension and their haemorrhoids. I spot one man who is thirty-five, but I just couldn't. Far too young. Where are the men in their forties? A decade younger is just about right, I think. I wouldn't want anyone to meet us together and ask how old my son is.

What the hell am I thinking? Am I doing this? Am I actually planning on dating a younger man? Where would we go? What would we do? You can't just meet up with strangers and go out for dinner these days, can you? They have to be in your bubble, don't they? Or is it OK if they're two metres away from you? You couldn't get up to much. Come to think of it, a socially-distanced date sounds perfect. Two metres away is the perfect distance for me.

I click on the first profile – Danny, 52, Essex. He looks promising. Muscular – his photo shows him on a mountain bike dressed in Lycra. He looks well groomed, a bit full of himself, but I can't deny it – attractive. I can imagine him pouring me a glass of wine in a candlelit restaurant, rubbing my feet at the end of a long hike. In addition to his profile portrait Danny has posted a few extra pics, which are lined up in thumbnail size under his main picture. I can't see any of them clearly – fuzzy pictures of him holding a sausage of some kind – so I reach for my reading glasses.

Jesus Christ. It's his penis. He is holding his penis!

I'm appalled. Bloody *hell*, is this a thing? 'Hello, would you like to meet for a cappuccino and a chat and just by the way here are several snaps of my tumescent cock?'

I click back on the main page and look at Clive, 61, Walthamstow. He is smiling at least, despite the fact that he is nothing like the toy boys promised here. Clive looks friendly, safe, intelligent. He is a maths teacher. Excellent. We will have teaching in common at least. Maybe we can talk about the crisis in the education system post-lockdown, and the cruelty of downgrading whole year groups to keep in step with annual results league tables. Maybe he will encourage me to go back to teaching, and his support could provide the confidence boost I need to make use of the rest of my life. Maybe Clive, although older than me, will be just what I need right now. I click on Clive's profile.

Oh God. Clive has four photos of his enormous engorged penis. He looks very proud of it, like a grandad holding a prize marrow. I shut him down, shocked. It's not even mildly titillating – it's just weird. He's a teacher, for God's sake! What if one of his students saw that? Not that any of them would be on a site like this, but you never know. Is this the Dark Web?

I feel so naive and silly. I've never seen pictures of other men's penises, not deliberately. I once had a porn website flash up when I googled 'good stuffing', but I didn't look. Not really. I scroll through a few more men. The younger ones – Steve, 41, Cheshunt; David, 46, Esher; Kendal, 43, Romford – are more overtly sexual in their language, saying things like 'I need too taste a womans pussy evry morning', and 'Cum and teach me a few of you're dirty trix u filthy mama' (all with terrible spelling and grammar) – but it's the older men who post the worst pictures. It's a grim gallery. Men with dreadful beards, hairy backs and pot bellies standing posing for selfies in front of cheap wardrobe mirrors, their backgrounds a riot of dirty laundry, dreadful '80s graphic bedlinen and dodgy lighting. Men with huge erections and sagging shoulders sitting on the edge of single beds in grotty divorcee flats. Men with grubby fingernails brandishing their weapons like swords – high sex drives and low personal hygiene standards.

To my horror, my inbox starts pinging. First one, then three, then seven men have already personally contacted me. Shit. I need to delete this. Fast.

Just as soon as I've had a look at what they have said.

It's only polite.

Hey sexy want some fun?

asks one. 'Not particularly, thanks,' I want to reply, but I don't want to commit anything to print – that would be dignifying it, wouldn't it?

Looking hot Angela 😜

Then, more prosaically,

SUCK MY DICK

I shut the website down, slam the screen shut and stare in disbelief at it. What the hell is wrong with men? I thought they grew out of this phallic obsession around the time they start shaving. Maybe I was just on the wrong site, but I thought I would maybe find someone to go to an Art House cinema with – it appears all single men want to do is sit by their laptops with their dicks out hoping someone will want to watch them masturbate for five minutes. I picture an army, thousands of sad and lonely blokes hunched over their penises, trousers round their ankles, all waiting for someone to say 'How lovely.' So much for fun and adventure with someone new. I'm in the cocoa years now.

10

19th July 2020

It's gone ten by the time I wake with a start. Slowly the events of the middle of the night come cringing into my consciousness like teenagers at a parents' evening. I must have been crazy. What was I thinking? I go downstairs and make strong coffee. Erin and Brendan have both left messages – sweet. They are having fun with their friends for the first time in months. They need it. They are both planning on backpacking this summer – why not? Nothing else to do. It's been a year of cancellations. The lost year of 2020. Earlier on in the lockdown some puffy-faced Tory Boy said that foreign trips would be out of bounds this year and we should all have 'Famous Five holidays' in the UK. Flapping tents, ruddy cheeks and lashings of ginger beer. Sod that. Erin and Brendan are off to the Greek islands. Me? I'll stay here with the dog.

I open the laptop to check my emails. The usual rubbish. At the bottom of the inbox there is a link to the cougar website. I have one hundred and forty-two messages. Urgh. I can't face any erect penises at this time of the day, so I ignore it. I'm just pouring my coffee and pondering when to make the scones for the tea party today when there is a knock at the door. Mona leaps from her seat and runs barking furiously. It's Jenni, dressed in the shortest white tennis dress I have ever seen.

'Morning!' she trills, pushing past me into the kitchen. 'Mmmm coffee smells good!'

'You look . . . sporty!' I say.

'Thanks. I picked this up in a charity shop a few years ago. Never worn it,' she replies, helping herself to a mug and my coffee.

'What about the red and blue?' I ask.

'Red bra, blue pants,' she says. 'And if Denise asks, I'll show her.'

I start getting the baking things from the cupboard. Should I tell Jenni what I did last night? It would give her a laugh anyway . . .

'Sleep well?' asks Jenni, catching sight of the burnt milk still in the pan.

'Not really,' I say, trying to sound breezy. 'Actually I was awake in the middle of the night and I signed up to a couple of dating sites . . .'

Jenni's mug stops in mid-air just short of her mouth.

'You WHAT?!'

I laugh.

'Tell me EVERYTHING NOW!' she shouts.

The horror of the night dissipates as I log in to my cougar account to show Jenni. Of course it's funny. In broad daylight the intimidation and repulsion I felt at the barrage of images softens and becomes more like pity. Silly buggers all desperate for attention and trying to get it the only way they know how.

I click on the messages folder. Jenni shrieks and gasps her way through the rogues' gallery of engorged sausages cradled by wrinkly knuckles.

'Oh my GOD!' she screams when she sees the eighty-year-old man with a long white beard who enjoys fisting and sado-masochism. 'This is HILARIOUS!'

She stops at the bottom of the list of messages – we haven't clicked on all of them, we know what they'll be – and peers closely at it.

'This one is good. No dick pic. Young. Well, under fifty. Quite cute. "Hello Angela – you look really nice in your picture. If you'd like to message me, I'd be happy to chat and maybe have coffee sometime?" '

'Where is he? Let me see,' I say, pulling the screen closer as I grab for my glasses. Nick is dark-haired, with soulful eyes and an angular face. His nose is long and he has a crinkly smile. It's weird to see someone smiling in their photo – everyone else looks so intensely focused on looking sexy. I click on his profile and read on.

> Hi – I'm recently widowed, no kids, and I'm looking for someone to chat to and maybe go for walks with. I like older women – my wife was ten years older than me – so thought I'd look here. I'm a bit shocked by the things I've seen here if I'm honest, but thought I'd leave my profile up anyway just in case. It's a jungle out there!

I show Jenni.

'Message him!' she says straight away.

'No!' I cry, horrified. I feel about thirteen, like she's just told me to go up to a boy at the school disco and ask him to dance. I wish I'd never started this, especially not with Jenni. She won't let it go.

'Why not? He doesn't want you to shag him he just wants to talk and walk! You can do that! Nobody will know!'

'No way! Why would I want to go out with someone who likes older women? That's just weird!'

'Why?!'

'Because it just is! The only men who say that don't mean that they actually *like* older women, they just mean they have an adolescent fixation on some Mrs Robinson-type teacher they once had and want to bang an old lady! They don't actually *like* them. Nobody likes older women. Not even older women like older women!'

'Speak for yourself!' says Jenni. 'I think we're pretty amazing!'

'Yes, I know we are, I know you are, but not in that way.'

Jenni stares at me, exasperated.

'Come on, Ang, where's your sense of fun and adventure? Where's your confidence?'

'Look, we might be wiser, kinder, more tolerant than younger women, but those are not highly prized attributes amongst men. Men don't want kind, nice, tolerant – not for sex – they'll put up with an absolutely vacuous cow if she's young and blonde.'

'I think you need to broaden your horizons, love. Not all men are like Robert.'

'Aren't they?' I ask. It's a genuine question.

'No! Some of them are nice! And there will be someone just like you wanting just what you want, who wouldn't dream of making you feel bad about yourself.'

I look at her intently.

'Sorry. No offence,' she says, flustered.

'It's all right. You're right,' I say, taking a closer look at Nick.

Should I?

'He lives in Brighton! That's not far! That's only fifty minutes on the train – an hour and a half tops if you drive from here!' says Jenni, egging me on.

'It's not exactly in my bubble, is it? And I'm not getting on a train either. Not at the moment.'

'Hello, Angela – this is the twenty-first century calling! You can meet him online. Just set up a Zoom!'

'I cannot be doing with all that nonsense!' I say, hating how old and out of touch I sound.

'Come on! It's easy! Erin will show you!'

'NO WAY! You want me to ask my *daughter* to help me hook up with a stranger online?'

Jenni grabs my laptop and hits reply.

'Hi Nick' she types.

'Hey! What are you doing?' I say, trying to grab it back.

'Come on, Angela – this will be fun, I promise!'

'Jenni! Stop!'

But it's too late. She's sent it.

She grins at me, delighted with herself.

'What have you done?!' I cry.

'Chill, it's just a hello!' she says. 'What harm can come from a hello?'

'But now he's going to think I'm interested in him!'

'You ARE interested in him! I saw the way you ogled his picture!'

'I was NOT ogling,' I say.

There's a sudden ping from the laptop.

'He's REPLIED!! OMG!' Jenni screams.

'Oh bloody hell!' I cover my eyes. 'Is it a dick pic?'

'No. He says, "Hi Angela – good to hear from you! How are you this fine Sunday morning?"'

'Don't reply!' I say, but Jenni is on a mission and is already typing.

I'm very well thank you Nick. I'm about to go to a street party with a Wimbledon theme

she types.

'Don't put that! Now he's going to think I'm a tennis fan and start asking me questions about world rankings or something!'

'He won't!'

'He will! Here, give it to me,' I say, grabbing the laptop. Before he can reply, I add 'It's not that I'm a loony Wimbledon fan but one of the neighbours is mad and thinks we need to commemorate it. I'm being forced to go, honest.'

Jenni smiles. 'You're hooked, then!' she says, irritatingly.

'No. I just don't want to be falsely represented.'

The laptop pings again. Nick has sent a string of laughing emojis. Then he writes

> Don't you just hate all the people who try to jolly you along and make you do things because they don't want you to be "sitting around all day grieving"? They're the worst. I feel like saying "I'd rather be doing that than having to go for a jog/have a picnic/join an online choir with YOU!"

I smile. 'Exactly' I type.

Jenni stands.

'I'll leave you two lovebirds to it,' she says, and I flick a tea towel at her tennis-skirted backside.

'I'll see you at the party,' she says, winking. 'Then you can tell me EVERYTHING!'

She goes, and I sit waiting for a reply. A minute passes. Then a ping.

> I thought it was just me. Don't get me wrong, I'm not sitting around crying all day (well not *every* day 😂) but sometimes I feel like I'm not allowed to be sad or angry, like it makes other people uncomfortable or something. Does that happen to you?

I smile. I reply,

Oh God yes. For years I felt like I wasn't allowed to be anything other than happy.

I don't know why I'm telling him. Any minute now he's probably going to ask to see my tits or something. But somehow I feel safe. I think it's his eyes – he looks trustworthy.

He replies straight away.

Sorry to hear that. I don't know why people find it so hard to let other people just feel what they need to feel. Why are people so afraid of other people's emotions?

God, this guy actually sounds like he has some (what Erin would call) *emotional intelligence!*

I reply again.

I don't know why. My late husband – Robert – was quite buttoned up emotionally. He wasn't really a talker. Sorry. Realise it's not really the done thing to talk about your ex, even if they're dead!

No problem for me – my late wife Alice was very emotional. She always welcomed me talking about my feelings. She was a very kind and sweet woman.

She sounds it. Lucky you.

Yes I was very lucky. I miss her terribly but it gets to the point when you have to say enough is enough and pick yourself up off the floor, don't you think?

I do. I think I'm there already.

Good for you! I think I am too. But this site, eh? All a bit desperate? I mean "rimming" "dogging" – what happened to a cup of tea and a nice slice of cake?!

I laugh out loud in the kitchen. He seems really nice.

Speaking of cake, I need to get going. I have to bake scones for the Wimbledon street party at four and if I turn up without them I'll get reported to the Bureau for Unpatriotic Thought Control or something. It was nice to chat to you.

Sure. Maybe we can catch up later? Can I get your number?

Wow. He's keen. I don't think I want to give out my number just yet . . .

Why don't we chat here later? About nine?

There is a brief pause. Have I offended him? I add

Sorry to be a bit . . . but you know . . .

No probs. I'll be here at 9. It's a date.

Oh bloody hell, is it? I send him a thumbs-up and shut the screen. A date. I didn't want a date. I haven't had a proper date in thirty years. But as I take out my mixing bowl and scales, I notice that despite myself . . . I am smiling.

11

'Come on, everyone – let's all wave our flags for Wimbers! Rain may have stopped play, but that's no reason to pull the covers over and go home!'

Denise is in full metaphor flow – it's a gloriously sunny afternoon so I can only assume that by 'rain' she means 'Covid'. Denise is a huge Wimbledon fan. And a royalist. And a huge cricket nut. One of the Barmy Army. At least, from a distance. She's never actually been, but she never misses an opportunity to get her bunting out. It must be exhausting. She is resplendent today in her Union Jack smock dress, matching floppy hat and frilly white ankle socks.

'There's the dress again! Suppose she has to get her money's worth with all that clobber,' says Jenni, sidling up to me as I arrange my scones on one end of the socially-distanced tea table. Denise has thought of everything. There are arrows marked on the road indicating a one-way buffet. Latex gloves are laid out at the start next to the plates, and a little sign says they are 'OBLIGATORY!' You must maintain two metres between fellow tea guzzlers at all times and use tongs for everything. Little bowls of strawberries and cream are lined up at the other end of the table with another sign saying 'STRICTLY ONE PER RESIDENT!' And dotted between each plate of sandwiches and cakes is a hand sanitiser pump. A more joyless spread you could not wish to see. And yet I feel happy to be here. Can a simple chat with a stranger flip my mood so completely that even Denise's little parties seem suddenly fun? I take a little plate and select a cucumber sandwich and a cupcake, but I don't feel hungry at all. I'm a bit skittish. My stomach keeps flipping over. I'm excited.

'So what happened?' says Jenni, waving her Union Jack napkin like a fan. She thinks she's in *Les Liaisons Dangereuses*.

'We talked,' I say, trying to play it cool. Jenni squeals.

'Ssssh!' I say, panicked. Too late. Denise is there.

'Hello, ladies,' she says, pulling her Union Jack face mask down over her little mouth as she approaches. 'What's all the excitement?'

'Nothing. I just really love scones!' says Jenni.

'Lovely, aren't they? These ones are mine,' says Denise, picking up a huge crumbly scone filled with currants. 'Are you two going to take part in the Mexican wave?'

Oh God. She can't let Wimbledon go.

'Well, I would do – but this dress is so short if I raise my arms everyone will see my Forty Love!'

Denise smiles thinly. 'Yes – very brave choice, I must say. Not many people your age can get away with showing that much thigh.'

Deuce.

Jenni grins and shoves a finger sandwich in her mouth all in one go. Thankfully Denise is called away to greet the jazz trio she has coerced into appearing.

'Stupid cow,' says Jenni, her mouth still full. 'I feel so sorry for Paul.' Denise's husband Paul is hovering around behind her in a pair of ill-advised tiny tennis shorts. In fairness, he doesn't seem particularly unhappy about it. He looks quite pleased with himself. 'And she didn't make those scones. They're Waitrose. I saw her stuffing the packaging down her bra.'

'So yes, we talked,' I say. 'We're going to talk again later.'

'You SLUT!' shouts Jenni, delighted.

'Ssssshhhh!' I laugh.

'Did you give him your number?'

'NO! I'm not mad! We just talked on the chat, on the website.'

'Did he ask for your number?'

'Yes, he did. But I thought best not until we know each other a bit better. If it gets that far.' I can't believe what I'm saying. What's happened to me?

'Bloody hell! Good for you!'

'He seems really nice. It's just a bit of fun. God knows I need a bit of that.'

Jenni goes to get us some Pimm's from her house and I look around at all the neighbours standing in awkward household bubbles on the street. It's actually very sweet, and I find myself filled with a feeling of goodwill. Children play hopscotch, chalking onto the road, and older kids ride their bikes up and down the pavements. It feels like the olden days, like we've gone back in time to an era when life was simpler, people more friendly and fun was self-made. 'Hi Ang – how are you doing?' says Ellis, appearing from behind me. He is doing that head-tilting thing – adorable.

'Oh, hi Ellis! Good, yes I'm good, thanks!' I'm aware how different – skittish – I sound, so I moderate myself. 'Well, you know, getting along OK, all things considered . . .'

'Hey – it's OK to be happy for a while, Ang. Have a Pimm's!'

'I thought we weren't allowed alcohol?' I say.

'Last-minute relaxing of prohibition – Denise persuaded Sebastian at number forty-seven that it was OK – turns out he was the fun Nazi!'

I take a glass and we wander around talking to people. He's so friendly and puts people at their ease. Jenni shouts over to him and he blows her a kiss. I want one like him. Maybe I've found one . . . We have a lot of fun when someone brings out a banjo and we have a singalong – cockney ditties and silly dancing. The evening draws in and it's almost nine o'clock by the time I look at my watch. I'm still out on the street chatting to one of the neighbours I have never met before. Apparently she has lived here as long as we have, but we've never met. She lives four doors away. Shocking. She says she is sorry about Robert. I nod. Then I realise what time it is and rush off.

Inside I can't find the laptop charger. It must be in Erin's room – she's always pinching mine. I rush around in a blind panic, imagining Nick waiting for me, a virtual bunch of flowers wilting in his hand. I find it under Erin's bed, plug in, switch on and log onto the site. Four new messages from Nick, the first at

20.59

Hi! How was the party? Straight sets 😂?

Then another at 21.01

Hello? Are you there?

21.03

Angela?

Blimey, he is keen.

21.05

OK well I guess you thought better of it. Shame. Hope to speak to you soon?

Oh no! He thinks I've stood him up! How can I have been so stupid? I scrabble to reply. Maybe he's still there.

Nick! So sorry! I lost track of time and then I couldn't find my laptop charger! Sorry! Here now!

It's 21.06. Only six minutes late. I watch for his reply. Nothing.

21.10.

21.16.

Still nothing. Oh well. I must have subconsciously self-sabotaged. I'm surprised at how disappointed I feel.

I go to put the kettle on. No flirty chat late into the night, then. Just a cup of tea and then bed, I guess.

21.19 the laptop pings. I rush to the screen.

Hi Angela. No worries. Sounds like you had a good time! Better things to be doing than chatting to some strange man you met online! Ha ha! Maybe chat tomorrow? Here's my number if you would like to call – 7pm?

Thank God! Thought I'd blown it then. I will call him tomorrow – bang on 7 p.m. And we can take up where we left off. I'm just relieved he got back to me. I tidy up and take a shower, shaving my legs for the first time in months. Stupid really. Inside my chest, deep within my ribs, something stirs. A fluttering. Like wings against a cage.

12

Monday. Brendan and Erin arrive back within an hour of each other and deposit dirty laundry and sleeping bags all over the kitchen, before collapsing into bed for the rest of the day. I dutifully load and unload the washing machine, taking advantage of the lovely weather to get some good drying done. I thought the years of domestic servitude were behind me, but the washing never ceases – the pants just get bigger. How humdrum my life is. Not for long. Soon I will be whisked away by a younger man for a glamorous Staycation. I allow myself to fantasise about where we will go first. Cornwall? No. They don't want Londoners down there, do they? I've seen signs on TV 'Turn round and F-off!' suspended over the A30. Southend? No, full of chavs. He lives in Brighton. Maybe he'll invite me down for a weekend? I start to feel anxious as I peg out my large beige knickers. I'm going to have to do something about those – can't be turning up in those passion killers. And the bras. It's all very well letting your elastic go grey and saggy when there's no one to see it, but I'd die if anyone spontaneously undressed me and found this sorry state of affairs. Like unwrapping a present and finding an old turnip.

I pass the day in a flurry of nervous energy, Mona following me up and down the stairs as if sensing an interloper is about to get between me and her. From six I start checking my watch every other minute. I mustn't be late today. The hour lasts a decade, so I drink tea, wipe the kitchen surfaces again and put lipstick on. It's just an audio call – I'm not going to FaceTime him yet, God no – but I want to feel attractive. At two minutes to seven I pick up my phone and dial his number. I hold my breath as I listen to the ringtone.

After three rings he picks up.

'Hello?' he says, an upward inflection making him sound slightly suspicious.

'Hi Nick? It's Angela! I'm not late!' I say.

'Hi Angela. I'm so pleased you've called. I wasn't sure you were going to!' he says. His voice is soft and kind.

'Of course! I really wanted to chat to you last night, but I just got a bit carried away at the party and lost track of time!'

Do I sound desperate?

'Good. Then we're both on the same page. I've been nervous all day! And breathe!' he laughs. I let out a sigh of relief. I haven't blown it. Yet. I'm flattered that he has been worrying about it.

'How are you?' he asks, and something in his voice makes me believe he really wants to know.

I let out a long sigh. 'Well, I'm very nervous too! I haven't spoken to anyone since my husband died – I mean, I have *spoken* to, you know, *people,* like the neighbours and people in Asda, but I haven't had any kind of . . . you know . . .'

'Dates?' he offers. He sounds a little bit like he's teasing and it makes me blush. Thank God it's only audio.

'Exactly. And you?'

'Well, I've been looking on a few sites for a couple of months now, but so far no one has quite interested me enough. So far.'

'Oh, so I'm honoured!' I say, blushing even harder.

'You are indeed. I mean, there have been some lovely women, but I think I wasn't really ready before. There was just something about you that looked – welcoming.'

I smile.

'Really? In what way?' I ask, keen to hear more.

'Well . . . I think I'm quite a good judge of character, and I can tell from your photo that you are kind, and you sound like a really nice woman. Your voice. It's . . . sweet. Does that sound wet?!'

I smile. Compliments.

'Not at all. Not at all, Nick.'

And we talk. We talk for two hours. He tells me all about his late wife Alice – she died of breast cancer two years ago and he's been on his own ever since. He tells me how they wanted children but had met later in life and then the cancer got in the way – and then she died. He's an architect and believes in social housing. He's passionate about helping the poor, and mentions that he gives a lot of his money to local charities. He doesn't do this in a showy way – he just mentions it in passing. He sounds so genuine, so down to earth. It's so refreshing. I tell him about Robert, stalling a little when I reveal it was just four months ago that he died.

'Four months is a long time when you're alone,' he says, and I'm relieved he is understanding. I don't tell him that the whole reason I signed up to this was as a kind of revenge against the cheating bastard. I think that might be a bit of a buzz kill, as Brendan would say. He tells me how he has been helping out at a local food bank during the lockdown, picking up food from supermarkets getting rid of old stock. He's started pottering in the garden and likes classical music. So far, so good. I tell him about Brendan and Erin, about how nice it has been to have them back and how much I am dreading them heading off for the summer. He is sympathetic but says I need to start thinking about myself, planning for my own future. He says he wants to do that too. It feels like a tentative offer. It's gone 9 p.m. when

Brendan comes crashing through the kitchen door looking for food. I dash out to the garden, guiltily, lowering my voice.

'I'm going to have to go,' I whisper. 'My son has just come downstairs.'

There is a short pause. 'OK, but you don't have to go just because of that,' says Nick. I'm torn. I don't want to hang up, but at the same time I don't want Brendan to see me flirting with a strange man just four months since his father died.

'No, I know, but I feel . . . a bit bad, you know?'

'OK, sweetie,' he says warmly.

'Sorry – can I – shall we speak again tomorrow?' I ask, suddenly shy and anxious to get off the phone. I feel like I've been caught red-handed.

'Sure, sure, whenever is good for you . . .' he says.

'Great. Same time tomorrow night?'

'Perfect. Sleep well. Bye, love.'

Sweetness. Love. I blush.

I slip back inside and start loading the dishwasher.

'Did you cook anything?' asks Brendan, sticking his head in the oven.

Phew. He hasn't noticed anything odd.

'There's some left-over soup in the pan,' I say.

'I think I'll just go to McDonald's,' he says, turning his nose up.

He heads for the door.

'Who was that on the phone? Looked a bit dodgy.'

Bloody hell, he doesn't miss a thing. I find myself blushing again.

'Nobody. Just a cold call.'

'This time of night? Bloody bastards. Bye!'

And he's gone. Thank God for that.

I pour myself a glass of wine and sit to mull things over. It was a really nice chat. I hope it didn't sound like I was trying to get off the phone. He sounds sensitive. I felt really listened to. Really cared for. It's crazy. I barely know him. But already I feel like we have a connection. Robert never asked me how I was feeling. It's not that hard to actively love someone, is it? You just have to care, then show them. Maybe that was the problem – it's not that he couldn't show it (the excuse I always made for him) but that he didn't actually care. I decide to message Nick, just to make sure he knows I really did have to go. I pick up my phone and think carefully about what to write.

> Hiya – sorry about that! I really enjoyed our chat. Looking forward to talking again tomorrow!

I hesitate then add a kiss. I sit with the phone on my knee, sipping my wine, waiting for his response. Nothing. Oh well, maybe he is busy. He'll probably reply soon. I tidy up a bit, waiting for my phone to ping. I sit again. How long do I wait? I switch on the TV. The news is about to come on, so I wait to hear about the bars and restaurants opening up. Suddenly it's not weird to see people being served from behind plastic shields like the ones they have in off-licences in the shadier parts of town. Having a meal out in such conditions doesn't really appeal. What if I get to actually meet Nick and we go for a meal and have to sit two metres apart with visors on? Hardly romantic. I watch the news. Half the population seems to be in the pub while the other half tuts. I hope we are not heading for a second wave. That would just about finish me off. The first one crashed ashore destroying everything it touched, took my husband and forty thousand others and then lay in rancid pools waiting for people to come out again. I stay up for *Newsnight*, but I'm too antsy to concentrate. Maitlis has a very bouncy blow-dry – that's about all I notice.

Newsnight ends and I switch off the portentous music before the credits are over. Still no message. I send another text simply wishing him a good night. I go to bed, cradling the phone under my pillow like a teenager. I sleep fitfully, waking up several times during the night to check for messages. Every time, I am disappointed. It makes me disproportionately nervous – two days ago I didn't even know he existed and now he is interfering with my sleep, affecting my equilibrium, such as it was, and making me feel anxious. I really am so silly. He's probably just busy, or asleep.

In the morning I wake early. I check my phone again. No message. It's only a quarter to six, but I get up and make tea. In the back garden the old lady's heart is grey, the sun yet to fill her solar panels with warmth and love. I know how she feels. Will I make things work with someone new? Or am I now a single woman, a widow forever? I contemplate the next thirty years on my own. I will be one of those old ladies who stop to try and talk to you while you're walking the dog or queuing at the till, because I'll be so bloody lonely. Brendan and Erin will have tortured conversations about whose turn it is to visit me in my care home. If I'm allowed visitors. Covid might have put paid to that forever. So I'll probably sit in a pool of my own piss, telling anyone who will listen how wonderful my children are. I'm just squeezing the teabag out over the sink when my phone pings. It's him!

Morning beautiful Angela! How are you today? xx

My heart skips a beat. 'Beautiful Angela' – two kisses. See? I was being silly! He probably just got tired and went to bed. I take things far too personally. Maybe this is Robert's legacy – a small pension, a half-decent house and a massive propensity for self-doubt. I am stupidly thrilled to get this message. Suddenly the day takes on a much sunnier aspect. Amazing how little it takes – another human reaching out across the abyss. I message back.

Morning! How are you today? Up bright and early! X

He is typing straight back.

Only one kiss?

he teases.

I smile and send 'x'

He replies with a loveheart emoji. I forget all about my tea and try to think what to say next. But he sends another message.

What are you up to today?

I wrack my brains for something funny or exciting to say. Nothing. Instead I tell him the truth.

Probably doing some ironing and making a salad! It's all go around here!

Good. I want to make sure you're behaving yourself! Not gadding about in the street drinking Pimm's! 😜

I like it that he remembers details about my day.

No not today – I'll be at home getting on with the housework.

And the kids?

Oh they'll be asleep half the day.

Lucky them! Well whatever you do, make sure you take a few moments to appreciate yourself. And don't run round after them too much! This is your time Angela! Speak later xxx

I smile. This is my time. Maybe it is.

And just like that I am something approaching happy again. We talk every night at 7 p.m. He's so sweet, remembering little things about my day, asking me about my life with Robert, wanting a tour of the house so that he can imagine himself visiting. A week goes by and I scarcely notice, my life just measured out in the hours spent either talking to him or waiting to talk to him. It's so nice to have some attention, someone asking me how I am and what I am doing. I realise Robert never asked me a thing, apart from how come I'd managed to spend so much money and buy nothing he wanted to eat. Every morning I set about watering the garden before the sun gets too high and burns the water on the leaves. Bees buzz hungrily around the lavender and the bird song seems sweeter than ever. Life could be about to get better. Perhaps better than it has been for thirty years. I am free. The kids will be gone again soon. Someone else thinks I'm worth talking to. I spend every afternoon getting ready to speak to him. After our second chat he wanted to FaceTime. I was so nervous I spent all day getting ready, trying out different tops and lighting – would a lamp hide my jowls? But how could I justify it in broad daylight?! I needn't have worried. He showers me in compliments and it never sounds cheesy or fake. 'Angela your eyes are so sparkly tonight! They are the most incredible aquamarine colour!' 'You look so sweet when you're shy!' 'I love how you've done your hair – you look fantastic.' He is even more attractive on video than his photo, so all these compliments make me feel giddy. To be lavished with praise like this by someone who is a very well preserved, successful and kind middle-aged man! Is this what it's like to be in a loving relationship? Is this what Jenni has? No wonder she's always so up for life. I feel like I was dead all those years. Last night he broached the subject of us meeting. He said he wanted to talk to me about something important and it would be better face to face. He asked me where I lived – we'd been talking about house prices, how crazy the market is in London, how ridiculous the prices are in some postcodes. He said he didn't understand why I wasn't thinking about selling up and getting a smaller space. He said I could invest the capital and live a life of luxury. He asked for my address and I gave it to him. He's going to research the history of the houses in my street – apparently you can find out what they have sold for over the decades. Not that I'm planning on selling. This is the kids' home after all.

It's Sunday again. We've been talking for a whole week. I'm in the garden with a cup of tea, doing some daydreaming and weeding, when the doorbell rings. It's only eight in the morning, far too early for Jenni, who has been vicariously loving what she insists on referring to as my 'internet lover'. I go to the door wiping my hands on a tea towel. On the doorstep there sits a huge bunch of baby-pink peonies, wrapped in soft pink tissue paper. The delivery man is getting back in his van. The new social distancing delivery rules mean they have to do this to maintain physical distance, and often they don't check the addresses properly, leading to so many mistakes. So far I've had books, sports equipment and gluten-free groceries all erroneously left on the doorstep and I've had to chase after them to take them back.

'Hey!' I shout after him. 'I don't think you've got the right address!'

He waves cheerily and drives off at speed. Bloody hell. Some poor sod won't be getting their birthday flowers today. I pick them up and smell them. They are stunning. There is a little card attached.

'Angela Happy One Week Anniversary! Love N xxx'

Nick? Nick has sent me flowers? I don't know any other Ns. I blush furiously even though nobody is looking. I am insanely thrilled. So that's why he wanted my address? All that talk about house prices! How utterly lovely. I push my nose into the soft fragrant blooms and inhale their sweetness. I can't remember the last time I received flowers. Just as I'm about to take them inside, Denise jogs over in some ill-advised running gear.

'Ooh who's a lucky girl! Secret admirer, is it? Birthday?'

Of course she would have to witness this. She never misses a trick.

'No no, not my birthday – they're for Erin,' I lie. I don't want to get the third degree later.

'Well, they're gorgeous. Byeee! I'm off to start my 5K jog! Wish me luck!'

'Good luck!' I shout to her retreating backside.

Inside I put the gorgeous flowers into a vase. I'm stunned.

Once again I spend all day waiting for 7 p.m. I've started to dodge the children in the house – they have noticed the upturn in my mood and I don't want them to know anything yet. If they were to suspect me of having – what? An affair? An online flirtation? – I would feel so shamed. Only by telling them the truth about their dad would I be able to justify it, and I cannot do that. Not yet. The tightly packed peony buds unfurl throughout the afternoon and by six they are big blousy blooms with frilly edges, flopping luxuriously all over the dining table. I get ready for the call by showering, styling my hair and putting on a nice shirt. I have been living in T-shirts and baggy trousers to help the denial about the weight gain in lockdown, but this past week I have been getting dressed properly, taking care to look as good as possible. It's years since I've really bothered. Any time I did change my appearance Robert would comment on it, asking me who I was trying to impress. I gave up in the end. At a quarter to seven I'm sitting anxiously in the kitchen. Erin comes in from a shopping spree – you'd think she'd never been in a shop, such was the level of her joy when they announced that non-essential shops could reopen – 'Non-essential? Fashion is ESSENTIAL!' she'd said as she skipped off to the sales.

'You look nice, Mum! Where are you going?'

'Nowhere. I've just got a clean shirt on, that's all. Is it that remarkable?'

'No. Just saying, you look nice. It's good! Good for you!' she says, trotting upstairs to try on all her purchases.

At two minutes to seven I go out into the garden and dial Nick's number. No answer. I try again. No answer. Odd. He always either calls me early or I call him. I can't believe how anxious it makes me that he hasn't picked up straight away. At seven I try again. He picks up after two rings. Thank God.

'Hi! I thought you were avoiding me!' I blurt. Stupid. Just be cool.

'Angela!' he says, laughing.

'I'm so relieved you're there!'

'Of course I'm here!' he chuckles.

'It's just I rang three times! I was beginning to think you weren't going to answer!' I try to sound blasé, but even I can detect the slight note of panic in my voice.

'We said seven, didn't we?' he says, sounding ever so slightly defensive. Don't blow this, Angela. Be cool.

'Yes, we did, it's just I didn't want to be late, because I know you hate that!' Nick mentioned last week that his biggest no-no is sloppy time keeping.

'I do. Bless you. Thank you for taking care of that. You took care of it so well you were early! Calling me at six fifty-eight! Then again at six fifty-nine!'

I laugh, but I register something. If he was there, why didn't he just pick up? I put it to the back of my mind.

'I'm just teasing, Angela,' he soothes, reading into my slight pause.

'How are you? How was your day?' I ask, keen to switch focus.

'Nice. Lovely. I went for a long bike ride. Thought about you. Wondered if you'd received anything . . .?'

I'm happy he has brought it up – I feel too shy to.

'The flowers are so beautiful. Thank you.'

'Flowers? What flowers? Who has been sending you flowers? Let me at him!' I can hear that he is playing dumb, so I play along.

'Well, of course I assumed it was you, but then I do have a long list of admirers so . . .'

'Oh, is that so? Should I just head to the back of the queue?' he says, playing hurt.

'Something like that . . . No seriously, thank you so much. They are absolutely beautiful. It's years since I've been sent flowers – apart from when someone dies, ha ha ha!'

'Well, more fool Robert for not treating you like a queen,' says Nick. It's odd to hear someone who didn't know Robert being critical of him. 'So you liked them?'

'I did. I do. I was a bit mystified – I didn't think for a minute they would be from you!'

'I just thought you'd like them. I'm so happy you do. I was worried it might be a bit . . . much. Too soon.'

'Not at all! It's never too soon for flowers!' I gush.

'Tell me about your day – tell me everything,' says Nick. So I do. And it's lovely. We talk for two hours, me hiding down the bottom of the garden with my new friends, the banjo-playing frogs. We chat and laugh, and Nick brings up the subject of us meeting. I gulp.

'I mean, as long as we stay two metres apart . . . We could meet up. I could pop up to London for the afternoon . . . we could have a walk and a chat.'

I balk. That's all a bit . . . real. But I can't deny the idea thrills me. A rendezvous with an online paramour – it sounds so exciting, a far cry from the beigeness of the rest of my life.

'OK,' I say tentatively.

'Don't worry – I don't bite! Not on the first date anyway.'

'How will I know you?'

'Meet me at Victoria Station next to platform twelve on Friday at midday. Wear a red dress. I'll find you.'

'OK. I've got a red dress but it might be a bit tight, ha ha ha! Might have put a little weight on in lockdown!'

'Well, you've got four days to diet.' I wait, but he doesn't laugh. He's so dry sometimes.

'And one more thing,' he says, just before we say goodbye, 'I've noticed that your profile is still up – are you planning on leaving it up there or . . .?'

'OK, yes of course, sorry, of course I'll take it down. I didn't think! I mean, I haven't been on the site since we've been talking, but . . . I don't want you to think I'm still looking!'

'Great. Let's chat again tomorrow night.' And he goes.

Friday. Four days. Oh God, what have I done?

Erin comes down the garden path with two gin and tonics and hands one to me. She looks curious.

'You're being a bit mysterious, Mum. What are you doing hiding at the bottom of the garden?'

I smile my best mysterious smile.

'Ask me no questions and I'll tell you no lies!'

I am bursting to tell her, but I can't. Can I? I need to talk to somebody! I gulp down the gin and rush out shouting 'Sorry, just need to ask Jenni something.'

Jenni will know what to do. I bang on her door and she opens it wearing a nurse's outfit.

'Sorry, is this a bad time?' What have I barged in on?

'No, ha ha! Ellis is more of a French Maid man! I'm just going through a charity bag that someone left. Denise is collecting for the homeless and has kindly designated my front garden as a drop-off point. Someone donated this. Can't see anyone wanting to wear it – unless it's to get a free coffee at Starbucks.'

'Can I come in for a minute? I need to talk to you.'

'Oh God, what have I done now?' she says, letting me in. I go through to the back garden, walking past Ellis who is hunched over yet another jigsaw, this one depicting a litter of white puppies in a basket.

'Hello, Ellis!' I say.

'Angela! How the devil are you? Pathetic, isn't it – a grown man obsessed with jigsaws. Oh well. Keeps me out of trouble!'

'Bloody jigsaws,' says Jenni, giving him a playful pat on the bum.

'Nurse! Nurse, I need my medicine!' says Ellis, reaching for her as she slips out of his reach.

Outside we sit and I take a deep breath.

'Is it your toyboy? PLEASE tell me it's your toyboy!'

I smile. Jenni screams.

'Tell me what, where, who, when!' So I tell her all about the last call, how we've made a date, about the flowers and the conversation about house prices and how many compliments he gives me. She smiles and nods. I can tell she is pleased. Ellis joins us and listens, tilting his head kindly when I express my worries about the dress and my weight.

'If he's a decent man he won't mind about that kind of rubbish, Angela – he'll like you for who you are. And I think you look great.'

'Thanks, Ellis. I think he is a decent man. He's going to help me look into what the house is worth.'

I notice Jenni shoot a look at Ellis.

'Why?' she asks.

I blink. 'I don't know. We were just talking about it. In general. He's an architect.'

'Yes, you said,' says Ellis, teasing. I must have been repeating myself all week, like a giddy schoolgirl.

'Just be careful, OK? Don't give too much away about yourself until you know him better. You've been through a lot,' says Jenni.

'Bloody hell, it was you that got me into this in the first place!' I laugh. I thought she'd be pleased, not *concerned*!

'Just be cool,' says Ellis.

'Of course I will. Cool as a cucumber, that's me,' I say. But my stomach turns a single flip.

Back in my own house I feel calmer. My stomach growls and I realise I haven't eaten since breakfast. It's just hunger. That's what it is. I open the fridge and go to pull out some left-over quiche, then I remember – 'You've got four days to diet.' I close the fridge door. Actually I'm too worked up to eat anyway. The peonies are in full bloom now and they fill the air with the most gorgeous sweet scent. A little cloying, maybe, but nice nonetheless. 'Play it cool,' Ellis said. Why should I? I want some passion and some fun. Sometimes you can be too careful. I've realised that since Robert died. Seize the day. My phone pings. It's a message from Nick. I hope he hasn't changed his mind. My hands start to tremble as I open it.

Hello baby cakes xxx

I smile, and send a single kiss back by return. My phone pings again.

Just a silly thing . . . I thought you said you were going to take your profile down? I don't like to ask again but . . . I really like you and I don't want to pursue this if you're not as into it as me . . . xxx

Oh bloody hell, in my excitement I forgot. I log on to my account and it takes me ages to find the delete button. They are very clever and hide it behind several other pages. I can't help but notice I have thirty-two new messages. All that time I put up with Robert treating me like a doormat when I could have been out and about with other men enjoying life and being . . . *wanted.* It is so nice to feel like I matter, and that my still being technically 'available' online has worried Nick so much that he has taken the trouble to message again. Finally I locate the delete button and in a few seconds I disappear from view. It's that easy to erase myself. If only there was a way to do that with the past. My future looks much brighter. I message Nick.

Done! Sorry – I was a bit giddy. Went to see my friend to tell her the exciting news! x

Nick is replying. I wait with bated breath for the rippling dots in the speech bubble to solidify into words. Words from my date. My date!

What did she say?

he replies.

I hesitate. Should I tell him they told me to play it cool?

She was very happy for me

I lie.

Good girl xxx

he replies. Three kisses. Three. I feel like a teenager. How will I survive between now and Friday? I rush upstairs and pull the red dress from the wardrobe. Tearing off my clothes I pull it down over my head and tug at the hem. It's polyester, so there is plenty of give in the fabric, but turning to look at myself in the mirror I am horrified at the lumps and bumps protruding from every angle. I look like a sack of badgers. I'm going to have to get some control pants. Do they do control body stockings? Ones that go up under your face so that you can tuck your chins in too? I experiment with various old shoes. I don't have any that match. I can't wear heels – I'll never make it down the escalators in heels – but the only decent flat shoes I have that aren't trainers are the nasty walking sandals Robert bought for me from the back of a colour supplement. I'm going to have to go shopping. Tomorrow. Just as I go to switch off my phone for the night Nick messages again. I open it already smiling. This is the effect he has on me. He's forwarded a link to a property website. When I click on it, a page with one-bedroom retirement flats pops up. I look through the images of tidy communal gardens and small, neat kitchens. Maybe he's right. What am I going to do in this big house once the children have gone for good? My phone pings again. Nick.

Above a picture of a cruise ship he has typed 'Think of all the fun we could have!' I go to bed with a smile on my face.

13

I'm in line waiting to get into the shopping centre bang on ten. A queue of eager consumers who look like they've not been out in months is chomping at the bit to get inside. I bet most of them are going to Primark. It seems the pandemic, the lockdown and the daily death toll has done nothing to dampen the enthusiasm for cheap goods made by tiny underpaid fingers. Maybe we will never learn from our past mistakes. Maybe we're just doomed to repeat them forever – the definition of madness. The security guard approaches the doors with an air of thinly veiled contempt and opens up. The queue surges forwards, social distancing forgotten. I make my way to M&S, thrilled by my secret mission – Operation Flab Attack. In the lingerie section there is a bewildering array of beige elastic pants – some that seem to go up the torso, some with large tummy control panels, and painful-looking thongs, some with bras attached. I'm not allowed to try anything on, according to all the signs, so I grab a pair of full brief high-waisters and shove them in my basket. Shoes next. I pick up a pair of nude patent court shoes. Very Duchess of Cambridge. Could I manage these? I can't buy them without trying them on. I take a furtive glance around. Nobody. Slipping off my trainers, I step gingerly into the shoes. They fit well, and I can see some calf definition I thought had long gone. But can I walk in them? I take a few steps. Not bad. But deep in my heart I know that buying them would be a triumph of hope over experience – I'd last five minutes before I'd be grabbing for the nearest handrail and toppling over down stairs. I slip them off and place them ruefully back on the shelf.

'Excuse me, madam!' says a voice drenched in opprobrium behind me. I spin round, guiltily.

'Did you just try those shoes on?' A grumpy-looking woman roughly my age is standing next to the summer sandals, her gloved hands on her hips.

'Yes . . . sorry . . . I didn't know . . .' What didn't I know?

'No trying on,' she says, pointing to one of the many signs.

'Sorry!' I simper.

'I'll have to put them in quarantine for three days now,' she grumbles, picking them up and carrying them off at arms' length like a pair of dead rats.

I pick up a pair of nude flats and shove them in my basket. They will have to do. Hopefully he'll be too busy staring into my eyes to notice my granny shoes.

Back home Erin is up and about. She and Brendan are going off to Europe on Thursday, taking advantage of two spaces in a car heading for France. Timing! If I want, I can invite Nick back here. The thought makes me feel sick and thrilled all at the same time. I could have sex with him! I'm at once appalled and delighted with my sudden raciness. I could bring him back here and we could rip each other's clothes off on the stairs, like they do in the movies, too keen to wait until we get to the bedroom. I could have Nick in my bed – Robert's bed, *our* bed – and nobody would know, but I'd be hoping that there is such a thing as an afterlife so that Robert would have to look down on us, me and my lover, tangled up in each other's bodies, heads thrown back in ecstasy. That will show him.

'Been shopping?' says Erin, sticking her nose into one of my bags.

'Get out of there!' I say, swiping the bag from the kitchen table.

'Ooh! What have you been buying, Mum? Being a bit secretive!'

'I needed some new pants,' I mumble, taking the bag into the hall and dropping it by the bottom of the stairs. I can't do anything without someone passing comment.

'Shouldn't you be packing?' I say, coming back into the kitchen. The sink is full – again – so I busy myself loading the dishwasher.

'It's only Monday Mum! I'm just going to shove everything into my rucksack the night before. Can't believe I'm actually going. Might be the last time we're allowed into Europe without visas! Will you be OK, Mum?'

'I'll be fine. You go off and enjoy yourselves. Don't worry about me.'

'Mum . . . I wanted to ask you . . . did Dad leave a will?' I look up at Erin. Strange question.

'Well . . . yes of course. You know Dad. He wouldn't have left any loose ends.' The idea that Robert would have left his affairs anything other than shipshape is ridiculous. His good friend Oscar, a shifty-looking solicitor with a slightly patronising manner, had everything tied up within weeks. The usual arrangement – surviving spouse inherits the estate.

'Why do you ask?'

'I was just wondering if he . . . you know, left anything to me and Brendan?' She looks sheepish. Is she asking for money?

'No. I mean, in the end you'll both get everything. When I die, I mean. You'll inherit.' I feel vaguely put out. Is she being mercenary?

'No, I know, I don't mean to be, you know, I just thought sometimes people leave small sums of money . . . you know, for people when they really need it rather than when their other parent dies, I mean, hopefully years and years later. This sounds terrible. Forget it.'

'No. It's OK. Dad didn't leave any money for right now, no. I don't think he was planning on dying while you were at university, so he probably thought you'd just have to wait for the inheritance until you were proper grown-ups. I mean, unless there is a stash of fifties under the bed.'

'Is there?' She looks genuinely excited.

'I doubt it. I mean, I haven't looked, but your dad wasn't really the money-under-the-bed type. All his money was properly invested and looked after.'

'Sure,' says Erin, picking at a croissant, 'I'll just have to get a job when I go back to Uni.'

This exchange leaves me feeling disturbed. I never got any inheritance when my parents died. They never owned a property, so me and my sister had to make our own way. Sally set up a business and moved to Australia. I married Robert. So why do my kids seem to think they can just wait for whatever I leave behind? Maybe they want me to sell up and downsize? Then they could get their hands on the capital from their family home and not have to worry for a few years. They could pay off their student debts. Buy cars. Travel. Maybe have enough for a deposit on a poky studio somewhere in the Thames estuary. All the things their generation say they have no chance of being able to do. I hadn't seriously considered selling up until Nick's comment. I always assumed I would die here. Is that what I want? To stay in this house until I'm carted out in a box? I picture myself getting ramps and grab rails installed. One of those high baths with a seat and a side door. Falling behind in home decor trends. Living in a museum of our family past for the next twenty, thirty years, the walls reverberating with the memories of the lives lived here as I sit silently wondering how it came to be Monday, Tuesday, Wednesday again. If I sold now, I could benefit everyone. The kids could come and visit me in my neat little flat. Maybe with Nick. I laugh at myself but it's true – who knows where this date will lead? I could be living it up by the sea, nicely settled into Nick's Brighton house, going out for lunch on a Thursday afternoon because why not? Stop jumping the gun, Angela! Silly woman. First things first – I need to shave what the magazines refer to as my 'bikini line' before Friday. I'll wait until Brendan and Erin have gone – I don't want the third degree about why the shower is full of grey pubes.

14

30th July 2020

They're up at six – or rather, they are dressed and stuffing hoodies into hastily retrieved rucksacks after a night spent crashing about in the kitchen keeping me awake. I'm sad that they are going, but I will try not to show it. I don't want them to worry about me – it's not fair on them. They've had the worst year so far – losing their dad, being sent home from Uni and being forced to stay indoors most of the time. But that's all behind us now – infections are dropping, thank God, the death rate has peaked and Brexit is just around the corner. Shame I never got to do my Grand Tour before I'd need a visa every time I enter a new country. So it's right that they are going. Plus, it's not as if I don't have something else to keep me occupied . . .

I get up to help, offering toast and tea, sandwiches for the journey, bottled water. They turn it all down, saying they will 'grab something' in France. Oh to be young and be able to turn down tea and toast because in six hours there will be baguette and wine.

'But you can't go all day without eating? Here – just take this packet of biscuits for the journey. Just to make me happy,' I say, stuffing a packet of chocolate Digestives in the top of Erin's bag.

'Thanks, Mum,' says Erin, who, despite the hour, is putting on a full face of make-up.

I'm starving. I pick at a punnet of raspberries. Tomorrow. I'm meeting him tomorrow. I don't know whether I'm sick with hunger or excitement.

'You'll be OK, won't you, Mum?' says Brendan, wrapping his arms around me and picking me up off the floor.

'Yes yes, put me down!' I shout. I love it when he picks me up. My little boy.

'Don't get too lonely. Call me. Go out. Have some fun.' I know he will worry about me. If only he knew. Would he be horrified?

'I should be in Greece by Sunday, so I'll let you know when I get there.'

We hug, and I feel my eyes filling up. I will miss them terribly. We've been quite a good little unit really and this will be our first separation since Robert died. A car horn beeps rudely outside.

'Bloody hell, is that Louis? He'll wake the whole neighbourhood!'

Brendan and Erin rush outside and there is an inappropriately loud conversation about boot space and who is sitting 'shotgun'. I bet Denise can hear them down the street. Jenni certainly can. 'We're going, Mum. See you in a month!' says Erin, breathlessly excited. I always wanted to 'do Europe' – I managed France and Spain as a student, but I was too timid to do the whole inter-rail thing. Robert would never have done it with me. So that's that. Will I have to be one of those mums that lives vicariously through her children, watching them conquer the world through a net curtain?

'Take care, both of you, and make sure you keep in touch!' I say, following them out to the street. Louis honks his horn to hurry them. They pile into the car and before they even have a chance to shout goodbye, Louis takes off down the street. Erin, having lost the front seat war, turns and waves from the back window. I stand at the front gate, every inch the empty-nester cliché. A knot twists in my stomach. I hope they'll be OK. This is what motherhood is, isn't it? A series of goodbyes. Watching them disappear over and over again. Their first steps, their first day at school, at University, watching their backs as they walk down the aisle. I stand blinking away the tears for a few moments, absent-mindedly dead-heading the lavender along the path. Tomorrow is the start of the rest of my life. Tomorrow is Resurrection Ground Zero. Watch out, world, here I come.

As I stand picking at the dried buds, I become aware of someone across the road. A presence. I've felt this a couple of times this week – like I was being watched. Someone is behind the white van that always parks there, blocking Jenni's light, much to her irritation. Who is out and about at this time? I don't look up – what if it's Jenni and she wants to have a go at me about the noise? What if it's Denise? I'm not in the mood to be pitied. I carry on plucking at the lavender. From across the street, just behind the van, I hear a baby cry. An early riser, clearly. Sometimes the only thing that helps a sleepless baby is a push around the block in the pram. I hear a woman's voice, shushing, urgent. She must, like me, be the sort of person who worries about waking the neighbours. But there is something in the situation that unnerves me. Why is she still behind the van? I look up, and catch sight of the buggy wheels and the edge of a coat disappearing. Why are they hiding? Am I being watched?

My blood suddenly turns cold. My body seems to know something I don't. 'This person is here for you', my adrenal glands seem to say.

Without thinking about it I open the gate and cross the road, my heart pumping. A thought rushes unbidden into my mind.

What if it's her?

I step onto the pavement and turn towards the van. The woman is walking quickly away, pushing a small buggy in front of her. She looks scared. I can tell by her pace, her hunched shoulders, the way every third step is off the ground like at any minute she might start to run for it. Before I know it, I am striding after her down the street in my pyjamas and slippers. She turns and looks over one shoulder without missing a step.

'Wait!' I shout. She doesn't stop. She keeps going, the baby letting out the odd wail.

'Wait! Can I help you with something?'

She carries on walking. Something about her pace, her gait, looks guilty. It must be her. Why else would she run away?

'Stop! You've come all this way, you've found me, you might as well get what you came for!' I'm shouting now, totally oblivious to the people asleep just a few feet away. I don't care. She is going to get it on all cylinders. How *dare* she? How dare she come here?

Something must have struck her because suddenly she stops. I stop too. We are about twenty feet away from each other. She doesn't turn but stands rocking the buggy, considering her options.

'I know who you are. And you've got a bloody cheek turning up here, spying on me and my children.' I am shaking with rage. I have never confronted anyone about anything in my life and it courses through me like lava now. All of it. All at once.

'What do you want? Who do you think you are, turning up here like this? You've got a bloody cheek! I told you he is dead. He's DEAD! You can't have him any more because he's DEAD. So if you've come looking for money or recognition or support or whatever, you're on a hiding to nothing because I've got nothing to show for the past thirty years apart from my children and my house. And if you think you're getting a penny from me just because you were his bit on the side for however many bloody years, then you are very much mistaken! So please just GO AWAY and NEVER COME BACK!'

I am crying now, tears of fury and humiliation. The baby wails too. The woman's shoulders slacken and her head drops. Good. Good. I have told her. Any minute I expect her to walk away down my quiet little street and out of my quiet little life. Good riddance. I stand panting in the street, aware of my own breath. A few seconds pass. She seems to be considering her next move. Slowly she takes her hands off the buggy and turns to face me. She has some brass neck. I stare straight at her. As she comes eye to eye with me I see the face of this woman who has sent an Exocet missile right through my so-called life.

She is black. I note this with mild shock. She is light-skinned, mixed race – what Robert would have stupidly referred to as 'half-caste' – but she is definitely black. It's hard to say how old she is but at a guess in her late twenties. Robert, with a young black woman? I'm not sure what I'm more surprised by – the fact that such a young and, yes I have to say it, *beautiful* woman was interested in fat, boring old Robert, interested enough to *procreate* with him, or the fact that Robert had a black mistress. Robert would never say he was racist, but he was at best extremely conventional, conservative even. He was from the sort of privileged background that would have seen inter-racial marriages as exotic – too exotic for the likes of him. We stand blinking at each other for a few moments and I can see that she is crying. Silent tears roll down her face, catching the early morning light.

'Don't you think you should just go?' I say quietly. 'You've seen what you came to see. You've had your fun. I don't need the whole street to witness his mistress on my doorstep.'

Then she speaks.

'For fuck's sake, I'm not his mistress, I'm his daughter.'

The baby screams and she reaches down to soothe it.

His *daughter?*

My heart starts to race and my blood rushes in freezing jets down to my toes and back up again.

His daughter? I panic. My hands start to shake. She looks at me and her face is softer.

'Are you OK?' she says as I grab hold of the gate.

'Yes, I'm fine,' I say, swaying slightly. I feel faint.

'Are you all right? Are you OK?' She comes nearer, her face now close to mine, her eyes searching me.

I stare blankly at her. What the hell is going on? Is this really the same morning in which I waved my children off on their holidays, anticipating a quiet day ahead of my big date tomorrow? How can it be? The world has changed in a moment. I stare at her eyes. They are green and brown and golden. They are Robert's eyes. Brighter, more beautiful, but Robert's, unmistakably.

'I'm fine,' I say. 'Just a bit . . . I mean, how do I know you're telling the truth?'

'Why would I lie about something like this?' She stares at me, incredulous.

'I don't know – money?' I say lamely. I don't know why anyone would lie about being the daughter of a dead man unless it's to defraud a widow.

'Look, I know this is a shock – I didn't mean for this to happen, I just wanted to see where he lived. I'm sorry. It was stupid. We'll go.'

And to my horror she bursts into tears again. I stare mutely at her. If she is Robert's daughter, what does that mean? She looks a bit older than Erin so that would make her *before*. I can't believe Robert knew and didn't tell me, if it was before.

If . . .

I need some answers.

'You'd better come in,' I say stiffly. I want her to go, but I need to get to the bottom of this.

I don't want to be here. I don't want this to be happening. I didn't ask for any of this. I want to know everything. I don't want to know anything at all.

She accepts with a nod and we go inside. His daughter. His daugher. We sit at the table opposite one another. Somewhere the baby gurgles. His . . . granddaughter?

'Sorry about that. Crying. Didn't mean to make it all about me,' says the young woman.

'How do you know you are his daughter?' I ask. It sounds a stupid question, but it's the only one I have.

'How do I *know*?' she repeats.

'Yes. Who told you? I mean, did you know him?'

She smiles a sad smile. 'I was starting to.'

'So you didn't meet?'

'No. He didn't want to. But we were talking.'

I sit and consider this. The other phone. He would have been so scared of me finding out that he had this other family. Her mother. Who is her mother? Oh God, did he have a secret other family somewhere? None of this makes sense.

'Your mother?' I ask, dreading the response.

'I don't know.'

'So . . . you were brought up . . .?'

'In care.'

'Oh. I'm sorry.'

It seems so inadequate, but I'm also irritated with my own need to apologise to this stranger who is biologically related to my husband.

'No, *I'm* sorry. This was a stupid idea. Totally insensitive. I was just thinking about me and Hery.'

'Hery? The baby?'

'Yes.'

I lean forward and look at the child still strapped into the buggy. She is just short of a year old, I'd say, chubby and sweet, and she grins when she spots me looking at her. I smile back. How can you not smile at a fat baby, even when she is the cuckoo in your nest?

'She's lovely,' I manage.

'Thank you.'

Mona emerges from the hallway and sniffs at the woman's feet, her tail wagging in first gear, awaiting some recognition before she will deign to show enthusiasm. The woman bends and scratches the dog behind her ears, and is rewarded with a fast wag.

'So she's . . .?'

'His granddaughter. Weird, right? This must be so horrible for you, us turning up like this.'

I don't speak.

'But you knew about us, right? You sent me those messages?'

'I knew about you only when I switched his phone on.'

'Oh. OK. That's deep.'

'But I thought you were – I don't know, I feel ridiculous but I assumed it was his . . . other woman.'

She lets out a small titter.

'Sorry. Yes, I can see how you might have thought that. I

hadn't even considered that you might not have been told *anything.*'

'Well. There we are.'

We sit in silence for a minute. The baby starts to fuss and the woman goes to her, taking her out of the buggy. I don't even know her name.

'Are you sure you are feeling OK now?' she asks, jiggling the baby on one hip.

'Yes, yes, I just, I don't know, it was a shock. Must have had low blood sugar or something.'

'Let me make you some toast, hang on,' she says, thrusting the baby at me. Instinctively I hold my arms out and collect the warm, soft bundle into my lap. Hery. She looks at me uncertainly then relaxes and starts to play with my glasses, reaching repeatedly for them as I duck away. She giggles. It's a good game. I smile.

'She likes you,' says the woman as she slips two pieces of bread into the toaster, totally at home.

'I don't even know your name,' I say.

'Zana,' says the woman. Zana. Robert's daughter Zana. I practise it a few times in my head, feeling a pang of guilt for all the curses I have poured down upon her head in my assumption that she was his mistress. The baby – Hery? Strange name – slaps her hands together and screeches. Zana butters the toast and offers the baby a slim slice. She snatches at it and rubs it over her fat cheeks, gumming at the edges.

'Shall we start again?' says Zana, resting her chin on her hands as she leans over the counter. Her long curly hair falls in thick curtains either side of her pretty face. She is tall – taller than me – and slim, dressed in jeans and a T-shirt, her long slim feet encased in tattered converse trainers.

'What to say?' I start. How do we move forwards from here? Typical of Robert to have made a mess and then walked away from it. I need some facts before I can begin to unthaw – although it's hard to remain frosty with a beautiful child on your knee offering you a piece of soggy toast like it's the best thing in the world.

'How old are you?' I ask. I need to know if she predates us, our relationship, or if she was some kind of accident after an affair during the early part of our marriage, when things were good – or so I thought.

'I'm twenty-eight,' she says. 'I'm sorry I don't know if I—'

I exhale. So it was before. Whatever it was. And he never told me.

'We met twenty-seven years ago,' I say. 'So you must have been before, I mean, I don't know who she was or how they met but I'm assuming it was way before . . . and I don't know if it carried on after but . . .'

Zana looks relieved.

'Oh good. Good. I was dreading you saying your kids were older than me. They didn't look it. But you know . . . I didn't know.'

Of course, she must have seen them leaving. I realise with a lurch that if she is indeed Robert's offspring, then Brendan and Erin have a half-sister. And a niece. This is huge. I pick up the baby and hand her back. I need to breathe for a minute. For weeks I have been holding in what I thought was his affair, when all the time it was a sister and a niece we had no idea about.

'OK, so tell me what you know,' I say. I need to get these facts straight.

'All I know is that my mother got pregnant young, that she wasn't married, she was poor, she was an immigrant, and my father was white and didn't want to know, so she had me fostered when I was about one – about Hery's age – and then I was adopted.'

'Right. How did you find all this out?'

'My adoptive parents told me and I thought maybe it was time to go searching. They never wanted me to look for my birth parents. I think they thought it would hurt me. But then I just sort of . . . drifted for a while. I only started looking last year.'

'And you found Robert. Your . . . dad.'

'Yes. I had his name – my birth mother had it put on my birth certificate – and a rough idea of where he lived. It was pretty easy to find him. His surname – your surname? – Loughty. It's unusual. I found him on the Council website. I wrote to him at work and after a couple of weeks he replied, giving me his phone number. Except it wasn't his regular number, he bought a secret phone – which I found a bit weird, but he told me he was going to tell you soon. I had both his numbers, but he only messaged me from the secret phone. Then suddenly he stopped replying to my messages. We spoke on the phone one day and then – nothing.'

'And that's when he went into hospital?'

'Yes. Well. I know that now. I'm so sorry for your loss.'

To my mortification now *I* start to cry, and so does Zana. The baby looks from me to Zana and back again, and her little bottom lip starts to tremble. We sit there for a few moments crying, all three of us. Zana consoles the baby and I try to think what to say. How can I tell her that my tears are not just sorrow, confusion and shock, but also rage? How could he have done this to us? To all of us? Who is Zana's mother and where is she now? How hard must it have been for her to be dumped, pregnant and poor, by Robert, who then went on to marry me and father two more children in relative luxury? I am thankful for my children but sorry for her. For a brief moment I was relieved to find out it wasn't 'another woman' – at least not while he was married to me – but now I sit here looking at this young woman and her adorable baby and I am cross with him all over again. Was he so concerned with keeping up appearances that he couldn't even tell me, *his own wife*, that this strange miracle from the past had surfaced? What did he think I would do?

'I'm so sorry your search ended like this,' I say finally, determined to try to do right by her even if Robert was too cowardly to. 'Did you at least get any kind of satisfaction from speaking with him before he disappeared again?'

'Yes. Yes, I suppose I did. He apologised over and over again. Not that that was what I was after. He sent me loads of Amazon parcels – things for the baby. I keep telling him that I didn't want all that stuff. He told me a bit about my mum, that he liked her but she wasn't 'the one' . . . He thought she was going to have an abortion. But he said he was glad she hadn't. Which was nice. He kept saying he was going to tell you – he wanted to tell you – but he was scared. I think he felt ashamed. He said he didn't want people to 'get the wrong impression' about him. He was pretty hung up on that. I never thought I'd actually be here.'

'So why are you here?' I ask. Maybe she really is expecting some money.

'I don't know,' she laughs, drying her eyes. I just wanted to see where he lived.'

'How did you find us?' I ask.

'I know it's a bit . . . I just . . . called his office and told them I wanted to take a parcel to you . . .' she says, sounding coy. 'We've been walking past for a few weeks now. I thought you noticed last week. I know it must seem really creepy to you, but I just wanted to bring Hery and say "That's where your grandad lived."'

I wince a little at the word. Am I Hery's de facto grandma now? I've always thought I would love the moment I became a grandparent. I never imagined it would be like this.

'And your mum? Have you found her?'

'No. No, I haven't. I know where she went but I haven't been able to go and look yet. I was going to, and then this one came along,' Zana says, stroking the top of the baby's head.

'Where did she go?'

'Home. She went home.'

'And where is home?'

'Madagascar,' says Zana, smiling. She says it like it's heaven itself. 'I never knew she was from Madagascar. When I saw it on her documents I had to look it up. I didn't know where it was. In my head it was somewhere near Australia. But it's not. It's east of Africa.'

'Incredible,' I say. 'I don't think I've ever heard of anyone from Madagascar.'

'Me neither,' Zana says. 'It's a massive island.'

'Well well,' I say, unsure how to proceed. What do I do now? What is the protocol for entertaining your dead husband's secret adult child and granddaughter? Do I show her around the house? Get the family album out? Invite her to stay for dinner? I want to lie down. I want to get back to yesterday when all I had to worry about was whether the red dress would look better by tomorrow. Zana seems to sense my uncertainty, and starts to gather her things. She straps the baby into the buggy.

'So anyway, I'd better go. I didn't mean to cause you any alarm, and don't worry I won't bother you again. Are you sure you're OK?'

I nod, and stand carefully. I follow Zana out to the hall. It feels wrong to be letting her go like this, but what else am I supposed to do? Am I not allowed to have my life now? Do I owe it to him – to her? – to tidy up his mess even after he has died? Zana stops by the front door and looks at a photo we have on the wall. It's been there for so long I barely register it now – I probably look at it once or twice a year when I'm spring cleaning – but she examines it like a forensic scientist. It's a photo of me, Robert, Brendan and Erin taken about ten years ago. We're standing in a tight unit, huddled together against the lashing rain on our Norfolk campsite. The kids are trying to smile, but you can tell they are fuming and would much rather be at home. I am smiling too, but is it just the wisdom of hindsight that makes me see the tension in my eyes? Robert has his arm hooked around my shoulders, just a bit too high, so it looks like he is about to strangle me. Maybe he was.

Zana looks wistfully at the image. Did she not have a happy family life – at least on the surface?

'Your children are lovely,' she says sadly. 'He was really proud of you all, you know . . .'

'Was he?' I say. Was he? The kids, of course, but me?

'He was. He said he knew he hadn't always been the best father, or husband, but that he loved you all a lot.'

I'm stunned. If only he had been able to say that to *us*. Not much good to me now. Zana is still inspecting the photo. It occurs to me how incredibly strange it must be for her to be staring at two half-siblings. Two white half-siblings. I feel a pang of guilt for not giving her more.

'Have you got far to go?' I ask, aware of the casual politeness of the question, like I'm chatting to a stranger on a long train journey and not my husband's secret daughter.

'No, actually. I know this is going to sound weird, but I actually moved in about a mile away a few months ago.'

Bloody hell. How long has she been watching us?

'Robert told me roughly the area he lived in, and then a place came up nearby, so I decided to go for it. I didn't know what was going to happen, but it seemed like serendipity.'

'Oh.' I feel even more uncomfortable now, knowing she is so close.

'Please don't worry. I'm not going to stalk you, and my place is only temporary, so there's every chance I'll be gone soon.'

'Where is your flat?' I bet she's renting one of those new builds near the station.

'It's the B&B on Heritage Hill.' Zana smiles at my confusion. 'It's temporary accommodation. We were sort of homeless, weren't we, sweetness?' she says, tucking the baby into the buggy snugly.

Homeless. Oh God. What do I say now?

'That can't be easy, being in a B&B with the baby.' I sound like the Queen trying to talk to a commoner, standing in my big house surrounded by my cosy family portraits.

'It's not great!' laughs Zana. 'But we get by. Hopefully something will come up soon. Before she starts walking.'

I open the door for her and she bumps the buggy down the step.

'Well, bye then,' she says brightly.

'Bye,' I say. I'm battling two thoughts –

1. Go away and don't come back ever again. I don't want to think about you or know about you or care about you!

And

2. Let me take care of you both and make it all better. It's not your fault you were fathered by a man that either didn't know or care about you.

It starts to drizzle in that early-morning soft summer way that turns the sky silver and the pavements grey. Zana is walking down the path. In thirty seconds she'll have walked around the bend in the street and I won't see her again. Then she may be moved from the area forever, and this unexpected chapter will be ripped up and thrown away.

'Wait!' I hear myself say as she starts to walk. What am I going to say next? I have no idea.

'Let me at least give you a lift.'

'It's OK really, it's not far.' But I can hear the relief in her voice. She wants me to help her, even if it's just for a mile in her life.

'I'll just get some shoes on, wait there.'

I scrabble for my sandals and my keys, pulling on my anorak as I head up the path. I zap the car door open as Zana wrestles with the baby and the buggy.

'Can you take her while I do this?' she says, offering me the baby. As Zana holds her out Hery grins and reaches her chubby little arms towards me. I melt. Zana expertly flips the buggy and it collapses towards the ground. She picks it up, opens the boot and throws it in amongst the bags for life and the dog-walking wellies.

'I don't have a baby seat,' I say, 'I got rid of all that stuff years ago.'

'I'll sit in the back and hold her, it's not far.'

We pull off and I check them through the rear-view mirror. The baby is all eyes. She must have been in a car before, surely?

'Is her dad . . .?' I ask. There's been no mention of a husband or boyfriend.

'Oh we don't talk about him. He's nothing. He's nobody.'

'Oh. OK. He didn't want to be involved?'

'He wanted to be involved all right. Mostly he involved his fists with my face.'

Oh no. Oh dear lord, no.

'I'm sorry,' I say, completely out of my depth.

'Don't be. We're better off out of it. As soon as we get a little flat, we'll be much better off without him.'

'Does he know where you are?'

'I hope not. He lives miles away. South London.'

I wrack my brains for any better option I can think of. Surely to God there must be help available for women and babies?

'Are there no refuges around here? They take you in, don't they? If you've suffered . . . you know . . .?'

'I wish. There is one not far from here, but it's rammed. The lockdown seemed to bring out the worst in quite a few men.'

I remember hearing this on the radio a while back. I probably tutted and got on with the ironing. Now the reality is in the back of my car.

'I should have gone last year, but then the baby came along and I thought it might help. But it got worse.'

'Well, you don't want her growing up in a . . . situation like that, do you?'

'No. Exactly. So.'

We have already arrived at the B&B. I've driven past this place on the way to the local refuse tip so many times and never given it a second thought, the shabby front with its dirty silk flowers sagging in the tatty window boxes. How bizarre that it now houses a homeless mother and child, forced onto the benefit system by abuse, who are, through the actions of my husband many years ago, now linked to my comfortable middle-class white family. They are governmental statistics, not *family.* Not my family.

Zana looks at me through the mirror. I try to mask my distaste for the place, for this situation. I am deeply uncomfortable.

'It's really not that bad,' she says. 'Why don't you come in?'

'Oh no, no honestly I should be getting back . . .' I say lamely. Zana raises her eyebrows as if to say 'To what?' She has seen Brendan and Erin wave me goodbye this morning. She knows there is only a little dog at home.

'I could do with a hand up the stairs . . . It's hard to carry the baby with one arm and the buggy with the other.'

'OK,' I say. What else can I say? 'No! Manage it on your own like you normally do'? Surely if I can help, I should help? I'm still in shock and I want to run away. But I can't do it. I can't.

We wrestle the buggy from the boot of the car and Zana hands me the baby. Once again Hery smiles and reaches out to me. Zana lets us in. Inside, the hallway is full of pushchairs and carrier bags full of nappies and baby milk formula. I trip on a wheel sticking out and nearly lose my balance.

'Careful!' says Zana, laughing. She leads us up the rickety stairs, dragging the buggy behind her.

'Why don't you leave that in the hall?' I ask.

'I use it to feed her.'

'You don't have a high-chair?'

'No. But this is fine. She doesn't mind so . . .'

On the first landing we pass three doors. A TV blares out from behind the first – children's cartoons, the manic cheerful voices contrasting luridly with the stale, sad atmosphere in the rest of the house. As we pass the second door a mum scolds a child in a language I don't recognise. Behind the third door a baby cries half-heartedly, as if it already knows it won't get what it needs.

'Next floor,' pants Zana, leading me up a narrower flight of stairs. The baby is heavy in my arms and I'm embarrassed by how out of breath I feel. It's been a long time since I've carried a baby.

Finally we reach Zana's room. She fishes around in her pocket for the key, leaning the buggy against the wall. A woman in the next room pokes her head out.

'Hi Zee – you're up and about early! Have you got any spare teabags? I've run out.'

'Yeah, hang on,' says Zana, pushing the door open. She takes Hery from me and lays her on the unmade bed. In a corner of the small, dark room there are cardboard boxes piled precariously on top of one another. A small TV sits in the other corner, its top acting as a shelf for two mugs, a bag of sugar and a small box of tea bags. Zana grabs a handful from the box and takes them to her neighbour. I stare at the magnolia walls, wondering how anyone can live in one small room like this, especially with children. I would have gone mad. It's clean enough, and there are a few small personalised touches that make it seem even more tragic – the little rug on the floor, the candles melted onto saucers, and on the wall opposite the bed, a laminated map. I peer at it – it's an island, but not one I recognise. The inscription says 'Madagascar', and I feel a lump in my throat as I imagine this poor woman staring at her mother's birthplace, longing for a connection with it, with her, with home. A crushing depression hits me like a tidal wave. I need to get out of here.

'Not so bad, is it?! Tea?' says Zana, coming back in and picking up the baby.

'No, no I really must be getting back.'

She looks disappointed but smiles anyway.

'Thanks for the lift. You know where we are if you ever want to visit . . .'

I nod my goodbye and stumble out of the door. I'm down the stairs and back in the car within seconds, pulling away without even putting my seatbelt on. It's only when I turn into my street

I realise I am crying. I'm angry. I'm furious – at Robert, at myself, at the bastard who beat Zana into that miserable bedsit existence. And sad. And inside something gnaws away at my heart. What is it? Duty? Why do I feel like I should do something? It's not my mess. Not my problem. I get home and go upstairs to lie on the bed. The red dress is hanging up waiting for tomorrow. The date. For an hour or so I had forgotten all about it. I'll put Zana out of my mind and focus on Nick. Should I tell him?

I pick up my phone. I don't want to talk. Not yet. I decide to send a voice note.

'Good morning, Nick . . . bit of a weird one . . . I've just found out that Robert had another child. Before he met me. He didn't know about her really until recently. She turned up here this morning. All a bit odd. Just wanted to let you know. Maybe we can chat later? Still in shock at the moment.'

I hit send and instantly regret it. You can't tell people you hardly know things like this, can you? In a voice note? But Nick just seems so trustworthy to me. So sincere. Maybe we can face this together. He will know what to do.

I close my eyes. What a morning. My phone pings. Nick.

Whaaaat? That's crazy! I mean, are you sure? Are you sure she's really his daughter? There are a lot of scammers out there Angela. I advise that you tread VERY carefully. She's probably after your money.

I text my reply.

Yes that's what I said but she seems genuine. She has a baby.

> Bloody hell. Still, don't panic. I'd insist on seeing a birth certificate, a DNA test or something. Sounds dodgy to me. Well . . . sounds like we've both had a heavy morning. I just found out I've been made redundant. As of now.

Oh bloody hell. That's awful. I call him, and he answers straight away.

'That's terrible news, Nick! What happened?! I thought you were high up there?' It feels strange to be brushing my revelation aside so quickly, but this has obviously knocked Nick for six.

'Yeah well ... the recession, I guess. Got a call from the lawyers this morning. The company has gone into liquidation. Effective immediately. Going to have to tighten my belt. No jobs around at the moment. I'm so angry. Why me? Why now? After all I've been through.'

Nick's voice starts to break and I realise he is crying. Poor man. At least I don't have those financial worries.

'Are you all right? I mean, financially? Can you survive?'

'Well, this is the thing, Angela – I invested all my savings into the housing project we had planned. Lost it all. No pension, nothing.'

'Oh God. That's awful. You poor thing! Is there anything I can do?' Funny how you can care for someone after such a short time. I feel genuinely bereft for him.

'No, no don't worry,' he sniffs, gathering himself, 'I'll be fine. But I totally understand if you don't want to meet up now. Not quite the catch you thought I was any more. Who wants to start a romance with an unemployed widower? I can't even afford the train fare to London!' He starts to sob quietly.

'Don't be ridiculous!' I say, worried that he is trying to cut me off. Is this an excuse? Has he had second thoughts? He sounds genuinely upset.

'Look – I can send you some money, just to tide you over, if that's really all that's worrying you?'

'No, no I don't want to take money from you. I'll be OK. I've got food, and the house is secure. For the moment. I'm renting, you see. I was waiting to buy somewhere new once my investments matured. Not going to happen now. I feel like such a fool. I poured everything I had into that project. Every last penny.'

'Won't you get a redundancy payout at least?'

'You don't understand, Angela!' he says, sounding impatient and cross. 'It's all gone! The company is worth nothing!'

I sit and take this in. Poor Nick. He sounds utterly broken.

'Listen, I know you don't want me to, but please let me help you.'

He stays silent. Sniffs quietly.

'Well . . . I feel so dreadful to ask but . . .'

'Of course! What are friends for?!'

'I was hoping we could be more than friends, Angela . . .'

I blush. 'Well, you know what I mean. But please, let me help at least to get you to London! How much do you need?'

There is a short pause.

'About . . . a thousand?' he says quietly.

'A thousand?' I blurt. I haven't travelled by train much lately, but that sounds a lot more than a super saver return to me.

'My rent is due and if I can just keep the flat for the next couple of weeks I can try to get back on my feet. I'll pay you back. I promise. I've never been in debt in my life . . .' He starts to cry again.

'It's OK,' I say. 'It's OK.'

I mean, it's not like I've got anything else to spend it on. Am

I being stupid? Probably. I feel a bit sick. What have I done? It's a huge risk to take on someone you have never met. But we feel close. I know in my gut that he is genuine. And if you don't take chances when they come your way, what is life? He gives me his details and I transfer the money. Five minutes later he texts me.

> I am so so thankful Angela. I'll never forget this. I will repay you – and more! Can't wait to thank you in person tomorrow. Much love N xxx

And despite my doubts, I smile. It feels good to help.

15

I wake with a start. Where am I? I pat the bed next to me. It's empty. Of course it's empty. I was dreaming. A man was pinning me to a wall. The wall was, it was . . . moving as he pushed at my shoulders, and I was out of breath. A baby was crying, but I couldn't get to it. Just a dream. I check the clock – 4.38a.m. I slump back onto the pillow. No point trying to get back to sleep now. Even though I was exhausted falling into bed at midnight after getting my hair done, my nails painted, my outfit ready on the chair, I will not be able to get any more rest. I'll just have to lie here getting more and more nervous. I wonder how Nick is feeling? I start to replay the events of yesterday morning – the bizarre encounter on the street, the baby's loving arms, the map of Madagascar. Nick and the money. Did that really happen? Thank God for the distraction of preparation yesterday, or I'd have been driving myself mad with guilt and worry. Every time I think of Zana and Hery a knot forms in my stomach and a fist twists in my throat. She has nobody. I wonder if they are sleeping now? The baby looks like the kind that sleeps soundly, gurgling gently when she wakes. Not like my two, who both complained bitterly if left alone to cry for more than three minutes. 'You've made a rod for your own back with those children,' Robert would say as I got up night after night to console them. Some father he turned out to be, abandoning Zana's poor mother. I think of all the mums in that stale little house, holed up in a single room waiting for a flat somewhere, anywhere. Surely there must be help available? Some charity that can lend a hand? I think of Zana lugging the buggy up two flights of stairs just so that she has somewhere to put Hery when she feeds her, all for the want of a high-chair. Maybe I could at least help with that? I could order one online. Send it straight there. But what then? Surely she needs help from people who know what they're doing? People who might be able to support her too?

I don't want to get too involved. I order a high-chair online and send it to Zana at the B&B. I can at least do that. I feel useful. I feel better. Lighter.

I get up, shower, taking care to avoid wetting my newly blow-dried hair. I was lucky to get that appointment – hairdressers have been swamped since they were allowed to reopen – so I don't want to undo the good work. My hair is normally a frizzy mess, but today it is smooth and luxurious, and the roots have been touched up nicely too, so for the first time since March I don't have a few inches of grey either side of my parting. I try to eat some breakfast, but I'm worried about the dress and looking lumpy. I'm too nervous to eat anyway. I take the dog for a walk around the block to steady myself. On my way home I see Jenni outside her house in a bikini top and tiny shorts.

'Hi Jenni!' I say brightly. I feel good. Helping. 'How are you this fine morning?'

'Good! You look nice – had your hair done?'

'Yes, yesterday,' I say, patting at it proudly.

'Good for you.'

'Big day today!'

Jenni looks blank for a moment. 'Ah yes! The Date! What time are you meeting him?'

'Midday.'

'Well, I hope you have fun. Sorry if we were a bit . . . you know . . . we just don't want you to get hurt, and I don't know, he's probably lovely and just what you need.'

I smile. 'Thanks, Jen. That means a lot.' Should I tell her about the money? Best not. She'll get the wrong idea. I know what it sounds like, but she doesn't know Nick.

'Come and tell me about it later – that's if you're not in a hotel room shagging your way to a weekend of cystitis!' she laughs.

'Stop it!' I say, blushing furiously. I'm about to go when I'm suddenly gripped by the need to tell Jenni all about Zana and the baby. She would know what to do. Dare I?

I told her all about the 'affair' that never was – maybe she deserves to know the truth? I take a deep breath.

'Actually there's something else on my mind,' I say.

'OK,' says Jenni, putting down the watering can and facing me.

'She came here,' I say.

Jenni blinks then registers what I am saying.

'The woman? She came here?!'

'It's not what we thought, Jenni—' I start, but Jenni is ready to explode.

'Oh yes they all say that! "It's not what it looked like"! Did she want money? The bloody cheek of it!'

'Jenni, Jenni, no – she's Robert's daughter.'

I let it sink in, my body letting me know via the jittery feeling in my stomach that I too am still in shock.

'His *daughter?*'

'Yes. And her baby. His granddaughter.'

'Shit. When? Who with? How old is she? Oh Angela, I'm so sorry.'

'It's OK. She's twenty-eight. So it was before.'

'And you didn't know? He never said? Did *he* know?'

'She says yes. But only just. She says they were talking. She was taken into care when she was little. Her mum disappeared. Robert didn't want to know.'

Jenni considers this for a while.

'Shit,' she says finally. 'Any details about the mum?'

'Only that she was from Madagascar, that they met over here.'

'So she's . . .?'

'Yes, she's mixed race.'

This piece of information seems to shock Jenni more than the fact that Robert had a previous child.

'Bloody hell. I always thought Robert was a bit . . .'

'He was!' I say.

'So what happened? Where is she now?'

'She's living in a B&B up the road. Temporary accommodation. Her partner was abusing her, so she left. With the baby. I've just ordered her a high-chair.'

'She's going to need a bit more than that!'

'What else can I do? I've been thinking what I could do to help her, but I don't really want to get involved.'

'Sounds like you already are.'

I sigh. I know she's right. Once people are in your family, they are in your family.

'You should come with me now – I'm delivering donations of nappies to the Magpie Project.

'I can't – I have to get ready!' I say. 'Can we go tomorrow?'

'No. They are only open Fridays and Wednesdays. It's a charity. It's run by amazing women who have their own families, but they still give up all their spare time looking after mums. They support women like Zana with young families living in temporary accommodation. They'll know what help she can get. Wait there – I'll put some clothes on.'

'Jenni, I can't!'

'It will only take an hour, tops! Wait there!'

And she disappears to get changed. Pointless saying no to Jenni. I might have known she'd get right on it about Zana. At least it might put my mind at rest a bit . . .

'Well, if we're quick . . .' I shout after her. It should be OK. I have time, and I need the distraction.

I drop the dog off at home and when I return Jenni is waiting in the car.

'Come on, Thelma!' she shouts, taking the hood down on her battered old Mercedes convertible.

'Thelma?'

'Yeah – Thelma and Louise.'

I jump in beside her. 'I'm definitely Louise,' I say.

We speed off and the wind whips my carefully blow-dried hair all over my face. So that's why Susan Sarandon wore a headscarf. Too late now. It feels good to be doing something.

16

We pull in to a small car park about three miles from our street but a world away in social class. It's only nine in the morning but already there is a small army of women sorting through piles of donations at tables dotted around the car park. A battered double buggy and a variety of well-loved baby toys lie strewn near the door waiting for collection. A cheerful woman in a trendy boilersuit and a face mask is at the front desk – a wallpaper table plonked in front of the doors of a small community centre. The atmosphere is jolly, everyone chattering and laughing. I don't know what I imagined – a circle of keening, wailing women despairing at the injustices of the world? – but it wasn't this. I feel shy and timid but Jenni leaps from the car and shouts hello to everyone.

'Hi Jen,' says the woman in the boilersuit. 'Come to help deliver?'

'Not today, Alison – I come bearing gifts of nappies! Hundreds of them!' Alison smiles.

'You are brilliant. Thanks so much!' She disappears into the building with some of the bags. A woman with green hair emerges with a huge Primark bag.

'Pants!' she says joyfully.

'I'm sorry?' I say, smiling.

'We're having a pants day. We have so many mums living in one bedroom with their kids, and they keep asking us for bigger and bigger nappies – they can't toilet train their kids because the nearest toilet is through two or three fire doors and they keep having little accidents on the way to the loo. We've got four- and five-year-olds still in nappies. So we thought, "Let's give them Big Boy and Big Girl Pants!" They will try really hard to keep them clean. It's a little idea but it seems to be working,' she smiles.

'Great idea,' I say.

'Yeah, it's gone really well. We put out a call for donations and we've had loads! This is the fourth bag this morning. All brand new, of course. The kids love it.'

To my mortification I realise I am choked up. What a brilliant thing.

The woman with the green hair clocks my tears.

'People can be pretty amazing,' she says. 'Sometimes they just need to be told what to do to help. The big things – the virus, the deaths, the NHS, the vaccine, racism, domestic violence – can be so overwhelming, can't they? But if you can just do one little thing, you're doing your bit, aren't you?'

I nod.

'Because if you're not part of the solution, you're part of the problem, aren't you?'

Her words cut me. She is right, of course. Although Denise is a pain in the arse, she is at least trying to do something good. I feel like a massively self-centred suspicious middle-aged cliché. Not in my back yard. I should do more. I could do more. I start carrying the loaded bags of nappies into the building. What a thing – to have to rely on the kindness of strangers for basic necessities. I think about my privileged life, the lives my children had growing up – the space, the parties, the long summers in the garden and the cosy winters by the fire. Then I think about Zana and the other women there – trying to bring up their little families in one poky room.

'Can I give you some money? For the pants?' I say, reaching into my purse.

'Thanks! Sure! Best to do it online, though. And if you're ever bored, come down and drive for us! There's always something to do here,' says Alison.

'I'm sure there is. You are brilliant,' I say.

'Actually, Ali, we have a . . . friend who is living up near us in a B&B – it's a bit far on the bus but can we tell her to drop in? You do the play sessions, don't you?' asks Jenni.

'We can't at the moment. Too many families mixing. Covid restrictions. Which is why we're doing all this collecting. But give her my number – if she needs anything, we'll try to help. You have to, don't you?'

It's a rhetorical question, but it hits me hard.

We drive off, leaving the Magpie women behind. I'm ashamed of myself. I have enough money to buy Zana new things, anything she wants, but something has stopped me. I want someone else to take care of it. It's not my fault. And yet. And yet.

The gnawing sense of responsibility is there. I know she is Robert's abandoned child from before I met him, I know I share no blood with her or the baby, but I feel a pull. What is it? Maybe he didn't know about her until recently, or maybe he did . . . but wouldn't it be wrong of me to turn my back on her now? If you're not part of the solution, you're part of the problem.

'Isn't it a cool place?' says Jenni.

I nod. I'm thinking. Thinking of all the times Robert made me feel useless. Or did he? Did I use his confidence and charm as an excuse to shrink back into myself? Should I have stuck up for myself more? Had a bit more of a spine? Isn't it high time I stopped using my rage at Robert as an excuse, and took a bit more control? I could do so much with what I have. Look at

Denise – we laugh at her, but she is like Alison – she makes a difference. I could do that too. I could. Should I?

No time to dwell on it now. I'm running late. I need an hour to get to Victoria station – at least an hour. I feed the dog, drag a comb through my now wayward hair and stuff some tissues and a lipstick in my handbag. Keys, purse, allergy tablets. It wouldn't do to come down with a hay fever attack today. Who would want to kiss a snotty-nosed, red-eyed sneezing old bag like me? It's ten thirty. If I can walk to the station quickly, I should be in more than enough time. I check myself in the mirror and grimace. I will have to do. I slam the door behind me and march up the road towards the station. Ten minutes and I'll be there. I'm not going to think about Zana and the baby now. I'm going to focus on Nick. Maybe he will have some good advice? I'm about two minutes away when I realise I've left my mask at home. Shit. They are compulsory now. I dash into the shop, hoping they have some paper ones. They do. I pay £5 for a pack of three, cursing the Covid entrepreneurs making money out of all this. I reach the station, but my Oyster card needs topping up. I punch at the buttons impatiently – of course I have forgotten my reading glasses, so it's hit and miss whether I get my PIN right. A couple of errors later I manage to add credit and push through the barriers just as I hear the rumble and screech of a train approaching. I rush down the escalator two steps at a time. I can hear the train pulling into the platform. If I don't make this one, there could be a ten-minute wait for the next – that's what it's like living out in suburban London. If I'm not there by midday he might leave, thinking that I am not coming. I don't want that to happen. I can hear the beeping of the doors signalling the train's imminent departure. I wait until we are three steps to the bottom and take a leap. And land heavily on my left foot. 'Ouch!' I scream. I buckle and fall to the ground just as the train pulls off. A young man comes to help me up.

'Are you OK?' he says, his face a mask of concern.

'I . . . I think so,' I say, trying to put weight on my foot. 'Ow ow ow!' I gasp. It's impossible to put my foot down. Shit shit shit – how am I going to get to Victoria like this?

'Let me help you to a bench,' says the young man, peering at my ankle. It's already swelling.

'I'd go to hospital with that, if I were you,' he says, handing me my bag.

'It's fine,' I say, 'I'll just get a taxi.'

'Well, if you're sure . . .' he says.

'If you could just help me back up to the station to call, that would be so kind.' He holds on to me, trying to maintain social distance while escorting me, one-footed, to the up escalator. At the top he lets go and heads back down. The next train is already rumbling in. Typical. I could have just waited. Now I'll have to message Nick and explain why I'll be late.

I reach inside my bag for my phone. Fuck. It's at home. I remember now, I put it on charge just in case it ran out and I needed it. Stupid stupid stupid. What the hell am I going to do now? I'll have to get back home somehow and pick up my phone. I attempt a hobble to the entrance but the pain is too intense. I hop outside and with the first bit of good luck today see a passing taxi. I hail it and miraculously it stops. I hop over and open the door.

'Where to, love – A&E?' says the cheery female cabbie.

I look down at my ankle. It's puffy and pink. There's no way I'm going anywhere today apart from Accident and Emergency.

'Yes, please,' I sigh, heaving myself into the back of the cab.

'Had a fall?' says the cabbie, looking at me through her

rear-view mirror. 'Don't worry, we'll get you there in no time. Wouldn't want to be going into a hospital any time soon, though. Not with all this. Still, at least you've got your mask.'

At A&E I note with a flutter of relief that the waiting area is almost deserted. It seems as though the idea of catching Covid is enough to put off the usual exaggerators and time wasters clogging up the system when they should just wait for a doctor's appointment. I still won't make it to Victoria, even if they tell me it's just bruised. The triage receptionist tells me it shouldn't take too long to be seen, and I ask her if I can use a phone. She points to a payphone on the wall and I hobble over to it, scrabbling around for change. I don't know anyone's number. How am I going to contact anyone to let them know I am here? The only numbers I know are Erin's and Brendan's. I punch in the number for Erin. Maybe she will have an idea. The foreign dialling tone rings out. I try Brendan. Same. They are probably sleeping off Retsina hangovers somewhere. I give up, deciding to deal with it all when I get home.

Two hours later I leave with my ankle in a little support boot.

'Nothing broken – just badly sprained. Rest up and you should be OK in a couple of weeks!' said the nice doctor. A couple of weeks?! They've given me some crutches to help me get about. As my taxi pulls into the street, I see Jenni out in her front garden with a Friday afternoon glass of wine. She spots me as I pay the driver and comes over expectantly.

'You're back early! Was it a disaster? Is he a psycho? I bet he was a psycho! Told you!'

I say nothing, but silently hand her my crutches.

'Bloody hell!' she says, taking them and helping me out. I tell her about rushing and falling and having no phone. She helps me inside and goes to fetch it for me.

'You poor thing. There was I thinking you were being wined and dined and all the time you were in hospital. What a couple of days you've had.'

I check my phone. Two missed calls from Nick at 12.02 and 12.09. No voicemail. Then a text. I take a deep breath before opening it. Jenni makes tea while I read it, my heart racing.

> Sorry Angela – I'm so sorry I wasn't there. The landlord came round this morning and took all the money you lent me. All of it. He says I still owe him £500 – truth is I'd fallen behind a bit . . . So I didn't have the train fare. I couldn't face calling you after your generosity. Don't hate me. Nx

I feel sick. He wasn't there! *He wasn't there!* Have I just been had? Surely not. Can I believe his story – or is it just that, a story to reel me in further? I'm so confused. There was no mention of rent arrears yesterday. How can he not have had enough money to buy a bloody train ticket? Even if my account was hacked and emptied right now, I'd be able to locate thirty quid down the back of the sofa or in the pockets of a few coats. This isn't right. With an acidic twist in my guts I realise that I have indeed been had. I can feel the blood drain from my face.

'Are you OK?' says Jenni, rushing to sit me down. 'You look like you've seen a ghost!'

'It's Nick,' I say. 'He wasn't there anyway.'

'Oh well, that's good, isn't it? You won't have stood him up!'

I hand her the phone wordlessly. She might as well know.

She scans the message quickly and gasps.

'You . . . gave him money?' she asks quietly.

I nod. 'No fool like an old fool, eh?'

'Oh Angela . . . oh bloody hell.'

'Yeah.'

'Well, we have to get your money back.'

'How? He's not going to just hand it over, is he? I mean, he's led me this far, he'll probably just ignore me if I call him out on it, won't he?' I feel so stupid. I am that cliché woman flattered into parting with her money. I could cry. 'And also,' I say, clutching at straws, 'maybe it's true, and he is in a crisis . . .?'

'Oh Angela, come on . . . I'm sorry, but I had a bad feeling about him after you told us about the property research.'

'But . . . but he was so nice to me, so genuine!'

'Yes, it's called Love Bombing – they schmooze you to make you vulnerable to manipulation,' says Jenni.

'I feel like such an idiot. Oh God.'

'Don't be so hard on yourself – you are a good woman, kind, trusting. You don't deserve this.'

She's right. I don't deserve this. I'm suddenly angry.

Action. Enough of this deferring to other people. Enough poor decisions based on what other people want.

I type my reply to Nick's last text.

Oh poor you! Don't worry, I completely understand. Is there anything I can do to help? Xxx

I press send and show Jenni. 'If he asks for more money, we will know he's on the make. Nobody with an ounce of decency would take a grand, stand me up then ask for more,' I say, my hands trembling.

We sit and stare at the phone. He is replying. It's a long one.

I am anxious, but in my heart of hearts I know what the rippling dots will soon confirm. Finally his message appears.

> Oh Angela you are exactly that – an Angel. Thank you so much for your kindness and understanding. I was so worried you were going to be upset with me. All I need is £500 and I'll be covered for two weeks until I get sorted. Then I PROMISE to pay you back PLUS INTEREST! xxx

'So now we know,' I say, feeling a strange calm descend.

'Bastard,' says Jenni.

'Yep. But he's the last. That's it. I'm done. Can't trust them to tell you the truth. They're all the same. I've been a doormat for years. I'm a pushover. I let the men in my life tell me what to do – I always have. And I always knew it, but I still let it happen. I obviously got something out of it – but what? Am I really so down on myself that I need a man to keep telling me I'm useless, just so that I can say to myself "See? HE thinks you're shit too, so you must be right!"? How can I have been so stupid? So weak? I need to start standing up for myself. Right now!'

Jenni stares at me for a second then punches the air – 'Yes, sister!!!'

I grab the phone and message Nick back.

> Gotcha. I want my money back NOW. Never contact me again. Shame on you!

I haven't the slightest hope that he will reply, but it makes me feel good to hit send.

'I'm going to get the wine. Wait there,' says Jenni, rushing to the door. 'This demands a celebration!'

I've just been fleeced for a thousand pounds by someone I barely know and Jenni wants to celebrate? I scroll back through all our conversations, me and Nick. If that's even his name. The dead wife – to garner sympathy? Or real? The 'charity work' to present an honourable front. The slight coerciveness, the hints and little manipulations. I even went on a diet. What a poor fool I was. I feel utterly ashamed, sitting here in my pathetic tight red dress, the control pants cutting into my torso. I've been a fool. Well, not any more. I stand up and wriggle out of the tight pants, easing them down over the ankle boot. It feels good to let my stomach expand and breathe again.

Jenni comes back with a bottle and two glasses. She pours me a large one and offers a toast.

'To Angela – no longer a doormat but her Own Woman!'

I sink the glass in one.

'That's my girl!' says Jenni approvingly. 'More?'

'No,' I say, the green shoots of resolve suddenly bursting through the darkness. 'We have stuff to do.'

'What?'

'We're going to bring them here.'

Jenni stops drinking and peers at me over her glass. 'What did you just say?' she asks quietly.

'Zana and the baby. They can come and live here. Just until they get a place of their own.'

'Are you serious? That's . . . a lot.'

'I know. And it sounds mad and I'm scared, but I have to do it. It's the right thing to do. It's what I want to do.' I am shaking, but I know I'm right. I feel it in my core. 'Well, if you're sure – I think that's incredible. Incredible.'

'I am sure. Because if you're not part of the solution, you're part of the problem.'

17

We are outside the B&B fifteen minutes later. I am trying not to think too hard about what we are doing, or I might back out. In my heart I know I am doing the right thing, but I am fighting my knee-jerk response, which is to defer, seek permission and approval. Jenni helps me out of the car and we ring on the doorbell. A large lady in a bright-pink dressing-gown comes to the door. We tell her we are there to talk to Zana and Hery and she scowls.

'Hang on – we don't really like visitors at the moment. Wait there,' she grumbles.

'That's OK,' I say. 'It's all a bit last-minute.'

We stand on the doorstep. It feels like the portal to another universe – a strange new world in which I house homeless women and babies who are the secret offspring of my dead husband at a moment's notice, a world where I am making decisions on my own about real things, things that matter, a world in which the beginnings of a spine is forming in my body.

'You OK?' says Jenni.

'I think so,' I say, leaning against the door frame. My ankle is throbbing, but the adrenaline is keeping the pain at bay. Suddenly we hear a window opening above us. Zana sticks her head out. She looks alarmed.

'Hello!' I shout, waving up at her. She frowns. She doesn't know who we are.

'It's me – Angela. We met yesterday. And this is Jenni, my friend.'

Zana smiles then. 'Sorry – weird angle from up here. Didn't recognise you! Is everything OK? Oh my God, what have you done to your foot?'

'Long story,' I say. What do we do now? I hadn't thought about the moment when I ask an almost complete stranger if she'd like to come and live with me. There is an awkward pause.

'Hi Zana, Angela has come to ask you a question,' says Jenni. She prods me and I wobble on my crutches.

'Yes. It's just – well, you're here with the baby living in one room and that can't be easy, and there I am in a big house all alone, and you know, you just found your dad and then he died, and it's the least he, I mean we, I mean I can do really . . .'

Zana squints down at me. The baby starts crying in the background and she ducks inside for a second. She comes back and shouts, 'Hang on, I'm coming down.'

'Well done,' says Jenni as we wait for Zana to appear at the door. I feel so nervous. Like I'm proposing marriage or something. The thought makes me burst out laughing. It's the nerves.

'Stop it!' says Jenni, but she's laughing too. Zana opens the door. She looks shy. A bit frightened. Are we being weird?

'Are you asking me to move in with you?' She is very direct. No nonsense.

'Yes. I am. I mean, if you want to. If that would be something you would like to do. You and the baby, of course. Until you get sorted.'

Zana considers this new information for a beat.

'But . . . why? Yesterday you seemed a bit . . . I mean, I assume it was you that sent the high-chair? Thanks for that. You didn't have to do that.'

'That's OK,' I say. 'I just had a think about it. And I want you to come. I mean just until you get sorted. However long it takes. I want to help.'

Zana looks at me, trying to suss out the situation.

'OK,' she says, 'I'll get my stuff. Can you help me?' she says to Jenni, before turning on her heel and heading back upstairs. Jenni follows her, giving me a thumbs-up as she goes. I'm surprised by a huge surge of relief. A minute later Jenni appears with a holdall and the high-chair. She has dragged it all downstairs without any help. Zana follows, carrying the baby, and retrieves the buggy from the hall. They are laughing and chatting. The large lady appears close behind them. She looks cross.

'It's £400 if she's moving out. Here are the bank details. She'll get it covered by housing benefit, so make sure you get it back off her.' She's all charm.

'Thank you,' I say, 'I'll pay it today.'

'You better – because they'll cut her off the housing list if she does a runner.'

'I will, don't worry. Look, I'll do it now,' I say, pulling out my phone. Jenni and Zana stand in an awkward tableau watching the transaction. I tap in the information and show the lady the transfer confirmation. I'm getting good at pinging large sums of money to virtual strangers – at least this one deserves it. And I have no doubt that at least this one will give it back. The woman grunts and trundles off.

'Thank you,' says Zana, 'I will pay you back. I get the cheque in two weeks.'

'OK.'

She nods, and climbs into the back of the car. I clamber awkwardly into the passenger seat as Jenni folds the buggy and puts it and the high-chair in the boot. She places the holdall in the back next to Zana.

'Where's the rest of your stuff?' I ask.

'That's it,' she says. 'I travel light.'

'All set?' asks Jenni, like it's a day trip to the seaside and not a rescue mission. The question is – who is being rescued? Jenni seems fired up by the whole thing. I feel weirdly elated. We are doing A Good Thing. Zana says nothing, and sits clinging on to the baby as the wind rushes through our hair on our way home.

Back at the house I feel shy letting them in. I'm going to have to camp out downstairs – I can't keep hobbling up and down. For a minute I consider giving Zana my room – our room – but I'm going to need my own place if this is going to work. I tell Jenni to take Zana and the baby up to the spare room – it's big enough, and much better than the single bedroom she has just left behind. Plus, she won't be confined to it. I can hear them upstairs talking about whether the baby will be safer on the floor or on the bed. I put the kettle on because I can't think of anything else to do. There's a knock at the door. Oh God, what now? A long-lost sibling from Mogadishu?

I hobble out to the hallway, clinging on to the walls as I go. Through the glass I can see the unmistakable silhouette of Denise. She is actually peering through the window, but jumps back when she sees me approaching.

'Hi Denise,' I sigh, opening the door. I try to keep my foot hidden – I don't want an interrogation about my ankle – but I'm aware that my peeping around the door must look very suspicious, especially to somebody like Denise.

'Everything OK, Angela?' she asks, making no attempt to hide the fact she is trying to look over my shoulder into the house.

'Yes, fine thanks,' I say, but she is having none of it. She's probably seen us all drive past.

'It's just that I saw you just now in Jenni's car—'

Here we go.

'And there was a woman holding a baby, no car seat, which I thought was a bit odd. I mean, everyone has a baby seat nowadays, don't they? This isn't the nineteen seventies any more, is it, ha ha!'

'Yes, it was a bit of an emergency. All sorted now.' I try to close the door, but to my amazement she jams her foot in it – casually, like she's just resting – and leans forward.

'Is there anything I can do for you?' she asks, desperate to be invited in.

'No no, I'm fine. Honestly, thanks, Denise.'

With perfect timing Jenni pounds down the stairs followed by Zana and Hery, who lets out a delighted shriek when she sees me. I make a 'go away' gesture behind my back but she misses it and comes to see who is there. I have to let go of my tight grip on the door.

'Oh Jenni! You're here!' says Denise, like it's a party she hasn't been invited to.

'Yes, I am here,' says Jenni brightly. 'Do you fancy a cup of tea?'

I shoot her a look – what is she doing, inviting the Gestapo in for tea?

Denise doesn't miss a beat.

'Ooh well, if it's not too much trouble – we can sit in the garden and stay distant!

She pushes her way in as I step back and comes face to face with Zana and Hery.

'Hello!' says Zana, and the baby gurgles.

'What a lovely baby!' coos Denise. 'And who are you, you little cutie?'

What to say now? Jenni comes to the rescue.

'This is Zana – Zana, this is Denise, and she is your Fairy Godmother.'

'I'm sorry?' says Zana, laughing.

'Let's get some tea and I'll explain,' says Jenni. 'Denise, can you help Angela into the garden? She twisted her ankle on the stairs this morning . . .'

'Oh NO! I didn't even notice! Poor you!'

Denise can't believe her luck. Strangers to interrogate, a dangerous merging of households to navigate, plus an injury to boot.

I hobble out to the garden. Oh shit. Now she's going to see my weird statue park. She's going to think it's Christmas.

'Oh! These are . . . wow, aren't they?' she says.

'It's OK. I know they're grotesque,' I say, lowering myself carefully onto the swing seat.

'Well, well, well!' says Denise, shaking her head in mock wonder.

Jenni comes out holding the baby, leaving Zana to make the tea.

'Right, before she comes out, I'll tell you what's going on because I don't want to embarrass her.'

Denise cannot wait for this. What the hell is Jenni going to say? Surely she isn't going to tell her the truth?

'Zana is homeless. We found out about her through the Magpie Project—'

'Oh yes, I know them, I did the pants collection—'

'Exactly. So she was living in a tiny room with the baby, because her twat of a partner was beating her up—'

'Oh no, that's terrible, I was reading that in the first few weeks of lockdown a woman rang a domestic violence report line every thirty seconds—'

'Yes, yes, so Angela has decided, since the kids are travelling and she's on her own, to put them up for a while.'

Denise looks at me with renewed interest, and yes, just a hint of jealousy. I bet she wishes she had a domestic-violence-surviving-mixed-race-single-mother to take in.

'Oh. Good. I mean, good for you. That's so lovely of you. But, I mean, are you *sure*?'

'Yes, why not?' I say.

'But – you don't *know* her. She could be *anyone* . . .' says Denise, her brow creasing with worry.

'She's not just *anyone*, Denise! It's fine, trust me! This is where you come in,' says Jenni, jiggling the baby on one hip.

'She's got nothing. I mean, *nothing*. She needs clothes, nappies, milk formula, a cot, a decent pushchair—'

I hesitate to point out that I could provide all those things – why would I do that for a random stranger? Jenni is trying to cover our tracks and also help Denise at the same time. It's genius.

Denise's eyes light up. A project. A real person to provide for.

'Leave it with me,' she says. 'I'll get whatever you need.'

Bang on cue Zana comes out with tea.

'Thank you, Zany!' says Denise warmly.

'It's Zana,' corrects Zana. 'And this is Hery.'

'Oh sorry – Zana. Pretty name! Where are you from?'

'Romford,' smiles Zana.

Denise laughs. 'No, I mean, *originally*?' I cringe inwardly. I'm sure I've said this before to a black person, but seeing Denise do it makes me realise how bad it sounds.

'Romford!' repeats Zana, still smiling.

'Ha ha ha, yes of course,' says Denise, taking an awkward slurp on her tea. It burns her lip and she winces silently.

Zana throws her a lifeline.

'It's actually a Madagascan name. Fanomezana.'

'Oh really? Interesting name. And you shorten it to Zana. I can understand why!'

'Yeah, bit of a mouthful for my parents, so they called me Zana.'

I flinch at the mention of her adoptive family. I hope Denise doesn't ask too many questions. Of course she does.

'Why did they give you such a long name if they didn't want to say it all the time?' chuckles Denise.

'They didn't. It was my name when they adopted me. They kept it. It's Malagasy. It means gift.'

I smile. Gift.

'Oh I see. Sorry. And the baby . . . what did you say her name is?'

'Hery.'

'And what does that mean?'

'Power,' says Zana, taking the baby into her arms.

18

Two hours later Denise returns. Zana is happily ensconced in her bedroom when I open the door. On the pathway there is a buggy, which looks as good as new (and much easier to handle than the contraption currently blocking my hallway), a travel cot and numerous plastic bags stuffed full of baby paraphernalia. 'Let her get her jollies being Mother Teresa of Calcutta – she can do your running around for you,' Jenni had said. But actually there is something incredible about this little woman. Nobody will say no to her. What power.

'There you go!' says Denise. She is red-faced and breathless.

'Bloody hell! Where did you get this lot from? Have you just looted Mothercare?' I ask. I am genuinely astounded.

'No. Of course not. I just put a few messages out. Called a few people. Got on the WhatsApp.'

'You are amazing!' I say, genuinely moved. I start to look through the bags as she brings them in. There are beautiful clothes, unworn, the labels still intact. Bags and bags of nappies, wipes, baby milk, little toys. The cot is spotless.

'This is incredible, Denise.' I can't help but feel a twinge of guilt at all the times I've laughed at her need to be Philanthropist of the Year, Chief Do-gooder. Maybe do-gooders are just good people after all.

'Denise – thanks so much. You're actually amazing. I don't know how you do it.'

'Thank you. Well, I'm just the conduit, Angela. There are a lot of good people out there. Everyone wants to help if you ask them.'

My eyes get a bit moist when she says this. Not everyone is on the make. Some are on the give, and I love this idea.

Zana comes down the stairs.

'Wow! Is this all for us? Incredible! Thank you so much! Is it all from your loft?'

'No. I never had children so . . . but we can all do our bit, can't we?'

'We can,' I say. 'We can.'

Denise leaves and Zana bundles all the bags upstairs. She has already put the baby to bed on a pile of pillows, so she will have to put the cot up and try to transport the sleeping bundle into it.

'I'm sorry I can't do much to help,' I say as she disappears upstairs.

'That's OK. I'm good. Have a good night.'

And she's gone.

I sit in the kitchen feeling comforted by the clunking about upstairs. I check my phone – radio silence from Nick. Guilty as charged. What an absolute bastard. And what a fool I was to fall for it.

I can hear Zana wrestling with the travel cot. I wonder what she is feeling? Surely she must be as discombobulated as I am? Is this the way it's going to be – me down here and her upstairs with the baby? But how could I have left her there – just down the road – knowing that Robert did not do right by her or her mother all those years ago?

What would he say if he could see all this right now? If he could witness his skeletons hanging their few items of clothing up in his spare room closet? Not once did he mention a liaison with a woman from Madagascar. You'd think it would have come up in conversation – you know, those conversations where you swap pasts with each other in order to build towards a future together? 'I have travelled extensively in Europe, I once got stung by a swarm of wasps, I always felt like a fraud at University and – oh yes – I fathered a child and then buggered off. How about you?' I wonder where she is now, Zana's birth mother? I'm sure she is keen to find out. What does she know? How come she came to England from Madagascar? What was she hoping for? Did she go back straight after giving her child up for adoption, or did she stay a while hoping to make it work here? Where even IS Madagascar? I pull my laptop towards me and google it. It's big. It's off the east coast of Africa. It's the world's second largest island country, and the fourth largest island. It took humans 300,000 years to discover it – probably why it's still so rich in animal and plant species; it's one of the most bio-diverse places on the planet. Its capital is a place that sounds like a stutter – Antananarivo. I say the name out loud, pausing after each syllable to get it right.

'An-ta-na-na-ri-vo.' It sounds so far away – each syllable a million miles. The google images are astonishing – rows of incredible architectural baobab trees. They look like cartoons of themselves – tall, thick trunks topped with small bushy hands reaching up to the blue sky. Like trees drawn by small children, bonsai magnified to the power of a thousand. They are mesmerising. I want to touch the trunk of a baobab tree and feel the heat on my palm, the sun on my face. They are so old. Like me. Thick trunks. Like me. And they have survived where not many others would have. Like me. The text underneath one of the pictures says that baobab trees are a prehistoric species. They predate both mankind and the splitting of the continents two hundred million years ago, when Africa and India formed either side of a thousand-mile strip left floating in the middle. For the Malagasy people, the baobab trees are a symbol of life and positivity, standing tall in a landscape where little else has survived. I'm filled with a longing to see them. I wonder if Zana's mum lives near a baobab tree? Perhaps she walked beneath them as a child, never giving them a second thought – as ordinary to her as lampposts are to me. I'm full of questions – the biggest of which remains: what did a woman from this beautiful island nation see in a controlling suburban Englishman like Robert? How did he get to father this mixed-race beauty now lying in his bedding upstairs?

And why did he never utter a word about it?

I hear a creak on the stairs. She's coming down.'All OK up there? Have you got everything you need?' I ask as she goes to the sink to refill her water bottle.

'Yes, thank you,' she replies, warmly enough but with just a hint of distance. What's that about?

'Do you need anything?' she asks briskly. The question sounds polite rather than genuine.

'No, no, I'm fine. I have a duvet and pillows. Toilet's just there. I'm better off down here until the old ankle deflates! Baby settled OK?'

'Yes, she's conked out bless her.'

Zana makes to go.

'Would you like a glass of wine?' I ask. I want to talk to her, try to get some answers to all the questions I have.

'OK,' she says, with not much obvious enthusiasm. Have I done something wrong?

I pour us a glass each and she plonks down next to me on the sofa. There is an awkward pause while we both drink. Then we speak simultaneously.

'So I don't—'

'I was think—'

'Sorry, go on!' I say.

Zana smiles. She seems nervous.

'Look, I'm not trying to be funny or anything, but this is all a bit . . . I mean, yesterday you were, like, "Nothing to do with me" and today it's, like, "Move into my house" – I don't get it. What changed?'

She looks at my foot – and I realise she must think I need looking after.

'As you can see I have great neighbours and everything I need downstairs, I just . . . wanted to do something good.'

I feel foolish. She must think I wanted a free maid. How awful.

'But why? What changed your mind?'

So I take a deep breath and tell her about the Magpie Project, how the women there were so kind, even though some of them had very little, and how it made me reflect on my own good fortune.

'. . . so what became clear today is "If you're not part of the solution, you're part of the problem."' I've grown very fond of my new mantra in the past few hours.

Zana looks underwhelmed.

'So, me and Hery, we're helping you "do your bit", or something like that?'

I squirm. 'That makes it sound very impersonal. Dutiful. I don't mean it to sound like that.'

'OK.'

She looks unconvinced.

'Honestly. It feels like the least I can do.'

'Because of Robert?' It's odd to hear her say his name, sitting on his sofa in his kitchen, where not so long ago he must have sat wondering what was to become of their fledgling but secret relationship.

'I suppose so,' I say.

'Sorry if I sound a bit . . . I'm just a bit wary, after everything we've been through.'

'Understandable,' I say. 'But I just thought, although it's you needing a decent roof over your head, it could be a mutually beneficial thing.'

'How?' she asks. I feel challenged, and I'm not sure what to say.

'Well . . . you can keep me company, now I'm all alone. I've been feeling a bit pointless since the kids went, and it's nice to feel useful.'

'So we're kind of like your little cuckoos? Your project?'

I wince. 'I think that's a bit . . . no, just, I don't know.' I feel my face burning. I thought I was doing a good thing. Why does it suddenly feel like I'm Miss Daisy?

Zana reads my thoughts. 'I don't mean to make you feel bad, honestly. I just need to know where we stand. I've had enough of being a pet project.'

I'm stunned. I feel like I've just been slapped in the face.

'No, of course not, it's not like that,' I say. Is it like that?

'No offence. It's just a thing white people do. It's what my parents did. Pick up a toy black person to patronise. Get them back on their feet. Ignore the bigger picture that put them down there in the first place. Feel like they're Doing A Good Thing. Buying off the problem. "I put a black child through Uni so I cannot be racist!" So I'm a bit, you know.'

We sit in silence for a minute.

Is this me? Have I got any other motive for bringing her here?

I take a deep breath. 'Can I see the messages? The ones you had with Robert?'

Zana holds my eye contact. Does she think I'm doubting her story? I'm not. I knew as soon as I looked into her eyes – Robert's eyes – that she was telling the truth. I just want to see. To see what he was like when I wasn't looking. What was his plan with Zana? Was he going to introduce me to her?

'OK,' she says finally, pulling her phone from her back pocket.

She hands me it and there they are – a stream of messages that began before Christmas. I thought he had become more moody than usual. I put it down to the new year blues.

He's down as 'Bob' on her phone. Maybe they were never destined to get to the 'Dad' stage. They have clearly spoken, because there is little exposition here – it's quite fragmented.

21st January Robert texts 'I will. I promise I will. I'm picking my moment, and the kids have just gone back so I'm sorry but you'll have to wait a bit longer.x'

'I had asked if he wanted to bring me to meet you,' says Zana, looking over my shoulder. 'But I think he was scared.'

'Scared to meet you or scared to introduce you to me?' I say. I feel shaky again – reading his secret messages when he is no longer here.

'Both, I think,' says Zana. 'None of these are very interesting – but you can see they stopped in March. That's why I rang his "real" phone.'

'What did he say about us?' I ask – I can't help myself from wanting to know.

'He said he'd been very lucky and that he was sorry I hadn't. That's the bit I remember.'

I hand the phone back. So he did consider himself lucky? Maybe the tragedy was not that he was really unhappy with me, but that he wasn't able to tell me that he loved us. Loved me. He could have said. He could have told me he felt lucky. That might have helped. Too late now.

'You were brought up in Romford? Your parents, how come you don't see them?'

'They were nice. They did their best for me. But I think they just couldn't handle it when I went off the rails. They couldn't "fix" me so fostered someone else. They don't want me near the house now. I was bad for a while – drugs. Booze. They don't want to know any more. I can't say I blame them. I did some pretty bad stuff. Stole from them. Usual junkie shit. Good Christians, you know . . . I went off to Uni somehow and that was it – they said I couldn't come back. But I dropped out before finals. Couldn't settle. I got it in my head that I would save the world instead of going into insurance like my dad.'

'Did you have siblings?' She glances upwards at me through her thick dark lashes, and we acknowledge the elephant in the room – we both know she has at least two half-siblings.

'No. Just me.'

'So why didn't you – come looking for your birth parents sooner? You must have felt very alone in the world.' I can't imagine Brendan and Erin cast adrift at such a young age. They wouldn't have a clue.

'I drifted around for a bit. Moved to Camberwell. At least there were a few more black faces. Not so much in Romford in the nineties. Got a bit lost. Drugs again. Worked in various dead-end jobs. It didn't feel like the right time to go looking for them – "Hey Biological Parents – bet you're sorry you missed out on this Hot Mess!" – when I was off my tits most nights living in a shitty shared flat and working in a crap call centre trying to sell people different energy suppliers.'

I squirm. I can imagine what Robert would have thought of her back then. She would not have wanted to hear it.

'So what did you do?'

'I met Lee. He was a social worker. Ha!'

'Is Lee Hery's dad? I mean, the one who . . .'

'Beat me up? Yes. He was my hero at first. Got me clean. But then that wasn't enough for him. He didn't want me talking to anyone. At first I thought he was trying to protect my recovery – no links with the druggy past – but then he started checking my phone, stopping me seeing friends from school. He said he didn't like socialising, he didn't want to share me. He controlled all my money, what I wore, what I watched on TV, and the odd time we did go out (always together, I couldn't go out alone) he made fun of me in front of people. Took the piss out of my accent, stuff I didn't know about in the news, things I said.' She shakes her head, smiling as though she can't believe her own story.

'Go on,' I say, glad that she is at last opening up a bit.

She glances at me and makes a decision to carry on. I try not to look too invested. I can see she doesn't want pity.

'So then I started just staying indoors all day, tidying up and all that. He liked things neat. I didn't mind – it was nice to not have to work. He drank quite a lot, so he was always tired, but he held the job down. I just wanted to make him happy. But that got harder and harder. He had a really tough case load, too many hours, too many tragedies, that's why he hit the bottle. Then he hit me.'

I gulp.

'Not much at first. A slap here and there. I just thought he was drunk, stressed. I've always been told I'm a bit much, a bit too intense, so I thought it must be my fault in some way. I can see now that it wasn't.'

'It wasn't!' I say, surprised by my own vehemence. 'Nobody has the right to hit another person!'

'That wasn't the worst of it really, the physical bit. By then I already thought I was a piece of shit who probably earned it. It was the emotional stuff.'

'Gaslighting?' I offer, keen to sound knowledgable.

Zana smiles. 'Yeah, that's what they call it, isn't it?'

'So what did you do? Did you try to leave?'

'It got gradually worse. I was going to go. Then I found out I was pregnant.'

'Oh God. What did he say?'

'He was chuffed to bits. He actually got his shit together for a while. Stopped drinking. Got on top of work more. We were sort of happy for a while.'

She falls silent.

'And then . . .?' I prompt.

'When Hery was born it was like she flicked a switch. He hit me in the hospital. He was furious that I wanted to stay in overnight. I was bleeding quite a lot and my blood pressure was low. But he wanted us to go home "to start our family life together straight away without anyone interfering". I gave in. Told the nurses I was OK, hid the blood by stuffing the sodden towels in my overnight bag. Drank a load of water to get my blood pressure up. Hery was OK and they were so busy they just said yes. He beat me up that night.'

To my absolute horror a tear falls from my glistening eyes. I brush it away with the back of my hand. I remain silent.

'So there we were – stuck in the flat with a new baby, nobody allowed in apart from the health visitor – oh he knew the drill, he was all smiles in front of her, changing nappies, stroking my back, they never knew a thing was wrong. I couldn't speak. That's when I decided to find Robert. I thought . . . I dunno, I thought maybe he could save me . . . stupid really . . .'

'Not at all. I can understand why you would want that.'

The poor girl. Why does life seem to heap misfortune on some people and not on others? How cruel that she should have started a relationship with her 'real' dad only to have him snatched away by Covid.

'So how did you end up in the temporary accommodation?' I empty the bottle of wine into her glass, but she doesn't pick it up.

'Things came to a head, I guess. When lockdown happened he got even busier. I was lonely. Even more lonely. I made friends with a young mum – Christelle – in the flat next door. He didn't like that. He came home early and caught us talking on the landing. Accused me of telling lies about him to get him sacked. We rowed. I knew the woman across the landing knew – she must have heard shit before. I mean, I could hear her kettle, the walls were so thin, so she must have heard us. And there was something in her eyes when we were talking. So I screamed. She came knocking on the door and he lost it. Told her to go away or he'd kill me and the baby. She called the police.'

'And they arrested him?'

She laughs. 'No. They didn't really care. They just told him to keep the noise down. But when they went, I made up my mind – the next day I was gone. He could knock seven shades out of me, but the minute I saw Hery in his arms while he sweet-talked the cops, I knew I had to get myself together for her. Waited till he went to work the next day, packed my bag, a few bits for Hery, as much as I could carry, and we went. I looked up at the flat as we walked away – Christelle was at the window watching us. She gave me a thumbs-up.'

'Where did you go?'

'Council. They put me in touch with Women's Aid but the refuges were all full. So they got me the B&B. I requested this area to live – far away enough for Lee not to find me, but close to . . . Robert.'

'And Lee? What happened to him?'

'He went on the sick. Said he had a breakdown. Twat.'

'And what did Robert say when you told him you were homeless?' I can only imagine what their conversation was.

'He was pretty shocked – I didn't tell him about the abuse. So he thought I'd just walked out. He was scared I was going to turn up on your doorstep, I think. And I knew my birth mother was in Madagascar. She told my foster parents she was going home.'

'What is her name?' I want to at least put a name to this poor unfortunate woman, wherever she is now.

'Fitiavana. Vana for short. It means love.'

'You said he never knew about you . . .?'

'Apparently not. She told the authorities she lost contact with him, but she gave his name. I don't know why she didn't pursue him. Maybe he wasn't telling me the truth. Maybe she was protecting me, so that I didn't think he rejected her. We'll never know, I guess.

So yeah . . . not been the best couple of years to be honest.'

'And then Covid!' I say with a bitter laugh.

'Covid has been the least of my worries. I was already locked in all the time, with no money, no job and nobody to visit anyway.'

I feel foolish again. Of course, for people in Zana's position the pandemic was probably not much change to normal life. You can't self-isolate if somebody has already made sure you're isolated. You can't socially distance if you have no social life. You just . . . carry on as normal, distant and alone.

'So what about your mum? Are you going to try to find her?'

'I want to. I don't really know how. It's hard over there. I looked into it. There's been so many changes over the past fifty years – who knows if their record keeping is up to scratch? But I want to try. I want to go there. Fat chance. I can't even afford a travel card.'

'I was looking it up,' I say shyly. 'It looks incredible.'

'Yeah?' She eyes me again. I feel like I'm trying to coax a deer out of the forest.

'Yes, the scenery, the trees, the nature. Such a stunning country. A scrap left when two continents separated.'

'Like me,' she says.

I smile. Maybe this is my calling now – to bring her back to the mainland.

We go to bed, but I don't sleep well. The conversation has unsettled me. Something about how Zana talked about Lee – his controlling ways – has made me really anxious. Is having a slightly controlling husband who sulks and withholds things, and occasionally puts you down in public, in the same arena as one who knocks you about and puts you in hospital? I'm uncomfortably aware of the fact that I have secretly judged women like Zana before now, assuming them to be weak, bad judges of character. Even after everything I went through with Robert, with the recent revelations about his past, the slow dawning that my marriage wasn't good for me, I still can't accept myself as one of *those women.* But perhaps I am. I was. I won't be now. I think about Nick, and how I walked right into another control trap. Never again. Never. Again.

19

17th August 2020

It's been more than two weeks since Zana and Hery came here. The time has flown by and I love it. I had forgotten how much I enjoy babies, and it's clear that Hery is very happy in her new home. My ankle is better, I've stopped drinking so much and I am not ashamed to say that five months after Robert died I am happier. I've started to feel so much more positive about my future. Perhaps that thousand pounds to Nick was a kind of down payment on my future – a one-shot therapy bill to finally kick me out of co-dependence! I'm going to make a difference in any way I can. I am looking into becoming a childminder. A job. Something to keep me busy and help working mums at the same time. I've already started an online course in childcare and I'm looking into all the insurance and certificates needed. I haven't felt this fired up since I finished my teaching degree. I love learning. This week has been a disaster for all the poor school kids. The exams are all a mess, with students left picking up the pieces of their futures courtesy of some stupid algorithm. Thank God my two are safely at University already. Although the way things are going, there won't be any jobs for them to go to.

I change channels. Enough of this depressing stuff. Let's look at some nice nature. Ah, David Attenborough. He always makes everything all right. His reassuring, mellow voice soothes as it instructs, adding commentary to aerial images of lush rainforest and deserted beaches. A turtle noses up the sand, and a lemur leaps from branch to branch nearby.

'Madagascar is home to some eighty varieties of lemur,' he says.

Am I imagining this? Is he in Madagascar? David – are you speaking to me?

I sit heavily and turn the volume up. I can't believe this.

'No big predators made it from Africa to Madagascar,' he continues, *'but the fossa, much like a mongoose, feeds on lemurs – so it has to be cunning.'*

The film shows a tiny, sweet-looking lemur balancing precariously on a bending reed.

'The lake lemurs of Madagascar cannot be found anywhere but here, and would struggle to live anywhere else.'

I sit taking it all in. The incredible landscape, the colourful birds and lizards, the trees – oh, the trees. In the south the flora and fauna have had to adapt to the most arid of conditions – little rainfall, harsh sun – but even in the tiny cracks between rocks, some hardy varieties still manage to produce a flower or two. It's incredibly moving, and I find myself sobbing. I'm tired. This has all been a bit much.

The kitchen door opens and I quickly swipe at my face with the back of my sleeve. Zana is standing with the baby, who grins and starts flapping her hands when she sees me.

'Morning!' says Zana brightly, thrusting the baby at me before heading to the kettle. 'I need a coffee – did this one keep you up as much as she did me?'

'Hery? No. I didn't hear a thing,' I say, grateful for the chubby little heap now in my lap.

'Well, she's a little madam! Look at you smiling and acting like butter wouldn't melt! She was awake half the night. Not crying, just chatting nonsense and making funny little noises.'

'It must be the new house, new bed.'

'She was having a great time, weren't you, missus!'

I stroke the top of the baby's head as she stares entranced by the lemurs on the shiny screen. I love how easy this feels. How life has changed.

'What you watching?' says Zana, coming to sit beside me.

'Oh, nothing, just—' I reach for the remote. I don't want her to see. I don't know why. It feels a bit close. Too coincidental. She might think I'm deliberately researching her.

She catches sight of a baobab tree and snatches the remote from my hand.

'Is this Madagascar?!' she says, delighted.

'Yes – I literally just switched on and there it is. So weird. I wasn't looking for it or anything . . .' But she's not listening. She's entranced.

'Isn't it incredible?' I say. Zana nods, and it's clear she doesn't want any interruption from her reverie. I get up and put Hery in the new high-chair. She slaps her little hands up and down delightedly on the plastic tray. I make some tea for myself, slotting two pieces of soft bread into the toaster. I butter them and without even thinking about it, cut the crusts from one and slice it into thin strips. I take the slices of buttery toast to Hery and she squishes them between her fingers before rubbing them all over her mouth. I hand Zana the other piece of toast and she chews on it, keeping her eyes on the screen. Outside the rain is lashing down, and the wind whips the barren wisteria against the window.

'You should go,' I say, sitting down next to her.

'Go? What do you mean?' she says, alarmed.

'There!' I say, pointing at the screen.

'Fat chance. I haven't even got the bus fare to the airport.'

'Well, I could help you . . .' I say. Zana says nothing, just sits and watches the rolling seas, the absurdly colourful chameleons and the strange long-necked giraffe beetles.

I watch with her, but in my head we are on the plane – me, Zana and Hery, on our way to Madagascar. We are going to find her birth mother. I picture us sweltering, pushing through crowds in over-populated slums, asking over and over 'Fitiavana? Vana? Fitiavana?' The locals would cluck at the light-skinned baby, and pull at my clothes asking for money. Finally someone would realise who we were looking for and lead us to a small but well-kept shack, where a gap-toothed woman with greying hair would be sitting on the floor shelling peas. We would explain who we were – Zana would have a baby photo of herself, and would have learnt how to explain in French Malagasy who she was. Cue tears, hugs, instant bonding as other half-siblings and grandchildren emerged from neighbouring shacks. We would leave money and gifts, and Zana would return happy to know where she came from. And I would have done something good.

'What good would it do anyway?' asks Zana, breaking my daydream.

I have no answer. I've played the Disney version out in my head, but as Robert never tired of telling me, 'REAL life isn't like that.' I have no other versions.

'I mean, really? What good would it do? I'd go out there and what? Find my mum? How? All I have is a name. An old address. I don't even know where she was born. When she was born. And what if I did find her? What would I even say? "I'm the daughter you didn't want. Hi!"'

Zana looks down at the crust of toast in her hand. I'm lost for words. I wish I could console her. She has been through so much. I want to help her but I don't know how. Perhaps this is enough – this roof over her head. A roof she is partly entitled to by birth.

'Look at you, mucky pup!' says Zana, plucking the greasy child from the high-chair and carrying her upstairs. 'Let's get you cleaned up.'

I switch off the TV. The kitchen is so quiet.

'Come on, Mona! Walkies!' I trill. At least one of us should be happy.

Outside the weather is bleak. August in the UK. Why do we live here? The sky is a dismal grey – not raining now but threatening, brooding. A big sulk. There are lots of people out despite the weather. Plucky Brits, planning picnics and trips to the beach in defiance of the clouds. A triumph of hope over experience. Early brunch parties meet and do comedy elbow bumps in a nod to social distancing before sitting less than a metre away from each other in crowded restaurants. No one is going away this year, so the cafes and bars look full. A few sparrows flit about from puddle to puddle, and a vigilante gang of seagulls guard a scattering of last night's chips on the grass. Mona runs at them barking her head off. The leaves, already brown from the extreme heat of a few weeks ago, are fallen now thanks to the recent high winds. There is that familiar sinking feeling in my chest – the end of the summer. The start of the school year. A feeling of containment, loss of freedom, grieving things long gone – the kids running in and out for drinks, their legs brown and their hair a tangled dirty mess. The sadness of having to relocate PE bags, pencil cases and school ties. Summer is almost dead. And soon I will be too. The contrast with the sun-soaked, technicolour island I've just been shown couldn't be more cruel. I long to go there. And I know Zana does too – despite her protests. I have no idea how we will do it, but we will try. I know this is what I want to do more than anything else.

But how?

I sit on a bench and get my phone out. A quick search on the internet and I discover that Air France flies direct to Madagascar from Paris. A nod to its colonial past, no doubt. The flight is around ten hours. I start to get excited. We'd have to book accommodation as well, but it can't be that expensive there, surely? I wonder what their Covid situation is? I note it's not on the government's 'safe' list, so we'd have to quarantine when we came back, but neither of us is going anywhere anyway. I'm tired of pussyfooting around in my life. I want to do something reckless, totally ill-advised and just . . . *different.* I'm suddenly filled with an excitement, an energy I haven't felt in years. I'm going to do it. I drag the dog home. She strains on the lead, letting me know she is not happy with this abrupt end to her daily walk. I have more pressing things to do now than sit staring morbidly at the dry, brown leaves.

Zana is still upstairs with Hery. Should I talk to her first? I know that if I ask her she will say no, so maybe I should just do it. I realise I don't even know her passport details. How can I book our flights without her official name etc? She has left her bag on the kitchen island. I can see a bundle of papers poking out of the top – no doubt collected in a hurry. I pull on an edge of paper. Nestled within the bundle are the unmistakable burgundy rectangles of two passports. I flip open the first.

Fanomezana Philips. Such a wonderfully exotic first name, followed by such a basic English surname. I open the second passport – Hery Philips. So she did manage to get the baby a passport despite Lee's controlling ways. Maybe she had an escape plan all along.

Is this it? Is this our escape plan? I want to go *now*.

My hands are shaking as I open my laptop and log in to the Air France website. I select London to Antananarivo from the dropdown menu. Strange to think I didn't even know the capital's name until a few short days ago. Travel dates. We could go really soon. Why not? Strike while the iron's hot. I don't want to give myself the opportunity to chicken out. I select September 10th to fly out, and September 20th to return. Ten days should be enough. I don't know where we will look for Zana's mother. We have a name and an address but that was thirty-odd years ago. Who or what will we find if we go there? I select two adults and a baby from the passenger dropdown menu and click 'search'. I watch the progress bar, desperate to see the flight that will take us out of here and into a land of lemurs and lost mothers.

The page loads.

A box is highlighted in yellow.

'Sorry, there are no flights available in the current month. You can view flights for the next available month below.'

No flights? Why?

I google 'Flights to Madagascar' and end up on a government website which tells me that Madagascar is basically – closed. 'Madagascar has suspended all international and domestic flights until further notice.' Not even cruise ships are allowed anywhere near the island.

Bloody hell. I feel insanely angry. I read on.

'On 21st March, the Government of Madagascar declared a Health State of Emergency, which is currently in place until 8th August and is likely to be extended further.'

Nice to know they keep it so up to date. It's almost the beginning of September now.

'It is mandatory to wear a face mask in all public places, including shops, parks and streets. The government has imposed restrictions on the Analamanga region, including Antananarivo. In this area, public gatherings are banned. Weekly markets, schools and bars are closed. District markets, banks, supermarkets, pharmacies, petrol stations and restaurants may open until 1 p.m. A curfew is in place from 8 p.m. to 4 a.m. Public transport is banned apart from taxis, who may operate until 3 p.m. and carry a maximum of three people. Only goods vehicles can travel in and out of the region.'

I'm going to have to think of something else. I have to help them. They need me. And yes, I need them. How has this little family landed in my life and supplied me with a focus at the precise moment the world shuts down? How can Zana find her roots when entire continents are furloughed? I slump back in my chair, defeated. Bang goes that idea, then. There are flights available from the middle of October but that's obviously a pipe dream. Already some European countries are reporting the beginnings of a second spike in infections. If 'developed' countries like France and Spain are struggling, what chance does a poverty-stricken island with no properly resourced health infrastructure stand? If I book for October there's every chance that I'll lose the money when the next lockdown happens. If the next lockdown happens. WHEN. So what am I looking at – the next six months with Erin and Brendan living at home, learning remotely and piling the sink full of dishes? Zana and Hery in my spare room? Will they accept her or will it all be weird and awkward? A long cold winter locked inside the house, cooking and cleaning like a glorified (unpaid) housekeeper, waiting to be let out into the sunshine to do what – watch them all bugger off again back to their real lives? Where is *my* real life? I want something to do too, somewhere I need to be, people who want to be in my bubble.

Who will be in my bubble when this is all over?

I hear Zana and Hery on the stairs, so I slam the lid of my laptop shut and jump up. She catches me just as I scuttle away from the chair. I must look like I've just been watching porn.

'What are you up to – buying more garden gnomes?' she laughs. Hery claps her hands as if that would be an excellent idea.

What to do? Do I tell her? Should I book for October anyway and hope the insurance will cover it?

Then I notice the passports. Shit. I have left them on the kitchen island. I lunge towards them instinctively, which of course means Zana looks. She clocks them. Shit. She looks from the passports to me, then silently picks them up and places them back in her bag. I smile sheepishly. I'm going to have to tell her.

Then she speaks.

'If you wanted to know anything about me you could have just asked,' she says quietly.

'Oh God, look I'm sorry – I wasn't being nosy, honestly, I just needed your details for something.'

'For what?' She looks suspicious now.

'OK look. I know this sounds crazy, we've only just met, and I know you're staying here because you don't have anywhere else to go – I mean, not really – but I just was thinking that I have to do something for you. I owe you it. He owes you it – Robert – and so after our chat this morning I . . . was booking flights for us to go to Madagascar.'

There is silence.

'Why?' she asks finally.

'Well, I thought it would be good for you, to, you know, see where you come from, maybe look for your mum. I mean, I know that's a long shot, but at least you will know you tried. You've lost all your other parents. I just thought it would be important for you.'

Zana speaks very slowly, her voice a constrained almost whisper.

'Important for me? You think it could be important for me?'

'Yes . . . you said you felt like the island . . . the scrap of land left behind when the continents were formed . . . I just thought if I could take you there, you might feel . . . put back together.'

I feel my cheeks flush. I sound silly. Zana stares at me angrily for a long beat. Then she bursts out laughing.

'What do you think this is – *Eat, Pray, Love*?!'

I'm confused. Hery slaps her hands delightedly on the high-chair table.

'Oh Angela . . . I know you mean well, and bless you, bless you for thinking of it, of us, but I don't think there's anything there for me now.'

'But your mum . . .?' Surely she must think there's a potential relationship there worth fighting for?

'Who knows where she is, what she's doing, but I can guarantee she's not sitting in a nice little house pining for me? Angela, I get what you're thinking, and it's sweet of you, but you really need to stop with the White Saviour stuff.'

'What do you mean?' I don't like the sound of this.

'I mean, trying to solve me, sort me out. You think we can just cruise into Madagascar, you with your big Missionary pants on, dishing out sweeties to the cute little black kids with no shoes, taking arty shots of shanty towns and plucky corner shops made from old crates. What good would that do? Really?'

I can see how it looks, but I'm hurt. She must know I mean well, even if I'm a bit clumsy sometimes. Maybe we've just been scratching at the surface these past few weeks. Of course, we don't really know each other.

'So better to not do anything, then – better to just stay where you are and complain about things?' I can feel myself getting upset. I don't know the right thing to say or feel. I'm trying.

'Of course not. God knows I've done my share of that. All we can do is try to put our own house in order. Keep our side of the street clean.'

'What should I be doing, then, if I want to help?'

Zana comes over and puts her hand on my shoulder. She can see the tears in my eyes.

'You put *yourself* back together. You think going to Madagascar will be all fluffy lemurs and spiritual salvation – making yourself feel less like a loser by gawping at people worse off than you, before chucking them a few quid? It's one of the poorest countries in the world – they've been screwed over for years by everyone. They're fucked. There is no easy way to fix it. Some things just can't be fixed. Not by us. Not by scattering a few crumbs from the white man's table. It won't help them. And it won't help you. Not really. No matter how good it makes you feel in the moment, it won't solve anything for you. Because wherever you go in the world you take yourself with you.'

I don't know if it's her hand on my shoulder, her brutal honesty or the fact that I know deep down she is right, but I feel the tears flowing freely, silently down my cheeks. She brushes them aside gently and puts an arm around my shoulders.

'Listen – I'm just saying what people have said to me. What do I know? I'm a complete fucking mess!'

And she starts crying too. I place an arm around her waist and we have a little laugh/cry. Hery shouts for attention – she doesn't want to be left out of a group hug – so Zana collects her and places her between us. She gurgles and laughs, pulls on my hair. We have a moment.

Eventually our tears subside and Zana pulls away decisively.

'Right. Enough of this. I'm going to cook some lunch. If that's OK. For all of us.'

'Yes, yes of course. But don't feel like you have to – for me, I mean.'

Zana laughs. 'Chill. I want to. I love cooking. I've missed it. It's what I love about being here. Now you concentrate on yourself – get that qualification and get on with YOUR life.'

And she knocks up the most delicious Spanish omelette I've ever had – caramelised onions, soft chunky potatoes, sweet red peppers, all perfectly seasoned. While she cooks she sings to the baby, the radio at full blast on some station I've never heard of. I could get used to this. She won't let me wash up either, and tells me to put my feet up. And despite the noise, the music, the clattering of pots and pans and the babbling of the baby, I fall into a blissful sleep on the sofa. I dream of Erin. She's a child again and she's asking me to read her favourite bedtime story – *The Old Woman Who Lived in a Shoe.* It wasn't the sanitised PC version but the original abusive one.

* * *

There was an old woman who lived in a shoe
She had so many children she didn't know what to do
She gave them some broth without any bread
And whipped them all soundly and sent them to bed

Later versions had changed it to 'with plenty of bread' and instead of whipping the children, she 'kissed them all fondly' before tucking them into bed. Ours was the original version, when whipping children was the only possible solution to over-crowding and the parental stress of an apparently single older mother. Erin used to love the illustrations – the children all spilling out of the lace holes, the rickety old chimney perched on top of the boot – but most of all she loved the bit where they all lined up to be whipped soundly, their little chubby faces creased with anxiety. I never could understand why she liked it so much. Maybe because it made her feel lucky – tucked up in her spacious bedroom, belly full and bottom smack-free. In the dream I look like the old woman, but Erin is just five or six years old. I am opening cupboard doors looking for missing children, worrying that they are frightened because they think I will whip them. But I won't. I desperately want to reassure them, but I can't find them. The cupboards are all empty. Erin follows me around calling for the children.

I wake with a start. There is drool on the cushion and the kitchen is empty. Zana has washed up and tidied the whole room. The house is quiet. I'm filled with that irrational waking fear that the dream is real, and I have to resist the urge to clamber out of my seat hauling my heavy foot behind me to open up all the cupboards.

'It was a dream,' I say out loud to break the spell. I sit and think about the quiet house. The rooms all empty, tidy, clean, waiting. For what? Robert is gone. Erin and Brendan will be leaving all too soon. I think they wanted me to sell up, but I have other plans. Not for me the little flat in a gated community, bowling club and shared launderette facilities with strict notices about not hogging the tumble dryers. Passive-aggressive laminates about not putting bins out too early for bin day. No guests. No children. No life. I shudder involuntarily. Not for me. I need to make a plan. I want to live the rest of my life, not just survive it. I'm going to be positive.

I am lucky. To have this house. This choice. It's what they call privilege, isn't it? I think about all the girls Zana left behind in the B&B. Waiting for exactly this. Wanting their own nest, no man to tell them what to do or how to do it.

If the last six months have taught me anything it's how precarious it all is. How full of shit it can be. How unconnected we are despite living inches apart. How we can live a whole life in the shadow of our true selves, not knowing what it is we really want because we were too busy conforming. School, career, marriage, house, children, death. All on our own little treadmills, looking anxiously from side to side to see if we're keeping up. Millions who've realised how much nicer it is working from home are now being pressganged by the government to go back to the office so that the inner cities, those temples to capitalism and conspicuous consumption, don't end up like Wild West ghost towns. They call it the Pret Effect. I know this because I read, and I watch the news. All the time. And so much makes me so angry. I feel it rising like lava suddenly spilling over the brim of a dormant volcano. Slowly at first – a few spurts, a gentle trickle, then in huge bursts.

*   *   *

I am angry about so much.

There is so much unfairness and suffering in the world. I am furious that so many died. Livid with the government and its lack of care. All those old people in homes up and down the country, sent back from hospital like unwitting Covid-carrying death stars. All those zero-hour contract workers lining up for the food bank, no hope of a job in the looming financial recession. It overwhelms me. I don't know what to do. I look at Denise scurrying around doing her bit for the war effort and I want to weep. She is trying her best, but in the end isn't it all a bit token? How can we fix this huge dysfunctional machine – one cupcake at a time? How can my few tins of top-brand beans in the Food Bank collection really help the starving millions? What good is it to supply hand cream for a nurse who is on her knees with exhaustion and about to sink into a pit of despair because she normally works in physiotherapy and can't handle all the death? These questions have started to haunt me day and night. What can we do? What can I do? What's the point of doing anything if you can't fix it all? Like putting a plaster on an amputated leg. If I give money to a homeless man, is that useful? Or will he use the money to buy the fix that might be his last? If I donate £10 a month to Cancer Research, it's not going to stop the deaths from undiagnosed cases due to the Covid crisis. If I sponsor a girl in Indonesia to go to school, it won't stop her from being forced into a marriage at fourteen. And yet. And yet I have seen how these tiny beads of kindness, strung together in quiet streets and repurposed community halls, can make all the difference to people.

I have learnt that despair is a luxury we can ill afford. I feel like I'm waking up. I can't slip back into an unwitting coma.

So what can I do? What do I have to offer? I don't have leadership skills. I can't change the world. But I care. I have learnt to care. I am being taught how to care. I am learning how to care *usefully.* If only that comes out of the last six months, maybe that's enough? Maybe it's just about being as practical as you can be, one day at a time. What can I do today to make something a little bit better for someone else? I have my house. I have room. Zana and Hery are here. I'm at least doing that. But what if . . .? What if I were to do more?

20

'But why?'

The woman on the phone at the Citizen's Advice Bureau is baffled. I am trying to find out how to offer my house as a day centre for women and their children who are victims of abuse. She has asked me lots of questions, but this seems to be the main one.

I'm not really sure how to answer. I feel like Scrooge at the end of *A Christmas Carol* instructing the pauper to go to the butcher's and bring back the biggest turkey in the window.

'Well, why not?' I say, trying to mask the giddiness in my voice.

'There's an awful lot of reasons why not. I mean, there are all the legal ones – like, you know, being registered so that the Covid restrictions don't apply, DBS checks, health and safety et cetera – but have you thought about what it will be like for you? I mean, it's not my area of expertise, but a lot of these women have lots of problems.'

'Yes – mostly their problem is they don't have anywhere to live where there isn't someone punching them, so they're forced to bring up their small children in one room.'

The woman clears her throat.

'Well, quite. I understand what you're trying to do. It's a great impulse, it really is. Apparently during lockdown a woman called an abuse helpline every thirty seconds.'

'I know. Everyone keeps saying that. But what are we going to do about it? The government doesn't care. They want to leave, these women, it's not that they like it. They don't leave because they can't leave – there is nowhere for them to go. The refuges are all full. Imagine that – having to stay in a house where you are literally *not safe* – not because of dodgy wiring or poor security on the windows – but because someone in the house is going to *actually kill you.*'

'What about drugs? Mental health issues? You're inviting these people into your home – how do you know you can cope?'

'I don't know. But I can get help. I'll get support. I just have a roof and some space and I want to offer it. Whenever they might need it.'

I can tell the woman is a bit stuck for how to help me. I hear her moving to another room, the phone crackling in her hands. When she speaks again it is in a hushed tone.

'Look,' she says conspiratorially. 'There is a system for all of this. We have a welfare state, we have social services, we have the police – but it's all evaporating, fast. I speak to women every day who want to know where they can go, how they can escape. EVERY DAY. It's a bloody pandemic of its own, but I don't see bloody Chris Witty or that clown Johnson standing at a podium telling us what they're going to do about it. If you want my advice – and this is very much without my Citizen's Advice Bureau hat on – just do it. Get people you trust to help you, and just do it. Otherwise you'll end up up to your neck in red tape and you'll never get anything done.'

She sounds like a resistance worker hiding in a bunker. I picture her holed up in the broom cupboard, peering through a crack in the door keeping look-out.

'OK, thanks!' I say.

'But you didn't speak to me, OK? You didn't hear any of this from me. Understood?'

'Understood.'

'Good luck.'

'Thanks,' I say, and I go to hang up.

'Wait! Will you let me know how you get on? Ask for Michelle D.'

'Will do.'

Jenni. I'm going to need Jenni. And Denise. I put a new WhatsApp group together and call it Operation Room at the Inn. I message them.

'Can you come to mine at 6pm today please – there's something I need help with.'

I've used the H word. They won't be able to resist.

Jenni messages straight back.

'What's up?'

I reply enigmatically, telling her she'll find out later. I'm going to need more cots. More high-chairs. A stair gate. Milk. Food. Toys! Denise will be all over that. She is a one-woman go-to general store. I'm excited. I can't wait to tell Zana. We can go and talk to her friends at the B&B – tell them that they can come here, use the garden, cook, do whatever they want. Once I've got all my Ofsted certificates and DBS checks done, they will be able to leave the children with me for short periods. Find ways out of the traps they've been put in. Maybe get jobs. And I will be able to sleep soundly at night knowing that four little families have access to a kitchen, a nice bathroom, a choice of loos. And a GARDEN. Outside space for kids. Maybe I can get a swing set? A slide? A sandpit! My kids loved sandpits.

* * *

I pace around all afternoon with the radio on in the background, unable to settle. I'm nervous and scared and thrilled. I feel purpose re-entering my veins for the first time in ages. I know it's mad. I don't care. It will be fun.

Finally Zana comes home. I hear her struggling with the buggy in the hallway, so I rush out to meet her.

'Hi! Sleeping beauty! You were snoring away when I left!' she says, handing me the baby.

'Are you free at 6 p.m.?' I ask. It's only an hour away now.

'Erm . . . let me check my diary . . . yes! I just so happen to be free. Why, what's up?'

'Meeting. Here. With Denise and Jenni.'

Zana's face darkens. 'Oh God, you're not going to chuck us out are you? If it's too much having me around we'll just stay upstairs.'

'No no no, God no – sorry – didn't mean to alarm you. Just come down at six if that's OK?'

'Phew. Yes. Of course. I'll just go and give Hery a bath.'

She slips upstairs like someone trying to be invisible. I can't help but smile at how horrified she was when she thought I wanted her gone. That means she must like it here. I like her being here. I can't wait to tell her what I'm planning.

At five forty-seven Jenni knocks on the door. I let her in and accept the bottle of wine she has brought. I get four glasses while she questions me, smiling as I pour.

'So, what's going on? How is it going? You're not having second thoughts are you, because that would be shit. How is the baby? Is it working out with them here?'

'All will be revealed,' I say, handing her a large glass of wine.

At two minutes to six Denise knocks gingerly on the door. Zana is running down the stairs and shouts 'I'll get it!'

She walks in behind Denise, who has brought a play mat for the baby.

'Someone donated this. Pet-free, smoke-free home, hardly used. I thought the baby might like it.'

'Thanks! That's so cute!' says Zana, taking the mat and inspecting the colourful dangling toys. 'She's fallen asleep on the bed. Knackered after the park and her bath. Bless.'

Denise and Zana accept the wine and sit expectantly on the sofa.

'Right – what's all this about?' says Jenni, eager to get straight to the point.

'OK. Wow I feel nervous. OK,' I say, aware of my heart fluttering around in my rib cage. I also note the tight, curled-up bat that has been housed in there for years seems to have spread its wings and flown away.

'So, it's lovely having you here, Zana, and Hery is just lovely.'

'. . . But?' says Zana anxiously. 'Just say honestly, because I need to know what I'm doing.'

'No but. More like *and*.'

'OK, *and*,' says Jenni. Denise looks from Zana to Jenni and then to me. It's clear she is loving being a part of this, even though she has no idea what *this* is.

'And I have a lot more space. Space I want to share. I want this house to be a safe space for play, like a sort of day centre. For you and your friends. I mean, I've got the garden, the living room nobody ever really uses any more. I've got so much space. I want to open up my house.' There is a stunned silence. Zana opens her mouth to speak, but nothing comes out. Jenni stares at me open-mouthed. Denise slowly reaches into her bag and pulls out a little police notepad, like she's about to take evidence.

Finally Jenni speaks.

'Sorry – what?!'

'I want to be helpful. I want to do more. I want to be part of the solution.'

Denise clears her throat.

'So . . . you want to get more mums and their babies to come and use your house as a play centre?' asks Denise.

'Yes. But once I'm a certified childminder they can just drop them off if they like.'

'And you'll look after the kids . . . what, for free? They don't have money to pay childminders,' says Zana. She thinks I've lost my mind.

'Yes. I don't need their money. But they need space, support, family.' I'm almost enjoying how baffled they look. It's almost funny how difficult people find it to believe that people want to do good with no agenda.

'I see, yes. But . . . don't you think it's a bit . . . risky?' Denise is biting her lip, pencil poised mid-air.

'Risky? In what way?' asks Jenni. Is she on my side? I was worried she would think I was completely mad.

'Well, you know, you don't know these women . . . and that's a lot to take on . . . a lot of work . . . at your age . . .?'

Zana snorts.

'What do you think, Zana?' asks Jenni. Oh God. It has just occurred to me that I hadn't thought about that. Maybe Zana won't want other women here. I'm such an idiot. What was I thinking? At last she has somewhere to spread out, relax, not feel afraid and here I am preparing to fill it up with more people and crying babies. I glance over to her. She is grinning from ear to ear.

'I think it's ace,' she says, and she comes over to me, wrapping her arms around my neck.

'Thank you,' she whispers. 'Thank you.'

I pat her on the back and swallow hard. I am not going to cry. There is work to be done.

'Right. So. First of all, we need things. Denise – take notes. I'll need three cots – good ones. New mattresses. Nap times are so important. We can set them up in the front room. There's good blackout curtains in there. Mums need a break during the day. Three more high-chairs, then daily supplies – money is tight for these girls. Food, arts and crafts stuff, toys. Educational things. Outdoor activities.'

'Yes, we have access to someone's garage locally – they have stockpiled donations. I can get the toys and nappies and so on.' Denise is scribbling furiously.

'Great,' says Jenni.

'The other stuff – it might be worth approaching the Magpie Project. I can do that.'

'We can ask, but I'm more than happy to cover it,' I say. 'Let them keep their stuff for those women who don't . . .'

'. . . have a Guardian Angel?' says Jenni, smiling.

'I'm sure we can get good stuff from local donations,' says Denise.

'Perfect, and what you don't have in your Aladdin's cave I will buy. They deserve new things too. The next big question is – who should we invite, Zana?'

'There are five girls there at the moment, but two of them were about to move on. They might even have already gone. I've kept in touch with the three I was closest to.'

'Annushka, Zainab and Lou. Annushka and Zainab have one baby each and Lou has twin toddlers – they're about two years old, I think.'

Jenni blows her cheeks out. 'Wow. Twin toddlers in a bedsit.'

'Not even a bedsit. No kitchen,' says Zana.

'But . . . how do you cook . . . for the kids?' asks Denise.

'We don't. Chips. Kebabs. Pot noodles. You can get quite good at heating up baby food for the younger ones in a kettle. Some of the rooms had a microwave and we'd share that. So, what with that and the one bath between five families, no outside space, no space at all really . . . yeah, I think they will come.'

21

The next three days are a blur. Denise and Jenni have their own keys now, and are in and out with what looks like the Mothercare warehouse contents. People have been incredible. We have duplicates of some things, so Jenni takes them to the Magpie Project in case anyone is in need of them there. They always are. Zana went straight to the B&B the night of our meeting. She told her friends about my idea of offering an informal day centre, and hopefully later down the line some childminding. There was some mistrust at first – I think they thought I was a weirdo trying to start some kind of cult. The Cult of Kindness. She must have been very complimentary because in the end they all decided that it was worth a go. I have told everyone to keep it on the quiet – I don't want anyone to know who these women are or why they are coming here. Zana assures me they come from far and wide – Zainab fled from Wolverhampton, Lou from Kent and Annushka from Chelmsford, so there is little danger of them being found by their partners in this quiet suburban corner of East London. Still, we don't want to put it out there. We will have to keep our heads down.

And now they are coming to meet me for the first time – this strange woman who has housed their friend and is offering her house and garden to their kids to trash. What must they think of me? I am nervous. I am standing in the garden waiting. Jenni and Denise have gone to pick them all up, using car seats we have been given. Zana has left the baby with me and has gone to help. Hery is sitting on a blanket next to the banjo-playing frogs. She slaps their little heads and giggles to herself. I smile. A knock on the door. Oh God, they're here. No going back now. I pick up the baby, straighten my hair in the hallway mirror and prepare myself. Here we go. My new life starts here. Their new lives start here. All will be well.

I take a deep breath and open the door.

And come face to face with my own children. Tanned, grubby-looking, exhausted. Brendan and Erin.

'SURPRISE!' they shout as I begin to open the door.

I freeze. For a mad moment I consider slamming it in their faces and hiding – from my own children! It's the shock! But it's too late. They've seen me.

And they've seen the baby. They said they'd be back at the end of August. They're early. Of course they're early.

'Mum! Are you going to let us in?' laughs Brendan, pushing at the door.

'Cute baby, Mum!' says Erin. 'Have you got something you need to tell us, ha ha ha!'

I stand back and let them heave their dirty rucksacks through the hall. Brendan's strap catches on the handle of the buggy and he pulls it along with him.

I follow them into the kitchen, Hery staring mutely at these new friends.

'Wow – that's a lot of baby chairs, Mum!' says Erin, noticing the row of high-chairs along the wall, 'What's going on?'

'You're back early!' I squawk, unable to control the panic in my voice. Erin stops fussing with her rucksack and looks at me.

'Yes – is that OK, Mum?! Bloody hell, I thought you'd be pleased, but you look like you've seen a ghost! Give me a hug! We had to come back because we ran out of money and we didn't want to risk Greece being put on the quarantine list.'

'Oh I see. Yes, very wise.' I smile, putting my arm around her. 'This is Hery,' I say.

'Hello, cutie pie! Isn't she lovely? Look, Mum, she's smiling at me! Ah she's adorable! Why have you got her? Who is she?'

'She's your niece.' Oh sweet Jesus, I've said it. Why did I just say that?

Brendan stops rifling through the fridge and looks from me to Erin, from Erin to Hery. The baby giggles, delighted with the attention.

I feel sick.

'What?' says Erin, laughing.

'Mum, have you been on the sauce already? How can she be our niece? There's only me and Erin. And correct me if I'm wrong, Erin hasn't given birth to a . . . mixed-race baby in the past year, I think we would have noticed!'

'Who's the Prime Minister, Mum?' says Erin, starting her 'you've got dementia' routine.

But she looks uncomfortable.

I'm in now. There's no going back.

'Sit down,' I say, in a tone serious enough to make any further jokes about my mental state off limits.

'Intriguing!' says Brendan, bringing the carton of milk he is swigging from to the sofa. They sit.

'I have to tell you something. It's going to be very difficult, but it's OK. It really is OK. So I don't want you to freak out and think anything bad about anyone, OK?'

'You're scaring me, Mum,' says Erin. Hery claps her little hands together and plays with my hair. Where to begin?

'Do you remember that weekend we went to the garden centre?'

'Yes, when you bought the freaks in the garden.'

'Well – there was a reason I was acting a bit strangely. I had just found some messages from a woman on your dad's phone.'

'Right . . .' says Erin, anxious to get to the point.

'I thought he had been having an affair. I was furious.'

'Dad? Having an affair?!' laughs Brendan. Erin is not laughing. She is looking intently at Hery.

'But he wasn't. I got it wrong.'

'Thank God!' says Erin. But she knows this is not the end.

And very gently I tell them the whole story – or as much of it as we know. They are stunned by the existence of Zana, looking to one another for confirmation that this is really happening.

'So Zana's . . . our . . . half-sister? We have a half-sister?' says Erin, her eyes wide with shock.

'Yes. She is Hery's mum. She is your half-sister.'

'Fuck,' says Brendan, taking a new interest in the baby on my knee.

'Jesus,' says Erin. She reaches into her rucksack and pulls out a bottle of Metaxa. 'I need a drink.'

'I know it's a big shock, but it's OK,' I say, keen to get to the smoothing things over bit. This must be a huge shock for them – a reconfiguring of the family unit not long since their dad died. Erin takes a large slug of brandy and hands the bottle to Brendan, who does the same.

'So – but, I mean . . . why did she come here? Oh my God, does she want you to look after the baby? Why have you got the baby, Mum?'

'She – Zana – was in touch with your dad – her dad – just before he died. She'd had a hard time and had to leave her relationship. Wanted to find her birth parents. She came to the house just to see, really. To see where her dad had lived. We talked. She's lovely. So I invited her to stay.'

'Fucking hell!' says Brendan, not unpleasantly.

'Where is she now?' asks Erin nervously.

'She's . . . out. But she'll be here soon. So I just wanted you to know. I'm sorry.'

'Why didn't you tell us, Mum?' says Erin. She looks shellshocked but also irritated.

'How could I call you while you were island-hopping? What would I have said? "Hi, how is the calamari, and by the way you have a sister you didn't know about?" I thought it would wait until you got home. I just wasn't expecting you today!'

'Clearly!' says Erin, casting her eyes around the cluttered kitchen. The stockpile of baby wipes and milk formula is stacked neatly on every surface.

'What's with all this? She's living here now? And why all the chairs?'

'Ah, yes—' I begin. But I am interrupted by a rowdy kerfuffle at the front door.

Shit. They are here.

'Hi!!!' shouts Denise from the hallway.

Erin and Brendan look at me, their eyebrows raised.

'Don't be alarmed. I've got some . . . people . . . coming with their kids. To have a play in the garden.' Denise bursts in, her arms full of toys, bags and huge packets of nappies.

'Oh!' she says, dropping everything onto the floor.

Brendan goes to help her and Erin catches my eye.

'*Denise?*' she whispers, her voice full of recrimination. 'You're hanging out with *Denise*?!'

'Sssh! She's all right. She's been helping. Hi Denise! Yes, they are back! Isn't that wonderful! The more the merrier! Ha ha ha!'

'Yes yes, lovely. Brendan, could you come and help Zainab please – she's trying to get the travel cot out of the boot and it's a bit stuck, ha ha!'

Brendan shoots me a look. 'Travel cot?' he mouths.

'Erin, would you mind taking this lot to the front room, please? Denise disappears with Brendan, and Erin gathers up the bags from the floor.

'Look, I know this is all a bit unexpected. I'm just trying to help a few people out. Some of Zana's friends. They've got nowhere to go during the day. They're living in single rooms. I've got the garden so . . .'

'OK . . .' says Erin, unsure. She looks at me like I've lost my mind. I feel like I've found it.

'How many of them are coming?' she asks as she carries a huge bag of toys into what is now the Play Room/Nap Room.

'So, we'll have Zana and Hery, Zainab and Amir, Annushka and Darcy, then there's Lou with the twins Charlie and Chelsea.'

'All those people? All those children? What, are you a nanny now?'

'Not a nanny. But I'm going to be a childminder! Soon. So that they can go to work or just have a bit of space.'

'Bloody hell, Mum. What's got into you? Are you bored? Is it money? You don't need money!' I can see she is struggling to work out why her dependable, under-confident old mum has suddenly become a carer of strangers' children.

'I want to help, Erin. I just want to help.'

She stares at me, shakes her head and dumps the bag on the floor.

'So where is Zana? Mum – I'm scared.'

I hug her close. 'I know it's a lot. It's OK. You'll like her. She's a bit like you.'

'This is all so weird,' she says, hugging me tightly. 'I need a shower. Get my head together.'

'Of course,' I say, following her into the hall.

Brendan and Denise are back, followed in by a tiny Indian girl holding a sleeping baby.

'Hello . . . I'm Zainab. You must be Angela? And this is Amir,' she says, tilting the sleeping baby to show me.

She stands awkwardly in the middle of the kitchen looking around at the walls, the garden, the photos on the window ledge.

'Yes yes, come in, come in, make yourself at home!' I say. I must sound deranged.

'Can I put him down somewhere?' she asks shyly.

'Come with me – I'll show you the Nap Room!' says Denise.

'The *Nap Room?* What the hell, Mum?!' says Brendan.

'I'll fill you in – Mum's basically Mary Poppins now. Welcome home.' And she heads upstairs, followed by a baffled Brendan. I haven't managed this very well. Why did I just blurt it out like that? The poor things. It's a lot. I've had a few weeks to get used to it all, but they have just had some earth-shaking news and come back to their family home about to be swamped with people they don't know. I'll talk to them later. I'm so anxious for them to meet Zana. She's the one that matters. They have to like her. I couldn't stand it if they didn't. For Robert's sake as much as hers. And with that thought I realise I am forgiving him. He did the best he could, I suppose. That's all we can do, isn't it?

There is an hour of chaos. Brendan and Erin stay upstairs, taking it in turns to pop down for reconnaissance snacks. Lou and the twins arrive, the children running excitedly into the garden, sending the dog into a fit of hysterical barking. Lou is tired, stressed, shouting at the kids not to touch anything.

'Leave the lady's nice flowers alone, Chelsea!' she says repeatedly.

'It's OK. She's fine,' I say. Lou smiles at me uncertainly.

'Thanks,' she says. Her eyes are hollow, and she is pale as winter.

Annushka is last to arrive. She is tall, capable-looking. It's hard to imagine anyone pushing her around. But then I guess other people never can tell, can they? Darcy clings to her leg like a limpet, and I try to coax her out with a chocolate biscuit. She is almost two but painfully small and unsteady on her feet. Not used to having the space to walk much, by all accounts. Maybe she will grow stronger here, with the garden to run in.

Zana is still not back. Jenni is with her, picking up a few bits for dinner. I wish she'd come home. I should forewarn her. I send a text.

> Not to alarm you but Brendan and Erin are here. They know. It's OK. When will you be home? x

Home. Yes, it is her home. But it's always been theirs too.

Zana replies instantly with a shocked face emoji. I busy myself with the children, trying to calm the rising panic I'm feeling. Fortunately toddlers are very good at claiming all the energy in the room, and I quickly rediscover my little-person voice, guiding them away from harm and distracting them from mini meltdowns.

Jenni has fitted a stair gate to stop the mobile ones from

getting into trouble on the stairs, and she has even child-proofed the doors and sockets. She has thought of everything. The noise is overwhelming – this many people, this many kids. I've grown too used to the solitude.

Where is Zana? I am anxious for her to return. To meet them. To show them that she is all right, that she is a gift, not a burden.

The rain starts to fall softly on the skylight in the kitchen. Annushka has shepherded all the children into the front room and put CBeebies on. The din reduces to a muted babble of little squeaks and cries. It's like dusk at the zoo. I start thinking about Nick – he took my advice quite literally and has not contacted me again. Of course he hasn't. He's probably moved on to some other sad sap. I feel like a completely different person now. These past weeks have shown me that I have plenty left to give – to the right recipients.

'Chips chips chips!!!'

Zana and Jenni are back. The kitchen is filled with the clatter of plates and the waft of vinegar. She shoots me a 'Where are they?' look. I point upstairs.

'Everything all right?' she says. 'Everyone behaving themselves?'

'Yes. Yes, everything is fine,' I say.

Zana comes over and speaks quietly. 'Should we go? I can get everyone back to the B&B in fifteen minutes. The van is still outside.'

I turn to Zana and take her face in my hands.

'Listen. It's OK. I want you here. I want you all here. Erin and Brendan will be fine. They are good kids. They'll get it. They just need some time to adjust. Don't worry about them. You've got enough on your plate.'

'Are you sure?'

'Totally.'

Zana hugs me. It feels good to be hugged by her. It's been a long time, and I've missed my kids. I hadn't realised how far two metres feels from another body, another beating heart.

Finally she pulls away.

'Right,' she says. 'Can you feed Hery for me?'

'Of course,' I say. 'I made some pasta for the children earlier.'

'Perfect. Thanks.'

And she goes upstairs. Oh God. What is she going to do?

'Zana? Shall I . . .?' I call after her.

'No. I'll just go and say hello. It's cool. I'll be cool,' she says, disappearing at the top of the stairs.

I hold my breath. I am scared. Should I follow her up, to smooth things over, to try to explain away their father's inadequacies, and his secrecy? Or is this something between them? There is little that I can say. I didn't know about Zana either. She didn't know about them until a few months ago. The only person who could join all the dots is dead and gone. I listen intently, oblivious to the clatter of plates and the sharing of hot chips behind me. The kitchen fills with people – Annushka and Zainab cheerfully dishing out sachets of mayonnaise and ketchup, the children screeching, the twins running round and round the kitchen island, giddy with the space. My nostrils fill with the smell of salt and vinegar and my stomach growls. I haven't eaten all day, but I cannot move. I have to keep watch at the bottom of the stairs. A few minutes pass.

'Excuse me – Angela? Do you want some chips?'

Lou is in the hallway offering me a bowl when I turn. She smiles nervously, unsure of the protocol regarding offering food to someone in their own house.

'No, I'm fine honestly – you sort yourselves out and I'll grab something later.' I hear a door open and quietly close again. Brendan has gone in to join the girls in Erin's room.

Hery starts to grizzle in her high-chair. She must be hungry. I take a small plastic plate with Peppa Pig on it – donated by a local family – and fill it with chips. She grabs handfuls and squishes them excitedly between her fingers. I need a drink.

'Would anyone like a glass of wine?' I ask.

'No, thank you,' they all reply in unison.

'Don't be shy! I'm opening a bottle!'

They shake their heads.

'I don't drink alcohol,' says Zainab. 'But you go ahead! You probably need it!'

I pour myself a glass of wine and head back to the stairs, taking the bottle with me. Just as I'm settling down on the bottom step Erin's door flies open and Zana comes hurrying down. Oh God – what's happened?

'Everything OK?' I ask as she comes down the stairs two at a time.

'Yeah – cool – just getting to know the fam!' she says. 'Mind if I take this?'

She swipes the bottle of wine from my hand and heads back upstairs. I sigh deeply. Things must be going OK. Should I go up?

I head back to Hery and help her polish off the chips and a yogurt. I give her a wipe down and take her up to bed, pausing at the closed door behind which my children are meeting their half-sister for the first time. Nothing. They are talking so quietly. I change Hery for bed and settle her down. She puts her thumb in her mouth and is gently snoring within a minute. She is exhausted. A big day. I tiptoe back down the stairs. Zainab is tidying up and they are getting ready to go home.

'I can do that,' I say as she starts to load the dishwasher. A pile of plastic plates smeared with ketchup fills the sink, and the floor is littered with the scraps from a toddler feast. Mona can't believe her luck, scooting around hoovering up the dropped chips and stray bits of pasta.

'No! Honestly. I love tidying up. It's nice to have a kitchen again!'

Jenni comes back with Denise and begins the arduous process of ferrying them all back to the B&B. There is a lot of kerfuffle in the hallway, with tiny wellies and raincoats being wrestled onto little tired bodies. The women thank me shyly, saying that the children have had such a nice afternoon. I urge them to come back tomorrow, or whenever they want to. I sweep the floor. The house is quiet once again, but reinvigorated by its recent visitors, as if it has remembered what it is to be a bustling home again.

Zana still hasn't come back down. It's eight o'clock now. The rain has stopped at least. Should I go up? Whatever they are saying to one another, it seems to be going well. A sudden burst of laughter – all three of them – makes me jump. I'll leave it another hour.

9 p.m. Still no sign of anyone. They must be hungry. Surely food will force them down. It feels like a siege. I am exhausted. I lie down on the sofa and pull a blanket over myself. I'll have to build my stamina up if I'm going to get this childminding thing going. There is talk on the news of different support bubbles – families being allowed to mix in one household. Who will be in my bubble? I close my eyes and listen to the shuffling about above me. I drift off to sleep comforted by the background noise.

It's dark when I wake up several hours later. I can hear noises in the hallway. Whispering. Giggling. Someone stumbles and laughter is stifled.

'Hello?' I say.

Brendan sticks his head round the kitchen door.

'Hi Mum,' he says sheepishly. He's grinning from ear to ear. He's drunk.

Erin appears behind him.

'Sorry, Mum – did we wake you?' She looks half-cut too.

'It's OK. What's going on? Where's Zana?'

'Hi!' she says, popping her head over the top of the drunken duo at the door. She looks merry as well.

'We just popped to the pub. While we still can!' she says.

'Oh OK. Is . . . everything all right?' I say. I'm relieved. I had imagined a resentful and difficult conversation upstairs. A Shakespearean showdown. A Greek tragedy. Instead they fall into the kitchen laughing and holding on to each other like the Three Stooges.

Erin sits one side of me and Brendan the other.

'Tea anyone?' asks Zana. It's somehow not strange that she is here and perfectly comfortable rummaging around for mugs and milk. It's at least partly her home.

'Mum . . . we've all had a long talk,' says Erin, her arm around my shoulder.

'Yeah, and basically, Mum . . . the upshot is . . . we love Zana!' says Brendan. I smile.

'And that's not the beer talking, Mum,' adds Erin. 'It's weird – we were saying, weren't we, Zee? – it's like the minute I saw you I felt like "yeah, she's my sister" – and I've always wanted a lovely sister.'

'So have I,' says Brendan. Erin thumps him and they laugh.

I'm amazed. And delighted.

'And also – we have a niece!' says Erin. 'So although we've lost Dad, we've gained two new family members.' I beam. This is better than I could have dared hope for.

*   *   *

We sit and sip tea and I listen to the three of them drunkenly rambling on, talking over each other, comparing childhoods, making connections. There is much hilarity when Zana and Erin discover they were both thrown out of the Brownies for being 'disruptive'. Brendan and Zana discover they both suffer from severe bouts of hiccoughing, and all three bond over a mutual loathing of peanut butter. And it's that easy. They are siblings. I feel a slight pang of jealousy – they share around twenty-five per cent DNA with each other. This new addition to the family is only Robert's. The baby – who I am growing very fond of – is not mine either. Not one bit.

As if sensing my sadness, Zana changes the subject.

'So. Angela. We've been talking – about what happens next. These two are off again next month, and you've been so kind in letting me stay here. And letting my friends come round. So we want to do stuff. To say thank you.'

'There's no need. Honestly. I'd just be on my own and that's boring.'

'We want to do bigger stuff. Help people. Give back. We're going to start a group. A kindness group. Like what happened in lockdown, but *forever*, you know? Why should it stop now?'

'Yeah – we're going to stage events. Stunts. Organise mass giving,' adds Brendan.

'We're going to do what we can to just – help people!' says Erin.

'Wow. I mean, that's amazing,' I say. I've never seen them this animated.

'Thanks, Mum. *You're* amazing,' says Erin.

'You are,' agrees Zana.

'You're not bad,' says Brendan, giving me a playful shove.

* * *

Zana hugs everyone and heads upstairs to bed, and I'm left marvelling at how what at first felt like a threat to our little unit of three has turned out to be the biggest gift. I was so worried that the kids – *my* kids – would react badly. It can't be easy. How has she slotted in so well? What magic dust has she sprinkled on them to make herself so instantly accepted?

'You OK, Mum?' says Brendan.

'Yeah. I was just thinking how nice this is. Is it real?!'

'Yeah, it's real. I mean I know we're pissed but – it's funny. This is all mad, but also it just feels kind of . . . right.'

'It does. And you know what else is weird? She's our sister because she's Dad's daughter – but she feels more like *your* daughter . . .' says Erin.

I smile. I know what she means. Zana has nothing of Robert's sudden coldness, none of his uptight self-importance, none of his controlling moods. Not as far as I can see. Her mum must be lovely.

22

22nd September 2020

I am exhausted. The past few weeks have been the craziest, most stressful and chaotic of my entire life. Yes, more stressful than the week that toddler Erin and baby Brendan both got Norovirus on a camping holiday in Wales when it rained all week, Robert was in one of his moods and slept in the car leaving me to mop up vomit all night whilst battling yet another urine infection, and our car broke down on the way home. More chaotic than the time the dog tripped Robert up on the stairs and we had to run around after for him a fortnight because of a 'swollen knee'. Crazier than my mum's funeral when Robert took us on a wild goose chase for the crematorium, insisting he knew the way, and when we finally crashed in we were in the beginning of someone else's funeral and he made us stay because he said it would have been rude to leave.

This stress has been incredible, though. I am energised by it. The more we do, the more I feel alive. The more I give, the richer I feel. Having the children here, helping their mums, doing my online course in childminding has lifted me higher than I could have ever dreamt possible. They come most days, and if the weather is nice we have picnics in the park, run around chasing the toddlers, having water pistol fights. Brendan is incredible with the little ones, and it's been so lovely to watch him grow as a man. A good man. Erin has become very close to Zana, and they cannot get over how alike they are. They have been hatching a plan to liaise closely with Women's Aid – they want to raise funds as well as awareness of the desperate state of affairs for abused women and children. But more than our own personal development, we have started something extraordinary. Following their drunken night in the pub, we had a planning meeting. The girls from the B&B were drafted in and we formed a collective. Me, Zana, Erin and Brendan have drawn up a 'Radical Kindness Task Force' with the kitchen as HQ. The whiteboard – normally home to dental-appointment reminders and shopping lists – has become our Kindness Matrix. The headlines, all colour-coded in wipe-clean marker pen, are giddying – 'Local Planting', 'Winter Street Outreach', 'Loneliness Liaison' and 'Promise Tree'. Denise, Jenni and Ellis have been fantastic too, driving us here, there and everywhere, as well as sourcing anything we need to make our plans work.

So far in the past few weeks we have

- taken the babies out in their buggies and planted over a thousand daffodil and tulip bulbs up and down the street. Around every tree, in every nook and cranny, they have pushed dry little husks into the ground to germinate ('It will be nice to see them coming up in spring when hopefully all this will be over,' said Zainab as she scrubbed the dirt from her fingernails afterwards.)
- put leaflets through the door of every house in the area asking for charitable donations for poor families ('It looks like the British Heart Foundation in here!' said Lou, sorting through the mounds of bin-bags full of good quality clothes.)

- drawn up a rota of Hit the Streets winter clothing and hot soup drops for the homeless
- accessed the membership list of a local social group for the elderly, long since closed down due to Covid, and knocked on all their doors to arrange socially distanced tea and cake in a movement called Tea for Two on Your Doorstep.
- organised a Jumble Trail for Women's Aid, and got the local MP on board with their refuge petition. They want to create more safe spaces for women and their children – properly resourced and funded
- started plans for a Christmas Gift donation scheme to help those families struggling during the pandemic.

Today Erin and Brendan are returning to Uni. They are spending their last day at home helping people tie 'Kindness Promises' to a large chestnut tree in the park. We have come down with lots of bright cards, a box of pens and long lengths of ribbon in order to start a local kindness epidemic. I sit with the dog and Hery on my knee like some old dowager, watching as local children, parents and passers-by, bemused by all the tree-centred activity, stop to have a look.

'Just take a card, write your promise on it, then tie it to one of the strings around the stump!' shouts Zana to the gathering crowd. Soon little hands are busy scrawling shaky vows on the coloured cards, and the adults follow suit once the children have paved the way with their joyful lack of inhibition. Erin and Brendan help the children tie their cards to the tree with colourful ribbon. Soon there are thirty, forty, fifty promises flapping in the gentle wind. An old lady stops and rests on her trolley, and Lou approaches her with a leaflet about the doorstep tea parties. Despite her mask I can tell that the old lady is smiling. Lou hands her a card and she rests on her trolley to write. I carry Hery closer to the tree over the bumpy ground, now littered with conkers and acorns. It's the autumn equinox and already the nights are drawing in. By eight o'clock tonight these colourful cards will be invisible from the road. But we will all know they are there, waiting for the sun to rise on them again.

I reach for the nearest card. A small child has drawn a rainbow and written 'I promis too smil at peepul'. The next one along reads 'I will be nic and help my brutha'. I smile at the cute misspellings. Zainab has just finished tying the old lady's promise to the tree. I can see her shuffling off into the distance pulling her trolley behind her. Is it just me or is her step a bit lighter, her pace a bit more jaunty?

I pull at her card and read the spidery handwriting. 'I promise to listen to my friends when they talk about their illnesses without interrupting them, especially Glenys who DRIVES ME MAD!'

A local florist has pledged to leave bunches of flowers in random locations for people to pick up. A hairdresser has offered free blow-dries for the over sixties. A local student will tutor kids struggling with maths for free. It's a beautiful thing.

'Right, Mum – we're off now,' says Erin, coming over and kneeling by my side.

'Already?' I feel suddenly bereft. I knew this was coming, but I've denied how much I've been dreading it. These two. These gorgeous two. We may have had a tough year, but we have come out of it so much stronger. They have grown into incredible young people, and my heart bursts with pride at how they have taken everything in their stride. I must be brave. I'm not going to blub. I want them to be happy.

'OK, love,' I say, bursting into tears.

'Oh Mum,' says Brendan, bending down and hugging me.

'Don't cry, Mum – we'll be back soon. And anyway – you've got this lot now!' adds Erin. We look at the gaggle of women and their babies who are our new funny little family.

'Not a bad bubble to be leaving you in,' says Brendan.

'I'll be fine. But be careful! No going mad at parties! Stay safe! I'll see you at Christmas – or maybe before, if this all dies down . . .'

But we all know it won't. Already the infection rates are rising again. Who knows if the students will even be allowed home for Christmas?

'Love you, Mum,' says Erin, hugging me tightly. We have formed a close bubble since the women have been coming and going. Erin and Brendan don't go out, so that we can all stay in contact without jeopardising the group. They have been selfless – but I suspect they will let off steam once they get back to their normal student lives.

I watch as they say their goodbyes to all the women. The twins cling to Brendan's legs, and Erin holds Hery close, breathing in her smell. Finally they go to Zana and encircle her in their arms. I am deeply moved and start crying again.

And then they go.

'Love you!' I shout after them as I watch their rucksacks disappear out of the park and round the corner to the tube. How will I cope without them? Zana appears beside me and takes my hand in hers. 'They'll be back soon, Mum,' she says.

'Mum?' I laugh, secretly thrilled. 'You've already got two of those, not that I'm not happy to be the third!'

'Great. You can be Three. Third time lucky,' she says. 'Now come on, we've got a lot of work to do.'

* * *

We head home for tea and cake before they take the children home to bed. I'm still waiting for my DBS check certificate – if I can get certified as a childminder I can keep helping out with the children. Who knows when they will change the rules about households mixing? I couldn't bear the thought of these little families being locked up again. I need to finish my course, do my first-aid certificate and get Ofsted to approve me – all before the next inevitable lockdown. Every day I wait for the post anxiously – I'm sure I have nothing to worry about – I'll get approved. I have a teaching degree, a good home, expert help from Jenni and Denise, who have been all over the paperwork. Denise is even thinking of joining me! Maybe there will be news when we get home. The post comes at all hours these days, our poor postie staggering under the weight of her deliveries. As we walk, talk turns to the housing list. Every week the women call to find out if they are anywhere nearer to finding a more permanent home; every week they are disappointed. They never contact anyone with good news – the deathly silence is enough communication to let everyone know that they are still months, years from any social housing of a decent standard. They do love to get in touch to tell you that you are no longer relevant, though – we get home to find a brown envelope on the mat. It's not my DBS. It's addressed to Zana. She rips it open and scans it quickly, before handing it to me. The bureaucratic language feels austere, punitive. Apparently because she has found 'alternative accommodation in the private sector' she is no longer in penury and has been taken off the housing list. We knew this was coming, but the confirmation has been delayed, and somehow seeing it in black and white makes the new permanence of our arrangement all the more nerve-wracking. We'll be all right. I'm sure we'll be all right.

Zainab, Annushka and Lou contemplate their own brown envelopes. When will they get out of that awful poky place? Before all the children are walking? Before they go to school? Before they leave home?

'It's a long shot for me anyway because they are questioning my right to remain,' says Zainab. 'Even though I was born here and my son was born here. I could be on that list for ten years. I could never be off that list. I could be living in a single room with no toilet and no kitchen until Amir goes to college. If he's allowed to go to college. If I could afford it.'

'We'll keep fighting on,' says Zana, getting the high-chairs set up.

'It's a crock of shit anyway,' says Lou. 'The housing list is an illusion – it's a mirage. Every time you think you might be near the top of the list it vanishes in a haze.'

Annushka slams Darcy's feeding tray down angrily. 'So what do they expect us to do? Just rot in a room going slowly mad? Just another number? What about the kids? It's not fair on them!'

'They don't care that it's not fair, do they?' says Zainab. 'As far as they're concerned, we're just stupid women who got battered and probably deserved it.'

'Meanwhile they keep building luxury apartments for "shared ownership" schemes. What a joke – you have to pay a shit load as a deposit then the mortgage on your 25%, PLUS rent on the other 75%! Who can afford that? I looked at a place near Forest Gate – studio flat, just dreaming really – and it would cost me fifteen hundred quid a month!' says Annushka.

'You're so lucky to have each other,' says Lou.

'And you've all got me too. You can come here whenever you want. You are doing such amazing things for other people – you deserve a share of our good fortune in return.'

Zana hands me a cup of tea. Her face is soft, kind. I know she is grateful to be here. Little does she know that it is she who has saved me.

That night I go to sleep wondering what it must feel like to have absolutely no agency, no control over what happens next, no financial cushion to fall back on. However shitty my life felt at times – and there were times I did wonder how my life had become so controlled – I never had to worry that I would be turfed out of my home on the whim of some landlord. Or that I would be evicted from the country on some spurious grounds or other associated with my parents' paperwork. Or that my ability to pay for food would be abruptly curtailed because I worked for three hours one week. It has been an eye-opener this past month or two, and I feel ashamed I didn't know more about how the underclass lives. The stress. The uncertainty. The feeling of absolute dependence on a capricious and asset-stripped welfare system. I have my house. I have a large sum in the bank from the life insurance and the healthy pension pot Robert guarded and pored over so religiously. I feel disgusted with the whole system. Merely by accident of birth I am all right and they are not. Hery, Darcy, Amir, Chelsea and Charlie are not. I am a wealthy woman with nothing to do.

But I can do something.

I can do good.

23

'I'd like to change my will, please – I want to sign my house over to my children and my late husband's other daughter, please.'

'Okaaaaay . . . that's not a problem, that's perfect . . . I'll just get your account up . . .'

The young man sounds a bit nervous. 'Perfect'?! Why do people say this all the time?

He puts me on hold and I listen to Vivaldi on loop. I'd much rather be doing this in person, but face-to-face meetings are so 2019. It seems like too momentous a decision to be administrating over the phone, but here we are. In the end it was a no-brainer. Of course Zana must be included in the house. She is part of the family, and deserves an equal share with Brendan and Erin. I want them to have the house now. It's worth quite a bit of money. I don't want to own it any more – I want to give it to them. Redistribute the wealth. It feels only right.

'OK, perfect, so I'm just going to hand you over to a senior here,' says the young man. He's clearly out of his depth. I know who he's going to get. Oscar Peterson. An old friend of Robert's. A golfing chum. Robert liked to do business with his mates. He had everything neatly tied up – which, even though I found it incredibly infantilising at the time, I have to admit made the will and all the other nonsense that goes with it run smoothly. Oscar and I have never got on. He's a patronising, smirking little creep who loved it when Robert was mean to me. I'm going to enjoy this.

'Hello! Angela! How are you bearing up?' says Oscar.

'Not too bad, Oscar,' I say, steeling myself.

'Good good. Keeping busy?'

'Oh yes, I'm—'

'Excellent, excellent. Now, my colleague has explained that you want to sign your house over to the children?' says Oscar.

'Yes, please!'

'And a third party . . . who is . . .?'

Here goes.

'Robert's other daughter.'

There is a short silence.

'Robert's other daughter? Ha ha, I think we would have known about her, wouldn't we? Correct me if I'm wrong but there was no other daughter mentioned in the will, as far as I remember?'

'No, that's right. She has come to light just fairly recently.'

'Right. OK. Erm . . . Angela – forgive me if this is impertinent, but are you sure you want to do this? Have you been able to verify her identity? We get a lot of scammers you know, probate chasers etc.'

'No, its all perfectly above board! He had another daughter. So now I'm going to do right by her. But thank you for your concern.'

The spluttering on the other end of the line is delicious. I'm trying not to laugh. How's that for pissing all over your cosy view of your dead old mucker? He thinks I'm like one of those silly dupes who sign their life over to a fraudster on a dating app. Well, I almost was at one point. But not any more.

'And are you completely aware of the implications? Are you cognisant of the fact that if you die before seven years is up, Erin and Brendan and . . . this other . . .'

'Zana. Her name is Zana,' I say helpfully.

'Quite, yes, they will be liable for inheritance tax? The full amount?'

'Yes, I'm well aware of that, thank you, Oscar.' He's starting to sound quite annoyed.

'So I assume, seeing as your children are living away from home, this Zana has put you up to this?'

'Nobody has put me up to anything. There's really no need to be worried.'

He allows himself a hollow, supercilious chuckle.

'And may I ask where do you plan to live? Because if you stay there you will have no rights whatsoever, and should this . . . Zana decide to throw you out, she will have every right to do so!'

'She won't.'

'Of course, you could always pay her rent, but then she would be liable for tax on that income, and it wouldn't help your security long term. I really must advise you to rethink, Angela.'

I take a deep breath. 'Oscar. Please organise the paperwork to hand the deeds over to Robert's three children. If you are unable to do that without embarking on further patronising little monologues, I am more than happy to take my business elsewhere. It is not your business, nor has it ever been, to question my intentions or my motives with regard to Robert's estate. The house is mine now. The money is all mine now. I get to do whatever I want with it, and if I was of a mind to sell everything and set up an Alpaca farm in North Wales, I would have every right to do so without having to listen to you bleating on about it.'

'Angela! You sound absolutely ridiculous! Robert was very careful with his money! He wanted to ensure he could provide for his family, and here you are acting in such a rash and ill-advised manner! He must be turning in his grave!'

'No, he isn't, Oscar, and I'm perfectly certain about that because he was cremated. Now are you going to do it or not?'

There is a huffy silence.

'Of course I will have to if those are my instructions.'

'They are. I will send Zana's details by email.'

'Fine. Is there anything else I can do for you?' he bristles.

'No. That's . . . perfect!' I say. And I hang up.

I haven't told them yet. I have no idea what Erin and Brendan will say. Will they be OK with sharing their inheritance with this new third party? I don't feel like there was any choice. They will have to just work it out between them. Everybody counts or nobody counts. That's my new motto.

'Come on, Mona – walkies!' The mums are all in the park. They are coming round for an early dinner later. I love to cook for them. Afterwards, I'm taking sandwiches and boiled eggs to a well-known homeless-person hangout. We go every week – to hand out boots, socks, whatever people need. I load the car up and one of the girls comes with me. Jenni and Denise go too. The boiled eggs are a huge hit – they are still warm when we get there, and people seem to love having something so homely and comforting to peel and eat while we chat to them. I've come to really look forward to these nights – that small, personal exchange – person to person. A scarf, a sleeping bag, a home-baked cookie. I feel fed by it. Deeply touched by their gratitude. Some are drunk, loud, high, grabby – but most are humble, thankful, dignified. People in need of justice, fairness, proper help – but who instead can only hope for kindness. Any cynicism I felt about charity being a part of the problem vanished in that first exchange of a warm boiled egg.

Lou and Annushka wave as I walk past them. Zana and Zainab are pushing Chelsea and Charlie on the swings while their own babies sleep in their prams under a chestnut tree. It's a beautiful autumn day – probably one of the last. The kids are screaming and running riot, and an ice-cream van has pulled up, hoping for some late-season profit. There is a sense of uncertainty everywhere despite the Indian summer. Will we be locked down again? Is this our last week of freedom before we are shut in for a long dark winter? It feels like the whole of London is grabbing this last hurrah in the sunshine – like the wild parties between bombing raids during the Blitz. Mona drags on the lead, stopping to sniff every lamppost. Jenni and Denise appear – each carrying bags of groceries for tonight's outreach.

'Cluck cluck cluck,' says Jenni, holding up a bag full of egg boxes.

'Oh well done!' I say.

'I'm going to hang on to these tonight – last week I turned my back for one second and some bugger took the whole box!' laughs Jenni. 'I was outraged! But then I thought, "It's not much to ask, is it, half a dozen boiled eggs when you haven't got a pot to piss in?"'

'I'm going along tonight – they won't get past me!' says Denise. She's right – I've seen her in action. She has just the right ratio of compassion and Headmistress. They've turned into the most brilliant double act, these two – Jenni is Eric Morecambe to Denise's Ernie Wise, the Laurel to her Hardy, the Cannon to her Ball.

'By the way, I'm glad I've bumped into you actually. I don't know if you've seen on the WhatsApp but a few of the neighbours have been asking questions, wanting to know who all the young mums are and why they are suddenly in the street. They've noticed they all come in and out of your house.'

Oh shit. Here we go. Neighbourhood Watch Covid Nazis.

'We're a bubble. That's not against the law.'

'I know, I know, don't worry. We've been through all this. Plus, soon you'll be registered and – maybe – so will I. We are perfectly within our rights to be mixing like this because we are providing childcare. I just thought you should know,' she says, 'because people can be mean, and I think you've had enough meanness in your life. So I told them.'

'What? What have you told them, Denise? Because these girls are vulnerable and I don't want it getting around that they are abuse survivors, because we don't want their partners to know where they are! What did you tell them?'

'I told them to mind their own fucking business.'

I've never heard Denise swear before. I burst out laughing. Denise laughs too.

'And you know what? It felt good. I think you're doing a brilliant thing. We're doing a brilliant thing. And I'll do whatever I can to help.'

'How did they take it – the neighbours?'

'It went very quiet for a day and now people are offering to help. Someone saw the girls planting the bulbs, and someone else saw them at the Kindness tree, so I think the general impression is they are some kind of hippy cult, but they are welcome because they planted daffodils!'

We laugh. This is great news. It's been playing on my mind, what the perception is in my street. To hear that Denise, one-time curtain twitcher and generous dispenser of disapproving tuts, is now standing up for our little band of survivors touches me greatly.

'You're a good woman, Denise,' I say.

'I want to be.'

'You are.'

'So are you, Angela. You're a good woman. A kind woman. And God knows we need a lot more like you right now.'

24

24th December 2020
Christmas Eve.

Normally I'd be wrapping presents now, panicking about running out of sellotape, trying to stop the dog from getting at the turkey, and worrying that Robert is already too drunk to go for drinks at Jenni's. It's all very different this year. There are five stockings hanging over the fireplace, but none of them are for my family. Not my blood family, in any case. They are ready and waiting for sticky little hands to pull them from the mantelpiece. Except those little hands won't be here tomorrow. We were planning a big spread. I ordered a massive turkey from the butcher and made sure I had borrowed enough chairs for Christmas dinner, only for Boris to cancel Christmas six days to go. Now the girls and their little ones will spend Christmas in their tiny rooms. I could cry. They are like family to me now and I can't stand the thought of them in their little rooms on Christmas Day. Thank God I still have Zana and Hery here. Hery, my sweet little cherub, who has started to talk and calls me 'Nan-nan-nan'. We have promised that when this is all over, when we can all be inside together again, we will celebrate. We could have bent the rules, but it's been so bad around here I couldn't bring myself to do it. Not after seeing the faces of all those poor nurses and doctors, their noses and cheeks bearing the red welt battle scars of tight masks worn during long, exhausting shifts. Thank God Erin and Brendan are allowed home – IF they get the negative test result they are waiting for. 'One visit back to your vacation address' said the government announcement. They had tried to make all the students come back within an early-December 'travel window', but my two didn't want to because of work and friends and needing to feel like there was some point in being back at Uni at all. But they have promised they will be here. They've assured me they will get negative test results in time to travel. I have no reason to think they will test positive – but this year has taught me to expect the unexpected. Where the hell are they? Why haven't they texted me to let me know? I start to panic that they have been apprehended on the motorway, stopped at the ticket barrier. People are paranoid. How will they police this? Arrest anyone carrying presents? Slap fines on anyone being festive in a built-up area? Knock on doors and count heads, comparing the guests to the electoral register?

Despite Christmas being cancelled, and the tightening of social distancing, we have managed to fulfil a staggering amount of charitable work. We had collected so many lovely things we had to deliver them, despite the restrictions – albeit with a top note of hand sanitiser and a side order of knock-down ginger. Yesterday we put Santa hats on and spent the day taking toys and gifts to the children connected to the Magpie Project. We all drove separately, then me, Jenni and Denise dashed up broken paths, up ill-lit stairs, along urine-soaked balconies to deliver a bit of Christmas cheer to the women living in temporary housing with their small kids. One family sticks in my mind. I had four bags of food and gifts, which I left on the doorstep. I rang the bell and retreated a safe distance before waiting to make sure they were collected. Three little kids rushed out to grab the bags.

'Thank you! Thank you! Merry Christmas!' they shouted, as their shy mum picked up the bags and waved. I cried more than once, I'm not ashamed to say, although I always waited until I got back in the car. A few spare treats donated to those with nothing. Why can't we *all* have enough *all the time*? I know charity is not the answer, but my God it can help in that moment of need. These kids can't wait for a socialist utopia to get a bag of chocolate coins.

Luckily this community has been incredible. We put posters up in the park a few weeks ago asking for nice toiletries, chocolates, new toys and games, and set up a trestle table in the front garden at the appointed time.

'Nobody is coming!' I fretted.

'Calm down, Angela! "Build it and they will come!"' said Jenni, cool as a cucumber.

And they did.

After fifteen minutes the entire lawn was covered. The street was backed up with cars trying to drop things off, but nobody tooted, nobody lost their rag. After half an hour the front room was full, so Jenni started taking stuff in too. Then we had to get a wheelbarrow to ferry more donations up the road to Denise's. They just kept coming. Children shyly offering chocolate, bought from their own piggy bank money when they were told there were children with nothing. Old ladies who had spent all week knitting adorable little teddies. Mums with arms full of luxury bubble bath and body lotion, happy to be able to help. It was the best day. A lot of tears. A lot of laughs. A deep sense of joy. At the homeless outreach we took mince pies as well as the eggs, and had collected enough money to give every man – and the few women – a pair of brand new boots. A local school had all the children write Christmas cards for them too. We finished the week off with a virtual carol concert for the elderly living nearby, with local school children, who had practised for weeks, acting as our online choir. All this charity around Christmas, all this division between rich and poor, has such Dickensian overtones. It's been the worst of times and the best of times. To see the goodness pouring out of people – the same people who, just nine months ago, would have chopped your hand off for the last loo roll on the shelves – has been truly uplifting. Despite everything that has happened this year – losing my husband (and with him my over-cosy view of our life – and the world), being duped by Nick, feeling lost and alone at times – I feel full of optimism for the future. Most people are good. Most people want to help.

I'm in the garden grabbing a moment's peace. Where are they? 4 p.m. and it's already dark – surely they must have their results by now? There is a hive of activity in the kitchen. Zana is preparing a little party for her new family while Hery bats at the baubles on the tree. She's mesmerised by it – the lights twinkle on and off – not the tasteful white fairy lights on the fake tree Robert insisted on, but big, gaudy coloured lanterns. Cheerful. Tacky. Too much. I love them. Tomorrow we'll sit down, me, Erin, Brendan, Zana and Hery, to have a family Christmas lunch – right after we deliver to our absent friends in the B&B. We've got the hot box ready, so we will load up and leave it at the front door. Shame not to use all that turkey. After lunch we'll be heading out to feed the homeless again. Feet on the Streets. We'll take food and clothes, and most importantly we will take ourselves – a chat and a laugh go almost as far as a turkey sandwich. But tonight we are having our little party. Just cups of tea, chocolates, mince pies and sausage rolls. It's bliss. No stress, no ridiculous consumption and waste, no one to avoid upsetting. I sip at my tea and wave to Hery, who has started to stand up recently. She leans heavily on the back door like a drunk, her little breath frosting the glass. Earlier I showed her the Santa tracking app – Santa is in Russia already. I smile as I remember the days when Erin and Brendan would rush up to bed on Christmas Eve, fearful of being found awake by Santa. It was the only day of the year they went to bed early. Just as well, because they would be up before dawn the next day. Decades ago now. So much has changed. The whole world has changed. 'Happy New Year!' we all said to one another as the clock struck twelve on 31st December 2019, the dawn of a new decade. Little did we know what a shitshow we were about to enter. If I could have foreseen what this year was to be like, what would I have done differently? Would I have paid more attention to the news from China in January? Would I have insisted Robert got his cough checked out earlier? Would I have bothered with the expensive coffin when only a handful of us were there to send him off? Perhaps. I certainly wouldn't have given any time – or money – to Nick. I wouldn't have been so mean about Denise. I would have backed myself sooner, and asked myself what *I* wanted for the rest of my life.

'What would you say if I said I wanted things to be a little bit different this year?' Robert had said. Had he been trying to tell me something? Did he already know about Zana? Maybe. Or maybe he just felt the past rushing up to greet him as his time on this earth was coming to an end.

'Go to sleep,' I said, shutting it down. I wasn't to know. None of us could have known what the year had planned for us. He started 2020 with a maudlin contemplation of his last years on the planet, unaware he had only weeks to live. Perhaps the knowledge would have changed him. Perhaps he would have introduced me to Zana, told me he loved me, hugged his children more. Perhaps not. That New Year's Eve he seemed almost to be foretelling something. He wanted things to change. Well, they certainly have. Only he's not around to show me what he meant. I was frightened – I didn't want to pick over our life together in case I didn't like what I found. Nevertheless, I have had to. And I am all the better for it. No, we didn't have the perfect marriage. No, he wasn't always nice to me. Yes, I let him put me down. His death has been an unexpected rude awakening I didn't know I needed. I don't want the trappings of happiness – I want the real thing, and it comes in unexpected ways. For me, this year has been the turning point it's been for so many. What use are statement holidays, fancy cars and prestige offices if you aren't able to enjoy them with people you truly love, and who love you back for who you really are? What's the point of life if it isn't to be with each other – kindly, patiently – to help each other and enjoy other people? *Now* I've found my people. *Now* I've found my purpose. *Now* I've found my family.

The back door flies open. It's Zana.

'Some people here to see you, Angela! Carol singers, I think . . .'

I shrug off my blanket and go through the kitchen, swiping a warm Rudolph biscuit as I go. Carol singers? On Christmas Eve? Haven't they heard – Christmas is cancelled and singing is just a fancy way of shedding the viral load in spadefuls?

Through the front door glass I can see two dark figures at the end of the path. As I open the door they start to sing. It's my favourite carol. My favourite verse. 'In the Bleak Midwinter'.

I switch on the porch light and there they are – Brendan and Erin, holding candles and wrapped in winter scarves. Their voices are full of spirit. Not the most tuneful but gloriously moving. I watch them as they sing, and in my mind's eye they are back at nursery, in their first nativity play, Brendan with a tea towel round his head and Erin with her tinsel halo.

'What can I give him, poor as I am?
If I were a shepherd I would bring a lamb.
If I were a wise man
I would do my part
Yet what I can I give him –
Give my heart.'

They are only two lines in when I am blubbing like a baby. The tears roll down my cheeks and I lean against the door frame drinking them in. They came. Of course they came home.

'Merry Christmas, Mum!' says Erin, waving her negative Covid result in my face as she rushes to hug me.

'Happy Christmas, Mum!' says Brendan.

'You're here! You're here!' I say. It feels like a Christmas miracle. 'Come in! You're frozen!'

'Is Zana in?' asks Erin, dumping a large bag of brightly wrapped gifts in the hall. They have been in constant contact – Zana shows me funny videos they send each other all the time. I don't understand TikTok, but it has them in stitches. They even got me to learn a dance once. Apparently I went viral. They rush in just as Jenni and Ellis come out onto the street. Jenni is, of course, in a sexy Elf outfit, her short red skirt blowing up in the breeze revealing frilly red knickers. She shouts over to me, clearly already quite well oiled. Oh well. It's Christmas . . .

'Is that them? Did they make it?'

'They did!' I shout back.

'Told you! Don't know what you were worrying about. That's brilliant. I'm so pleased for you! How lovely!'

'Here, we got you this,' says Ellis, appearing behind her with a bottle of champagne. 'I'll leave it on the bin. And there's some silly bits and bobs for the kids too,' he adds, placing a Santa sack next to the bottle.

Bang on cue, Denise appears with a plate of sausage rolls.

'So this is where the party is?' she laughs, leaving the plate on the gate post. Her Christmas jumper has flashing lights – so do her earrings and her stripy knee-high elf socks. Nobody can say she doesn't make the effort. One by one we help ourselves, retreating with our piping-hot pastry. 'How is everyone doing?' asks Ellis.

'Good. We're good,' I say. In the early days after Robert's death, when I contemplated this first year without him, I would never have dreamt I'd be standing here now with our neighbours – my friends – celebrating Christmas Eve out on the street with a new step-daughter and, yes, granddaughter inside. Christmas drinks around the bin is an unexpected glory.

'Merry Christmas, Angela. What a fucking palaver it's all been, eh? But I think you've come out of it all right, you know?' says Jenni, raising a glass.

'I think I have. Thanks to you guys,' I say, tears in my eyes again.

'Well, the best thing we can say about this bastard year is that it's nearly over,' says Ellis.

'I don't know – I know this sounds weird but . . . I've sort of enjoyed it,' says Denise.

'I know what you mean,' I say. '*Enjoyed* might be a bit strong, but it's certainly had some good points.'

'This year can just FUCK the FUCK OFF!' says Jenni. 'Because next year is going to be OURS! Get ready 2021, because these bitches be coming to get you!'

Back inside Zana is shrieking and hugging Erin. Brendan is throwing a delighted Hery up into the air, Erin is catching up with the lives of our friends at the B&B. They are doing so well. It doesn't take much to make a difference, one life at a time. Zainab has a new part-time job at Tesco. Annushka is going to catering college next year and Lou is hoping to train as a nurse. Erin stands with her arm around Zana's waist, taking Hery into her other arm. After helping with their CVs and doing a bit of advocacy via Women's Aid, Erin is deeply invested in these women's futures. They are getting back into the world. So am I. Brendan has turned the music up.

'Mum, you look amazing!' he says, spinning me round.

'She *is* amazing,' says Zana.

'She's glowing,' says Erin. Champagne is popped, and they talk over each other, words tumbling like water from a broken dam. I watch them, grinning from ear to ear. They are right – I am happier than I have been in a long time. Possibly ever.

It's hot in the kitchen, so I take Hery out to the garden. Outside the statues stand in a silent circle. The children love them, and even though I was clearly off my rocker when I bought them, I have grown to see them as friends. I sit and stare up at the sky, wondering what my quiet little life will be like next year. If I have the strength and the means, I will go on helping wherever I can.

Everybody matters or nobody matters.

It's a clear night, and the stars twinkle obligingly. Hery points up at them, her breath billowing out into the cold night air like angel mist.

'Star!' she says, delighted with herself.

'Star!' I repeat, kissing her little head.

In the darkness the old lady holds her hand out to the robin and her heart glows red.